AND BABY MAKES SIX
Linda Markowiak

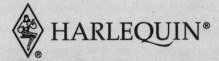

HARLEQUIN®

TORONTO • NEW YORK • LONDON
AMSTERDAM • PARIS • SYDNEY • HAMBURG
STOCKHOLM • ATHENS • TOKYO • MILAN • MADRID
PRAGUE • WARSAW • BUDAPEST • AUCKLAND

ISBN 0-373-70920-X

AND BABY MAKES SIX

Copyright © 2000 by Linda Markowiak.

This edition published by arrangement with Harlequin Books S.A.

Visit us at www.eHarlequin.com

Printed in U.S.A.

AND BABY MAKES SIX

CHAPTER ONE

MITCH OLIVER WAS FAST on his feet, could face down a two-hundred-and-sixty-pound bully, give a glib talk on national television and handle being a hometown hero with class.

So he certainly shouldn't be scared of an eight-year-old girl.

Remember, she's got to be a lot more scared than you are, pal.

The social worker went ahead of him down the hallway to the office. It was here that he'd sign the final papers, and bring Crystal home with him.

The funny thing was, his niece hadn't cried much when they'd had her mother's funeral yesterday. Mitch had thought he'd have to do more...comforting somehow, but...the kid had just sat there with that Litton woman, staring straight ahead. And afterward she'd hardly said a word to Mitch.

It had been that way over dinner last night, too. The only person the child had talked to was Jenny Litton, who hadn't had too much to say to Mitch, either.

The social worker paused at the closed door to her office.

Mitch said, "It's just that it took me so long to get here." Seeing the look of puzzlement in the woman's eyes, he clarified. "It would have been better for Crystal if I'd got here sooner. I could have helped with something. Made…you know, arrangements. The funeral." After all, his own wife, Anne, had died four years ago. He knew there was a lot to do, sad decisions, kids' tears to wipe.

That thought got him back to Crystal and those dry eyes of hers.

Alma Winters sighed. "I don't know, Mr. Oliver. Miss Litton took care of everything. I mean, I don't know if a day or two earlier would have made any difference."

"Mitch. Please call me Mitch." He'd told her that a couple of times now, but he knew people were more formal down here.

He'd never visited his baby sister in South Carolina. He'd never been close to Kathy, even though she was the only family he had anymore outside of his kids. In fact, he'd only seen Crystal once. About six years ago Kathy had made a short visit to Ohio. He and Kathy had loved each other, he guessed. But he'd already been on the road by the time she'd hit junior high, and as an adult she'd always lived so far away… In fact, he'd seen little of Kathy even before her young husband died and she'd moved to South Carolina to raise Crystal alone. A sense of loss filled him. His baby sister was gone and he hadn't really known her. Now he wouldn't have the chance. His memories were from long ago, child-hood ones. Armloads of lilacs, Kathy going out to the big old bush by the pond and picking more than she could carry up the hill.

He raked a hand through his hair. No use in sugar-coating it. He'd been too busy for his kid sister, and now it was too late.

Once he'd been too busy for them all—playing professional hockey, managing his endorsements and his investments. He'd become a rich man, but he'd missed out on family life. Four years ago he'd made a promise that that would change.

"If we hadn't been camping so far out, and if I hadn't had to make an unscheduled stop in Memphis, I would have been here sooner." Mitch stopped. He had to quit explaining.

The older woman smiled at him, her eyes warm black-brown, her skin a shiny mahogany. "You can't help the fog. It's like that on Hilton Head. It's an island. We get fog."

Kathy had liked the South Carolina island for the warm climate and proximity to the seashore. Crystal had a real southern drawl that made her seem even more strange to him.

"I'll do my best with Crystal," he promised suddenly.

The social worker sighed. "I believe you. But it's always a sorry time when a baby's momma dies. Fortunately, she's had Miss Litton. Miss Litton has been a good friend, done the right thing by taking Crystal in and arranging for Kathy's funeral. I want you to remember that." Her eyes crinkled with kindness even as she hesitated. "Look, Mr. Oliver—"

"Mitch."

"Mitch. Thank you. Mitch, I need to tell you something before you go in there. Crystal keeps saying she doesn't want to go with you."

Ah, hell. The greasy breakfast he'd eaten went sour in his stomach. "She doesn't even know me."

The social worker put a light hand on his arm. "Right. I understand that. She needs to give you a chance."

He swallowed. "What if she isn't in the mood to, ah, give me a chance?" He needed to know exactly what he was up against.

"Try not to worry too much. Just take her home, ease into things."

"I'm good at going with the flow."

She smiled again. "Listen to her, maybe try to do things in your home that will make her feel welcome. Your sister named you guardian in her will, and you're the only close family Crystal has. Her father died about eight years ago, and his parents were never really involved with Kathy or Crystal. In fact, I gather they're relieved to have you handle the situation." There was a slight pause. "We'll have a social worker in Ohio stop in and do a couple of quick checks of your household, but it's just a formality, really."

"A formality?"

She hesitated again, and Mitch got impatient. "Just break it to me. What are you trying to say here?"

Alma Winters touched him on the arm again. "All right. Jennifer Litton has raised the issue of whether you're the proper person to care for Crystal.

That's why we're having an Ohio social worker check. You see, Miss Litton was under the impression that Kathy's will named *her* guardian.''

Mitch stared at her, bewildered. He and Kathy might not have been close, but they'd stayed in touch. She hadn't trusted him to care for her daughter?

The social worker said, ''Miss Litton claims Kathy had mentioned changing her will a couple of times.''

''Well, she never did it, did she?''

''No, she never did. Look, I'm a southerner, and nobody believes in family like a southerner does. You're blood. You're kin. But you have a lot of responsibility. It's not too late to change your mind. If you can't see your way to providing a home for your niece, Miss Litton would—''

''No. I believe in family, too.'' He looked her directly in the eye.

There was a second's pause. Then she said, ''Ready to take your niece home?''

''Sure.'' Crystal was just a little kid. A little girl.

A little...*girl.* He stepped through the door Alma Winters held open.

Crystal was sitting on a chair by the window. She wore her hair long and wavy, and was dressed in shorts that made a yellow bib kind of thing over a T-shirt. Sandals on her feet, those feet swinging up and down as if she were on an imaginary swing. Mitch's sons' legs were full of scars, scratches, insect bites in the summer, but his niece's weren't. A scrap of a cat, as orange as her hair, lay curled in her lap. A cat so small his dog, Face-off, was likely to have it for lunch and then look for more.

She was just a little kid.

His gaze was caught by the blonde who stood with a hand on his niece's shoulder. Jennifer—Jenny—Litton. Miss Jenny Litton was real pretty, like some high-class southern belle right out of an old movie. He'd had trouble not looking at her last night at dinner. He glanced away now. After all, he was used to looking—and then not looking—at attractive women.

He addressed himself to his niece. "Hi, Crystal."

Her legs swung higher. The kitten woke up and stretched.

"We're going home today. On the airplane, remember? You haven't ever been on a plane."

Those bare legs kept swinging. He clenched a fist in his pocket, painfully conscious of the social worker behind him, and the silent woman next to Crystal. The pretty, uppity woman Kathy might have preferred to him to raise her kid.

"You're going to like it in Ohio. We talked about it last night. We live in an old farmhouse and we do a lot of fun stuff, like sports. In the spring, you can use that mitt and baseball I got you last Christmas."

The cat turned to stare at him.

Jenny spoke for the first time. "Crystal doesn't like sports."

"Oh."

"Kathy used to say you were a big hockey star. Rich and famous." There was no admiration in her voice. That voice was low and feminine, and she drew out the syllables until she sounded as southern as fried chicken and biscuits. Mitch frowned. No, not fried chicken. More like a cool glass of iced tea.

He wasn't a big hockey star anymore, and he wasn't that famous anywhere outside of North Shore, Ohio, these days, but his sporting-goods store, Serious Gear, was doing well and he didn't have to answer to this woman.

Belatedly, Mrs. Winters came forward. "Crystal, maybe you'll learn to enjoy baseball, and here you are with your own mitt and ball."

Her voice was so falsely cheerful that even Mitch winced.

Crystal shrugged, and her movement must've startled the cat. It leaped to the floor. "Jewels," she called and scrambled down after it.

But Jenny was quicker. She took a couple of steps and bent to keep the cat from scurrying away. "Here, Crystal. Your baby landed on its feet." Jenny ran her fingers down the kitten's head and back, her long, polished nails scratching behind its ears. The cat set up a purr so loud even Mitch could hear it.

The floor was dusty, but she got down on her knees despite those expensive-looking silky stockings she wore, and petted the tiny animal. Crystal sat beside her. Jenny stroked along the kitten's backbone, and its hind end came up as her fingers reached it, its skinny tail in the air like a flagpole. Crystal turned and looked up at Mitch. "My momma named him Jewels because I'm Crystal."

Huh? Well, at least she was talking to him. "Ah, that's a good name. For a cat. Jules." He tried harder. "He's a cute cat."

"He's a *she*."

Jules was a weird name for a girl cat, but Mitch decided to let it go. He said, "Okay, a she then."

But he must have said something wrong, because his niece turned then to Jenny. "Do I have to go with him, Miss Jenny?"

Jenny's fingers on the cat stilled. In her position on her knees, her jacket was hiked up a notch, showing the fullness of her curves beneath. The fact that he noticed so...intently made him more uncomfortable than ever. Maybe he should have been the one to get down on the floor. But somehow today he had a hockey stick for a spine, and so he stood there like an idiot, looking down at them both.

"Well, then," he said to Jenny when the silence got so long he couldn't stand it. "We'll pick up Crystal's suitcase and be on our way a little early. The plane leaves in a few hours."

A *really* heavy silence fell over the room. Mitch finally added, "I want to thank you for helping out until I could get here." He really was grateful for that part. He tried a smile on her, though nothing about her manner encouraged one. "You...did a good job. You had things Kathy would have wanted. I knew she liked lilacs. She always did."

Emotion flickered in Jenny's eyes for the barest second, so quickly that he almost missed it. But he knew in that moment that his sister had meant a lot to this woman.

Crystal had been scratching the cat. Now she looked up from the floor. "I want to stay with Miss Jenny," she whispered.

Oh, hell.

Instinctively now, he squatted. At his movement, the cat leaped up in the air and took off. Crystal jerked, wrapping herself around Jenny. Jenny hugged her, whispered something into her ear that Mitch couldn't catch.

The social worker cleared her throat. "Your uncle is family, sweetie. He lives in a big house in Ohio, which is a very nice place to live, and you'll have four cousins." She spread her hands helplessly. "He loves you. He told me so."

Mitch had told her that, over the phone when he'd got the shocking news of his sister's death in an auto accident. Had that only been two days ago? Saying he loved his niece wasn't really a lie. He was sure he would love her...just as soon as he got to know her.

Jenny gently disengaged from Crystal and stood. "Why don't you find your kitty and see if she's hungry? You know how hungry she gets, and how much she relies on you to take care of her." Surprising Mitch again, she pulled a little plastic bag of cat treats from the pocket of that yellow outfit.

"Can we talk?" It was Jenny Litton again, her eyebrow raised in polite inquiry.

He nodded, out of his league. He wanted to do what was best for Crystal.

Jenny stroked Crystal's hair. "Will you be all

right with Mrs. Winters for a while? Just for a minute? I need to talk to your uncle Mitch.''

"Do I have to go with him?" she said, her eyes filling with tears.

Jenny hesitated.

Mrs. Winters said, "Sweetie, we've talked about this.''

Mitch seized on a sudden inspiration as the kitten munched on a cat treat. "I have a dog at home."

A flicker of interest crossed his niece's face.

"And ponies."

"Ponies are big." She frowned.

Mitch figured it was best not to mention that Face-off was about as big as one of the ponies. "I also have a hamster, and some fish. They aren't big."

Crystal no longer looked as ready to burst into tears as she had a moment ago. He was just mentally congratulating himself when Jenny Litton motioned him toward the door.

He got to his feet, too, but thought about not following her. He was in no mood to be ragged on for not being a better brother. But the alternative was for her to speak her mind in front of his niece, so he followed her out. The hallway was hot—the air conditioner in the social worker's office didn't cool the air out here. Hard to believe it was October.

Jenny motioned him toward the window, out of the way of the few passersby. "I'm sorry for your loss," she said politely. "Kathy—" She stopped and moistened her lips, and Mitch realized she wasn't as cool about this whole situation as she pretended to be. "I was your sister's best friend."

"Like I said, I appreciate your handling the funeral." He'd been camping with his sons in Colorado, when he'd got the news of Kathy's death. It had taken a while to get to an airport and book the kids on a flight home with nineteen-year-old Luke in charge.

She smoothed back her already-smooth hair. The sun caught a little gleam from her round gold earrings. She had a nice chin and dainty ears—*don't look.*

She said, "From what I know about you, your life is pretty complicated. Like you said at dinner last night, you're a widower. You have three teenage boys and an eleven-year-old. I can make things easy for you. I'm prepared to take custody of Crystal today. She'll have a good home, and your conscience will be clear."

"I'm her uncle."

"Crystal doesn't know you. And quite honestly, Kathy didn't talk about you much. As far as I know, you never came for a visit."

Guilt pinched him. "I didn't have time."

Her chin tilted in a sort of southern belle arrogance. "You didn't have time?"

"No. I didn't."

"What makes you think you'll have time now?"

"I'll make time"

"I have the time. I live alone—" Abruptly, she bit her lip.

"Crystal is my family."

"She doesn't want to come with you."

"As you said, that's because she doesn't know me. Yet. She's family. I'm sorry if you had…plans to keep her. I don't know how much time you actually spent with Crystal—"

"I've known her for three years. I've baby-sat. I've spent days at the beach with both Kathy and Crystal. I've had dinner at their house—I've had them over to mine. We've rented videos—I got her *Mulan* last week. *Your* interaction with Crystal was to send her a ball and glove that she's never used." Though her voice was carefully polite, he heard the criticism in it.

He told himself not to react—either to her tone or the fact that she knew a lot more about Crystal than he did. There must be a book or something out there on how to raise little girls.

She looked him full in the eye. "Kathy intended to change her will."

"But she didn't. Or are you going to try to prove in court that she did?"

Her mouth went slack. There was a long pause. "No," she said softly, so softly it was almost a whisper. "Not now…" Her voice trailed off.

He was going to win. Suddenly, on what should have been a surge of satisfaction, Mitch felt like a bully. Jenny Litton cared about his niece and she knew about little girls. Mitch only knew about raising boys. On top of that, Crystal liked her.

"Look, I…" He shut his mouth before he could admit his insecurities aloud. "Listen, you don't have to like me. But think of Crystal. It's obvious she trusts you. If you tell her things will be okay with me, I think she'll feel better.''

She shifted her little purse from one hand to the other, and there was a long, uncomfortable pause. ''She loves the kitten. You're going to let her keep her kitten, aren't you?''

''Of course. I'm not a jerk, no matter what you think.''

She flushed a very becoming pink, a wash of color on her perfect, pale skin. ''I can help you take her to the airport.''

He was impressed. The woman was a good loser. ''Thanks.''

''I'm doing this for Crystal. Not for you. I mean—''

''I know exactly what you mean.''

She blushed harder. ''I'll give her my phone number. She can call me anytime. Collect.''

''She doesn't need to call collect.''

''Collect,'' she said firmly.

Whatever. ''Okay. That sounds like a plan. Let's go.'' He turned to head back into the office to break the news to Crystal.

He held the door to the office open. As she passed by him on her way inside, she whispered, ''Listen. If I hear there's a problem, either from Crystal or the social worker in Ohio, I'll be on the next flight to come and get that little girl. And believe me, if I have to, I'll take you to court and fight you for her.''

They were almost in the office. She added, ''I'm only giving her up because my lawyer and Mrs. Winters are telling me that's what I have to do. But it won't take much to push me into changing my mind.''

Her voice was soft, a drawling whisper, like a slow fall into dusk on a hot summer night. But her words were fighting words, and he respected that. ''I wouldn't have expected anything else, Miss Jennifer Litton.''

JENNY LITTON HAD BEEN true to her word, talking with Crystal, hugging her, reassuring her. If she resented Mitch, she didn't show it in front of the girl.

When they were finally on the plane, Mitch let out a long breath of relief. So far, so good. There had been one bad moment when Crystal had discovered that her cat had to ride in the cargo area. But there'd been no crying from the little girl, which would have been bad, because then Jenny would have looked at him in that prissy, judgmental way.

But he didn't like how quiet Crystal was now as she looked out the window of the plane. His kids always crowded around, making jokes about how small the cars down below looked, and talked loudly and happily about the prospect of aircraft trouble. This kid just sat there.

''Can you see the clouds?'' he asked.

She didn't answer. She didn't even shrug.

''The trees looked real green when we took off. All pines, like Christmas trees, and now we're so high we can't see them at all.''

Nothing. Her head was turned away; he couldn't read her expression.

O-kay. He was getting a little desperate when he had a sudden thought. "I'll buy you a dog."

She turned to him. "A dog of my own?"

"Sure." Although he was elated that she'd spoken at last, he groaned inside. Another dog. Yeah, *that* was sure an inducement to get a housekeeper to stay more than a week.

Crystal said, "When you get me my dog, I want one of those with a ball of fur on its head and little balls on her ankles."

That stumped Mitch for a second. Then he said, "A poodle?"

She wrinkled her nose, thinking. "Yeah, a poodle. A white one, one of those little ones. The real tiny kind."

"Ah, honey? I think you might want a bigger kind of dog. Our house is sort of rowdy—"

She got a fierce frown on her face, and he stopped.

An awkward silence fell. Mitch searched desperately for things to say. She'd put on a pair of jeans, and sneakers had replaced the sandals in preparation for the colder Ohio weather. But even in these clothes she seemed small and frail.

They traveled in silence, and by the time they landed, Mitch felt so uncomfortable his throat ached. Maybe he should have left her with Jenny Litton.

No! He'd make this work, he wouldn't take the easy way. Never again. He'd promised Anne he'd take care of everyone, and that meant taking care of them *all*.

Luke had used Mitch's Jeep to take his brothers

home from the airport. So Mitch rented a car for the short ride. As they climbed the hill to his house, he said, "There's where you're going to live."

He glanced at her out of the corner of his eye, and he saw her bite her lip.

"It's big."

He didn't know if that was good or bad in the eyes of this kid. The old, rambling farmhouse, white with green shutters, had seen many additions by the time he and Anne purchased it. The land hadn't been farmed in years, and had been seeded to grass. Behind, out of view, was the pond where he'd learned to skate as a kid. If you stood in the backyard and looked across the pond, you could see the small house where he and Kathy had grown up.

In the front, the yard sloped down to a huge old red barn that he'd had converted into a garage and stable, with a new tack room attached to it. In the pasture were the kids' ponies.

Crystal said, "Those are your horses?"

Thank God for animals, Mitch thought. "They're not horses. They're the ponies I told you about. I can teach you to ride them."

"No thank you," she said in that southern drawl. "They look too big."

"Maybe when you get used to them—"

"They're too big."

"Okay," he said quickly.

As they pulled into the driveway, the boys spilled out of the house. Jason was first, eleven, with dark hair like Mitch, an anomaly in that he was small and wiry in a family of big men. Behind him were the fifteen-year-old twins, Ryan and Tommy. The twins were blonder, like their mother had been. The oldest, Luke, was dark, too.

Jason jogged up to the car, Ryan right behind him. Crystal scrunched up in the seat.

Mitch reached over to ruffle her hair and stopped at the last minute. He settled for a pat on the shoulder.

"They're big," Crystal said. Tommy and Luke, who was big by anybody's standards, had followed Jason and Ryan. All four boys came to a halt in front of the car. There was some shoving as they peered into the car. Without looking, Ryan reached behind him and put an elbow in Tommy's gut. Then Ryan tried to push Jason aside. Crystal scrunched up even farther.

Mitch sighed. At least there was no sign of Face-off.

He touched his niece's arm again. "They're nice boys, once you get to know them."

"I don't like boys."

"I live here, honey. We can sit in this car for a while, but sooner or later you've got to get out and meet your cousins." At that moment, Jules let out a mew from her cat carrier in the back seat. "Jules needs to get out of that carrier and explore. It's not good for a cat to be locked up too long."

Crystal bit her lower lip and nodded. Then she reached around and pulled the carrier toward her. She got the little wire door open and scooped the cat into her arms. "Okay. I'm ready."

"It's going to be fine." Mitch reached over to her side and flipped her door handle open.

He got out of his own side of the car as Crystal opened the passenger door. "Listen, guys," he said to his sons. "Give the kid a break. No roughhousing for a minute, you hear?"

"Sure, Dad." As usual, Luke, his oldest, was quick to size up the situation. He said to his brothers, "Now shut up and make nice for your cousin."

Crystal slowly got out.

Jason said, "You don't look like Dad."

Ryan said, "Uh, hi."

Tommy said, "A cat."

And Luke, bless him, said, "It's going to be okay. We're not as bad as we sound." He gave Crystal his million-watt smile, the one that always worked on the girls of North Shore, Ohio. It apparently impressed eight-year-old girls, too, because Crystal took a tentative step toward him.

Just then the front door exploded and a blur of black came blasting out. Face-off ran toward them at breakneck speed, ninety-five pounds of fur and mutt, barking like the beast he was.

Crystal screamed.

Jules sprang from her arms.

Face-off headed straight for the little girl. As she cowered and screamed, the dog caught sight of the kitten and veered.

Jules tore off across the lawn, Face-off at her heels.

"Shit," Mitch muttered, hampered for a moment

by the fact that he was still on the far side of the car. "Get that dog!" he shouted.

Luke had already begun the pursuit. Jules made a dizzying circle around the huge lawn, followed by dog and four boys. Around and around, faster and faster, Face-off barking his head off, Luke and Mitch shouting, the other boys yelling in glee, Crystal standing by the car screaming, a shrill, high wail that went on and on.

Mitch veered right, trying to block Face-off. The dog saw him and put on the brakes, skidding toward Mitch in the wet grass. Mitch tackled him. Jules skittered under the wire fence and into the pasture, where she was lost in the tall grass.

The kids skidded, too, ending up in a messy tangle.

Face-off licked Mitch's face. Ice-cold mud seeped through his jeans.

Slowly, Crystal's wailing tapered off into silence.

Mitch got to his feet. The dog jumped up, planting a couple of muddy paws on the front of his jacket. "Down!" Mitch said, and the dog—reacting to the no-nonsense tone—obeyed. "Sit." A quivering sit. "Jason, come get this dog!"

Jason untangled himself from the other boys and grabbed Face-off by the collar. "I'm sorry, Dad," he said quietly. "I thought I had him locked in the laundry room, but the door doesn't work too well since Tommy broke it last week."

"We'll talk about this later," Mitch said. He turned to look at Crystal who was sobbing quietly. "You guys are going to have to do better. She's not used to boys. She's a little girl, and she's just lost her mom. Don't you remember how that felt?''

''I remember,'' Jason said in an even quieter tone, and suddenly all the anger left Mitch. He walked over to Crystal and picked her up. She felt skinny, warm and fragile, and her hair spilled over his arms.

Despite the mud, she threw her arms around his neck and sobbed in earnest. ''Jewels is lost.''

''No, she isn't. She's just hiding, because she doesn't understand that Face-off only wants to play. Listen, we'll lock up Face-off better this time, and put a bowl of milk on the stoop, and Jules will come home. I promise.''

There was a pause. ''I hate your dog,'' she finally sobbed.

She might as well have said, *I hate you. I hate your family. I hate that you've brought me here.*

Mitch held her tightly. He was still breathing hard from chasing the dog, but that didn't explain the peculiar ache in his chest.

CHAPTER TWO

TWO WEEKS LATER, what was left of Jenny Litton's world fell apart.

She stood at the sink in the ladies' room at Kyle Development and pressed a cool, wet paper towel to her cheek. That helped some. A moment before, she'd been in the toilet stall with dry heaves, and her whole face was flushed. She swallowed, trying to quell the nausea. As the manager of the real-estate development company, she had no time to be sick.

Perspiration was beaded on her upper lip and she dabbed there, too. Then she wadded the paper towel and took out her lipstick. She smeared Plantation Rose across her lips with a hand that quivered slightly.

Giving in to a sudden impulse, she leaned forward and pressed her forehead to the glass of the mirror. Cool and smooth, it felt comforting. She opened her eyes and stared at her own face a fraction of an inch away. Apart from the redness in her cheeks, she looked much the same. Her makeup understated and carefully blended, her silver-blond hair well cut and turned under at the ends. Small studs in her ears. Nothing flashy for Jenny Litton. Nobody from here to Savannah would ever accuse her of flash.

But even as she looked at her own reflection, even as she should have felt satisfaction at that last thought, her eyes filled with tears.

Sad tears, because she missed Kathy. Kathy had been her best friend, the only one who'd known about the baby. And she missed Crystal. She'd talked to the little girl every night by telephone. Crystal didn't have too much to say, and the words unsaid bothered Jenny a lot.

She straightened, wishing she hadn't let Crystal go with Mitch Oliver, even though Jenny's lawyer had insisted it was the only thing she could do. *You don't have a case. You'll hurt the child more if you fight for her—let her think she's going to stay—and then lose her anyway. If Kathy really hadn't wanted Mitch Oliver to be Crystal's guardian, she would have changed her will.* The lawyer had reminded Jenny—as if she'd needed any reminders—that she had enough to worry about in her own life.

Jenny's stomach gave another quick heave, and she pressed a hand to it. At any moment one of the other women who worked at Kyle Development might walk through that door, and it wouldn't do for the polished-up and buttoned-down Jenny Litton to be standing in front of a mirror watching herself cry.

She pasted on a smile and headed out the door.

"Oh, there you are." Her secretary, Yvonne Rolland, looked up from her desk as Jenny passed. "It's eight o'clock. I thought maybe you weren't in yet. That would be strange, *non?*" Yvonne had a French mother and was given to sprinkling in a little of the language.

Jenny nodded, taking a stack of mail Yvonne handed her, wondering when Yvonne would notice how much time she was spending in the ladies' room. In a few weeks it wouldn't matter anyway; everyone would know her secret.

She'd told Kathy. *Kathy, I'm pregnant and I'm scared. Delane doesn't want the baby.* Kathy had looked shocked for less than a second and then she'd hugged her friend. *Well, I never thought this would happen to you. Okay, I know how much you loved Delane. It's going to be tough seeing him at the office, but you'll be okay. Women have babies on their own these days.*

Well, maybe other women made those kinds of mistakes, but Jennifer Litton didn't, and the shame of it washed over her.

She'd slept with her boss.

She bit her lip, took a few steps away and pretended to sort through her mail. As office manager, Jenny supervised a relatively small staff—just a couple of secretaries, the payroll clerk and the eight-person sales crew that sold upscale properties in Hilton Head. Her co-workers knew she'd broken up with Delane a month ago, but not why.

"Uh, Jenny?" Yvonne hesitated, then said, "I thought you'd like to know. Delane is back in town. He's coming by the office today at ten. He wants to have a meeting with everyone. It's important, he said. You'll need to be there, too."

She squeezed her eyes shut for a second. *Not today,* she thought.

"I'm sorry," her secretary said softly.

"It's all right." She'd fallen out of love with Delane Kyle for good the day he'd offered to pay for an abortion, but not offered to take any responsibility for their baby. Reflexively, she put a light hand on her belly. *Don't worry, baby, I want you very, very much.*

"Well, I'm glad you're not mooning over him. I know it'll be awkward." Yvonne averted her eyes.

Jenny put her chin up. "I can handle it." She'd known that if she kept her job at Kyle Development, she'd certainly see Delane from time to time.

She wanted more than anything to turn tail and run, to go someplace where nobody would ever need to know about the circumstances of her pregnancy.

But she was hanging on to her job. Overseeing the Hilton Head office was a respectable job, one with good pay and benefits. Benefits the baby would need.

Besides, she wasn't the only one who ought to be ashamed. Let Delane Kyle feel the good hot scald of it. Let him watch her belly grow and go home and try to sleep at night!

The thought of his discomfort gave her some satisfaction, and by the time she and her co-workers gathered in the large conference room, Jenny felt more in control.

"Wonder what's up?" That was Rick Caldwell, one of Kyle's best salespeople. He poured himself a cup of coffee and took his seat at the shiny conference table facing Jenny. "I mean besides the obvious."

Sales of the expensive condominiums ringing Hilton Head's newest golf course had hit a bit of a snag.

Rick stroked his mustache. "I can't understand it. The economy's good, and the population's aging and playing more golf. Hilton Head's been overbuilt, but hell, when hasn't it been?"

No one answered. People stirred their coffee or shuffled papers. Jenny finally spoke up. "Things will work out. I really think this slump is just a hiccup."

Rick gave her a thumbs-up. "Yeah, you're right. Not like me to be so down, and really, I do think with some more time, some more advertising in the bigger newspapers... Hell, maybe if Delane would stop being such a playboy in Charleston and pay a little more attention to what's going on down here—" He stopped abruptly.

"That's all right," Jenny said quickly. She looked around the room, and realized people were watching her while pretending not to. "Don't worry about it. I told you, Delane and I aren't seeing each other anymore." She swallowed. She was respected at the office, but she knew what people thought—she was a good manager, fair and organized, but a little cool, a little unapproachable. Even though she'd got used to it, the realization sometimes hurt.

One of the sales staff, an older man, cleared his throat. "I wish Delane didn't have so much on his plate. So many projects going forward so fast, we could use him here..."

There was some generalized grumbling, and Jenny was grateful she was no longer the center of attention. She checked her watch. Ten after ten. De-lane was late as usual. The conference room was glass on three sides, bright with a nice view. But the sun streaming in made it warm. That was the reason she had perspiration on her lip again. She took a quick swipe with her finger and her eye caught the portrait that hung on the one solid wall.

Delane Kyle, the youngest son of one of Charles-ton, South Carolina's, premier families. He'd appar-ently been considered a bit wild in his younger days, but when he'd come into his trust fund, he'd turned into quite a businessman, with holdings here and at Myrtle Beach to the north. Kyle Development, the company he'd founded, had grown very fast.

Delane Kyle was handsome in a lean, smooth kind of way.

Not like Mitch Oliver.

Jenny's mind conjured Mitch. He was not smooth. He was tall, with shoulders as wide as the island, and everything about him was big. Dark hair, a little shaggy, an emphatic wedge of a nose, a faint scar below his eye. Though his features were blunt, they were as regular as if they'd been carved by a sculp-tor who'd really known what he was doing. She pic-tured his unmanicured, competent-looking hands, that masculine, barest stubble of a dark beard—

For heaven's sake! She'd been thinking about Mitch Oliver for two weeks. Didn't she have enough on her plate without mooning over a man she barely knew? She pulled out the schedule of the week's sales presentations and made herself concentrate.

At ten twenty-five, Yvonne opened the door and

stuck her head in. "Sorry, folks. I just got word. Delane isn't coming."

There was some low-key grumbling before Yvonne continued, "His lawyer's here."

At that moment, Timothy Suddington stepped around Yvonne and into the room.

The staff exchanged glances as Suddington went to stand directly in front of the portrait of Delane.

He plunked a briefcase down on the table, and an eerie kind of quiet settled over the room. "I think y'all know who I am," Suddington said. "You know that I handle Delane Kyle's legal work, both business and personal. This morning, Kyle Development filed for bankruptcy in the U.S. District Court, Bankruptcy Division, in Columbia, South Carolina."

There was silence. Hot shock ran through Jenny, and she pressed a quick hand to her lower belly.

Then everyone spoke at once.

"Hell, I knew we were down on sales but—"

"How can he be bankrupt? He's got a Ferrari and a yacht docked right here in Harbor Town—"

Jenny's thoughts were racing, but she managed to put up a hand. "Wait, everybody. Wait, this can't be as bad as it sounds—"

"Easy for you to say," one of the women said. "You don't have a kid to watch out for."

This isn't the time for another trip to the bathroom! Jenny told her stomach firmly. "Nobody's said anything about our jobs. Tim, you need to tell us more. I happen to know Delane came into his trust a few years ago. It was a lot of money."

They were all looking at Timothy Suddington now. He said, "Jenny, you know I can't talk too much about Delane's personal matters. I'm his lawyer. Just his lawyer." He looked genuinely sorry to be fulfilling that role today, and in that second, Jenny realized that any money Delane had had was gone.

She pressed a protective hand to her stomach again.

Suddington made a fist, brought it down lightly on his briefcase. "I'm sure you all know that appearances can be very deceiving. Delane—with good intentions—tried to play with the big boys. He expanded Kyle Development too quickly. The business was fundamentally sound, but no matter how hard he tried, Delane had cash-flow problems—"

"Skip the bullshit." It was Rick, the man who had been concerned about sales. "What's happening here?"

"The office will close at four today. Please make sure that when you clean out your desks, you take your personal belongings home. Anything left here at the close of business today will be tagged and taken by the court as a business asset."

There was a roaring sound in Jenny's ears. She managed to say, "At least I have the payroll checks done."

Suddington said, "I'm sorry, Jenny. You can't distribute those checks. I'm sure if there are any assets, the bankruptcy court will eventually see that everyone's paid—"

Dear God, the man was saying they couldn't even

meet the last two weeks' payroll. As the reality of that sunk in, people gasped. One of the women started to cry.

Jenny felt like weeping, too. She had a big mortgage and a baby on the way.

Emotions zoomed through her: anger, fear, determination, fear, fear, fear. Shame again—after all her work and planning, she was out of a job! Then for a second, she felt hysterical laughter well in her, and she fought the sensation down, scared anew at how out of control she was.

It was a good thing after all that she'd let Crystal go with Mitch Oliver. At least he could give the little girl a place to live. Which was more than Jenny might be able to do.

WHEN CRYSTAL GOT HOME from school, she saw that Jason was in his room. Jason wasn't as big as the other boys. And he was pretty nice except he didn't like it when her cat sat on his desk and looked at his hamster. He always said, "That cat looks hungry. Get that cat outta my room."

But the kitten wasn't around today. Crystal thought maybe she was hiding from Face-off again. So maybe it was okay to look in Jason's room now, and see his hamster. She really liked Nosy. Nosy had eyes like shiny black beads and fur that was very soft. Jason let her pet him sometimes.

She stopped in the doorway to see if Jason would ask her to come in. All the boys went in and out of each other's rooms, but she didn't know if she should. Her momma always said to knock, but here if the door was shut and you knocked, the door would probably come open just from your knocking. Most of them were busted.

She stopped in the doorway. Jason was sitting there looking at the computer real hard. Then he looked up at her and said, "Whatcha looking at?"

That was just his way of talking. Crystal said, "Can I see Nosy?"

"So, like what's stopping you?"

She came into his room. Jason was kind of her friend. Uncle Mitch was nice, he let her call Miss Jenny every night. Crystal was happy to call Miss Jenny, but sad too because she didn't know when she'd get to see her again. Miss Jenny had said Crystal had to come here and Mrs. Winters had said Crystal had to come here, and once, she heard Mrs. Winters telling Miss Jenny that the judge would say Crystal had to come here and live, and so she knew it didn't matter if she wanted to stay with Miss Jenny.

Uncle Mitch said maybe Miss Jenny could come for a visit some time. Crystal was happy and sad about that. She didn't want to cry when Miss Jenny left and she was pretty sure she would.

She was trying and trying not to cry about anything.

Besides, Uncle Mitch was nice, and when he came home from work at night he always asked her about what happened that day, just like her momma used to. It wasn't Uncle Mitch's fault that even if she felt like talking, one of the boys would talk first.

Luke was nice, too, but he played hockey and that

seemed to take a lot of time for a game. The twins were big and wild and she didn't like them at all. But that very first night when she came here, Jason had said, "My mom died, too, and I was sad," and then Crystal knew he would be her friend even though he was a boy.

Now she looked into Nosy's cage, but he wasn't running on his Ferris wheel or sniffing at his wood chips. He was just sitting there breathing. So she looked at Jason. "Are you doing your homework?"

"Nah, sending e-mail to my friend who lives in New York. I'm good on the computer. See, I'll show you."

Jason sounded like he was bragging, but she looked anyway. E-mail looked boring, not like the games they played on the computer at school, but when Jason said you could write things and send them and they got there in seconds, she changed her mind. It was neat how you could send stuff to your friends.

"See, this is the address line. It looks weird but it works. Want to try it?"

So Crystal tapped out the address and pushed the buttons that Jason told her to and then she pushed Send and Jason said in a second his message would be in New York.

"Hey, hey, hey! We're playing football. Come on, Squirt." Ryan was standing in the doorway with Tommy, and Tommy pushed him into the side of the door, but Ryan only laughed and punched him in the stomach. Squirt was what they called Jason.

Jason jumped up and bumped Crystal's chin real

hard and didn't even say he was sorry. Crystal said, "You hurt me."

"Oh. Sorry." For a second, he looked as if he'd forgotten she was there.

"Come on. We need another body to crush." That was Ryan, who was bigger and had blonder hair than Tommy, and a bigger nose, and that was how you could tell them apart. Because other than that, they acted the same. Two big boys who were always pushing each other.

"I'll whip your butts," Jason said, bragging again.

"Oh, did we say we were going to let you on a team?" Ryan laughed. "We're going to let you be the football, Squirt."

Jason said, "Cut the crap." *Crap* was a bad word, but nobody paid attention.

Jason grabbed his sweatshirt. When he pulled it over his head, it was like he noticed Crystal again. "Hey, guys. Remember what Dad said. We gotta be nice to our cousin." Then Jason looked at her and said, "Do you want to play? We'll go easy on you."

Crystal couldn't believe that. Nobody wanted to play with her here, not even Jason. Her chest kind of pounded. They wanted her to play. But they were all so big and football was rough. She said, "I don't know how to."

"We'll do touch. No tackling. We'll go easy and then when you get tired and quit we'll do tackle."

"But I'll get knocked down."

"She'll get knocked do...wn," Ryan said in this

voice that made fun of the way she talked, and then he and Tommy laughed.

All of a sudden, Crystal couldn't stand it. She said, "Cut the crap." Her face went hot but it felt good because Ryan and Tommy stopped wiggling and they all stared at her. She knew her momma would be mad that she'd said a bad word, and Miss Jenny wouldn't like it, either. But her momma was in heaven, and Miss Jenny was in Hilton Head, and Crystal was in Ohio, and even the judge said she had to live here.

It seemed like a long time that they stared at her, and Crystal felt so funny with them looking at her that she almost took it back. But she didn't.

Tommy finally said, "Well, okay, you can be on Squirt's team."

They went downstairs, and Jason said stuff like it's not fair to have the big kids against the little kids, but it didn't seem to really bother him a lot. When they got out in the yard, Jason said, "Tommy, you're on Crystal's team." Tommy came right over to Crystal. She couldn't believe it.

Tommy stood behind her and held her arms and showed her how to hold the football. The football was big and hard. Then Tommy showed her how to pass the football. He stepped away and Crystal tried it. The football went up sorta high and then it squiggled and fell down not very far from her. The boys laughed. Crystal thought about saying cut the crap again, but decided once a day was enough.

They told her the rules, which didn't make sense. But that almost didn't matter—now they weren't laughing at her any more and they were playing with her. She felt better than she had since she came here. The sun was shining even though it was cold, and the sunshine felt good, making the top of her head warm.

Ryan and Jason went into what they called a huddle, and then Ryan came running. Before Crystal could blink her eyes, Tommy had touched him, which was a tackle when you played touch football. Well, Tommy did more than touch—he grabbed Ryan on the arm and twirled him around.

Football was rough.

They played some more. Once Crystal got the football and she held it to her stomach even though it was covered in mud, and ran as fast as she could. It took a long time until Jason touched her and she had to stop. That felt good, especially when Tommy said, "All *right,* kid. You gained us some yards."

Then the football was up in the air, and it was spinning, spinning down toward her. Tommy yelled, "Catch it," and Crystal held up her arms.

Wham!

Something hit her hard in the shoulder. She fell and went skidding along the stiff, frozen grass. She finally stopped and was lying on her side, her cheek in the grass, staring across the yard.

All these feet were coming toward her. Big feet, running.

"Are you okay?"

"Are you all right?"

"Hey, kid, are you hurt?"

She sat up, though she felt weird, like shaky inside.

Tommy was looking down at her. "Ryan hit you."

"Well, I was trying to get the ball, you dork. Not hit the kid."

Jason got down by her. "Are you hurt?"

She looked where he was looking, and saw that the sleeve of her sweatshirt had come up and her arm was all full of cuts. When she touched them, they hurt.

"Oh, man, Dad's gonna be pissed this time." Ryan stood there, and he was shaking his head at Tommy. "You knew she was too little to play football. How could you have been such an idiot?"

"Well, you wanted to play, too." They went on arguing, and Jason said what Ryan said, that his dad would maybe get mad. Crystal just sat there on that horrible rough grass in the cold. All she wanted in the world was to be back home.

"She's not hurt that bad," Jason said, pushing at her arm and making it hurt more. "See? She can bend her elbow." He bent it back and forth.

They all looked at her, all those big boys, and she thought of saying cut the crap again, but she didn't feel as though she could right now because it was so hard not to cry.

"I want my momma," she said instead, and her voice didn't sound like it had when she'd said cut the crap. Now it sounded tiny.

"Listen." Jason got down beside her. "You aren't hurt that bad. We were only playing. The thing is, we might get in trouble if you tell Dad.'' He stopped for a second. ''You don't want us to get in trouble, do you?''

She didn't care. She wanted her momma. She wanted Miss Jenny!

Tommy got down by Jason, and he had this kind of frown on his face. ''Jason's right, kid. There are things Dad doesn't have to know, and we don't rat on each other. We just get even when we can. If you live here, you've got to learn the rules.''

That was a bad rule. ''He'll find out. My sweat-shirt is all torn.'' She was *not* going to let them see her cry!

''Nah,'' Ryan said. ''Just throw it out. Dad'll never notice.''

That was maybe true; some lady came in and washed the clothes and put them away. But Crystal didn't know what to do. If she told Uncle Mitch, he would maybe get mad, and she didn't know what he'd do if he got mad. He was big; she didn't want to find out. Would he maybe blame her for playing with the boys? Or would he be mad at the boys, and then they'd get even with her?

She looked down at her arm, and now the most terrible thing was happening. The red scratches were starting to bleed. Did that mean she was really hurt?

She started crying, and she jumped up and ran to the house. They followed her, so she ran up to her room and shut the door. Her door shut fine. The boys stayed outside the door, calling to her, but she sat on the bed and watched her arm bleed. Finally she said, ''Go away! I won't tell!'' and after a while they went away. In a few minutes, she looked out the window and saw them out in the pasture by the ponies. Face-off was out there, and she saw her kitten sneaking around the bushes.

She felt so alone. Everything was quiet, and she didn't think it had been quiet since she got here. She almost wished the boys were still outside her door. She touched her arm and blood came off on her finger.

That scared her, and she went down the hall to the phone and tried to call Miss Jenny even though she always called Miss Jenny at night before she went to bed. Nobody answered, and her arm kept bleeding. Wasn't it supposed to stop?

Her momma had been in a car wreck and been so hurt she died.

Something squeezed her in the chest then, and she started crying harder and tried to think what to do.

Miss Jenny would come and get her. She just knew it, and if Uncle Mitch and the judge knew that she was almost dying they would let her go home, wouldn't they? If she could just talk to Miss Jenny!

Then she had an idea. She went down to the kitchen and got this piece of paper off of Uncle Mitch's desk. The paper was Miss Jenny's paper from work. It had her address on it, and then some stuff at the bottom that had never made sense until today. Now she looked at it again. Just what she thought. It was an address like Jason's friend had.

She took the paper and went to Jason's room. His computer was still on. She did everything he'd told her to do. She thought about how e-mail was kind of like magic, and she wished you could send e-mails to heaven. But instead, when the square came up, she carefully typed in Miss Jenny's address. Then it got to the part where you could write the message.

Mis Jenny they hurt me. im bleeeding From Crystal.

Then she found the Send button and pushed.

CHAPTER THREE

MITCH WAS running late again. He had an eight-thirty appointment this morning with one of the high-school coaches to discuss the possibility of Serious Gear supplying all the sporting equipment for next year's football program. Setting the meeting so early this morning had seemed like a good idea when the guy had called yesterday. Mitch had figured to get a jump start on the day, make a good sale before he'd even opened for business.

But last night, he'd been out until after 2:00 a.m., working on Luke's slap shot and helping Luke's minor league team, the Northern Lights, with practice.

Now he stood in his kitchen and raked a hand through his hair and tried to shut out the sounds of his kids. They were arguing again—or goofing around—who could tell the difference?

"Gotcha, Squirt." Ryan put another Froot Loop on his spoon and flicked it at Jason. The bit of cereal hit Jason on the nose.

"I'm gonna get you for that." Jason jumped off the counter stool and grabbed the open box of cereal. Dancing away, he held the box out temptingly, then snatched it to his chest when Ryan made a grab. "I've got the ammo."

Ryan dodged Tommy, who was going to the refrigerator for another gallon of milk. Ryan grabbed Jason by the shoulder and swung the younger boy around. Jason kept up the taunts.

Mitch had finally had enough. "Cut it out," he said at the same time Luke said, "Quit that." Mitch looked up from where he was loading the dishwasher and shrugged at his eldest son as Jason and Ryan kept at it. Neither Mitch nor Luke were big on mornings; too many late-night practices at the rink had done in mornings long ago.

The kitchen floor was sticky; Mitch had felt it on his bare feet. The kids must have spilled milk again. Someone must have turned down the furnace; the air in the house felt chilly on his bare chest.

Weren't millionaires supposed to live better than this?

Jason was still teasing Ryan. When Jason's elbow hit Tommy's cereal bowl and sent the empty bowl skidding across the counter, Mitch finally said, "That's enough!" He marched over and held out his hand for the cereal box.

"Aw, Dad, I was finally getting to him," Jason pleaded. Face-off was begging at his feet. Face-off loved Froot Loops.

Mitch ruffled the hair on his youngest. "You'll get him next time."

Ryan did a sneak attack and grabbed the box. Cereal flew. Face-off gleefully chased the windfall. Crystal's kitten—which had been observing the shenanigans from the safety of a chair back—puffed out her tail and took off.

Mitch turned to Ryan. "Give me the box. Now." After a couple of moments to see if Mitch really meant it—*why* did they always do that?—Ryan finally handed it over.

He peered inside. "You guys are done here. You've eaten your way clean through two boxes, and you're going to be late for the bus. Luke doesn't have time to drive you, and neither do I." Absently, he scooped up the crumbs of cereal from the bottom of the box and fed them to Face-off, who'd finished his vacuum routine and sat before Mitch with his big wet tongue hanging out. Then Mitch crumpled the box and tossed it toward the trash.

As he started for the stairs, it dawned on him that Crystal was missing. "Hey, where's Crystal?"

For a second, the boys, arguing about something, didn't seem to hear him. Then the room got very quiet.

Not a good sign. He looked at the boys, who were looking at each other.

Luke said quietly, "Okay, what happened?"

"Nothing."

"No clue."

"How would I know?"

They were looking everywhere but at Mitch or Luke. From the bottom of the steps, Mitch bellowed, "Crystal!" She didn't answer, and alarm ran through him. Before he even realized where he was going, he was halfway up the stairs.

She appeared at the top of the stairs. Slacks and a flowered sweater, a toothbrush in her hand.

He stopped dead. She looked so normal. "Are you all right?" he asked foolishly.

She nodded, but she had this fearful, pinched look on her face, the one she often got around him.

"Oh. I just wondered—" She was still looking at him. He said, "You're running late."

Her face crumpled. "I slept too long," she said in a small voice, and Mitch had the horrible thought that she was going to cry.

"That's—uh, okay." *Don't cry.* "Listen, I can drive you if you miss the bus."

"You're not mad? You yelled."

"I didn't yell at you."

"Yes, you did. I heard it from the bathroom. You yelled real loud. *Crys-tal.* I dropped the toothpaste." Her lower lip wobbled.

"That was to see if you were okay," he tried to explain. She didn't look convinced, and he didn't know what else to say—they seemed to have no conversation, no common ground at all, and she was so sensitive.

The doorbell rang.

Barking from Face-off, a call to the dog, the closing of the laundry-room door. Heavy, clumping feet heading for the hall. Then one of the boys called, "D—aaa—d."

He was so relieved to have a reason to escape his niece's scrutiny, he didn't even consider the oddity of someone at the door at eight in the morning. He turned and headed back down the stairs.

"It's some lady," Tommy called as Mitch passed the kitchen doorway on his way to the front hall.

He had an appointment with a woman who was applying for the job of full-time housekeeper, but that interview was supposed to be at the store later. The door was agape a fraction. He pulled it open.

Jenny Litton stood on his doorstep, a small carry-on bag in her hand.

He froze, his hand on the doorknob.

"Is she all right?"

He blinked. "Huh?"

She said impatiently, "Crystal. Just tell me, is she okay? What's wrong with her?"

"Nothing's wrong with Crystal." Hadn't he determined that not two minutes ago? *What in hell was Jenny Litton doing on his doorstep?*

"Was she in the emergency room? What did the doctor say?"

Her southern drawl was hurried. He realized belatedly that the woman looked white as a ghost, and that her eyes were round and intent. That previously smooth-as-glass hair of hers was in tumbled disarray. She was wearing a suit, but the jacket was unbuttoned, and a silky scarf had come loose from some mooring or other and fluttered in the breeze. She looked like a pale butterfly.

A pretty butterfly. A sexy butterfly, if butterflies could be sexy.

An angry butterfly.

She was so pretty. That made him suddenly conscious of the fact he was bare-chested and bleary-eyed, and that he needed a shave. Besides, he didn't have a clue what she was talking about.

"Please." She held out a hand. "I won't get you in trouble with the court. Just let me see her."

When he didn't immediately respond, Jenny seemed to make up her mind about something. Then she...charged him. She marched on him like a rookie defenseman, determined to send him flying into the boards. Stunned, he held open the door, certain that if he hadn't, she would have shoved him aside.

Once in the doorway, she called, "Crystal. Crystal!"

"Miss Jenny!"

There was clatter through the house. Commotion. Then his niece was in the hallway, running so fast she skidded on the hardwood floor.

Jenny dropped her bag and knelt and grabbed her, hugging hard. "Oh, my Lord, you're all right. Oh, my Lord..."

Mitch raised his eyes. All four of his sons were in the hallway now, and all of them were watching Jenny and Crystal. Jenny was rocking her, and there were tears on her cheeks. "Oh, sweet baby, I was worried sick. The phone was busy all night...I almost called the police... I caught the first plane I could... You're okay..."

There was something about the scene that gave Mitch a stab of pure guilt. "Of course she's okay," he said gruffly. "You didn't seriously think we'd hurt her, did you?"

She looked up at him, her blue eyes capturing his. "I didn't think so, but when I got her e-mail—"

"E-mail. Crystal sends you e-mail?"

Crystal looked up at him fearfully, but when she spoke, she sounded just a touch defiant. "You never said I couldn't send e-mail."

He stared at her.

"It was only because I thought I was dying," Crystal explained.

Dying?

He said, "Uh, Jenny, why don't you come in and we'll talk about this."

Even as she straightened, he saw Ryan and Tommy start to slink away. "*All* of us."

Before he could suggest the living room, which was the cleanest room in the house because nobody used it, Tommy motioned Jenny Litton into the kitchen.

He followed his sons, Crystal and Jenny, and then stood behind Jenny in the doorway. He was standing so close to her he could see the distinct colors of gold in her hair. Its disarray had exposed part of her neck. He saw the clasp of her pearls on skin that looked tender and white.

Quickly, he raised his eyes. That was a mistake, too, because he found himself seeing his kitchen through her eyes. A kitchen that probably horrified Miss-Perfect-Pearls. There was a scratching sound intermingled with whines as Face-off begged to be let out of the laundry room.

Six cupboard doors were open. Four bowls of milk were on the counter. Splashes everywhere. Errant Froot Loops. A crumpled cereal box. Two teaspoons, upside down in little puddles of milk. An empty cardboard box that had held last night's pizza—it was too big to fit in the trash can, so the boys always waited for him to carry it to the garage. Schoolbooks, backpacks on the table. Lunch fixings—peanut butter and an open jar of jelly, chips, yogurt—he'd learned that it was best to pack the kids' lunches the night before, but who could remember? One of the cords that held the draperies back on the big sliding doors in the eating area had come loose, and the draperies just…hung there on that side. When had that cord come undone?

Jenny moved into the kitchen, and any minute now those high heels of hers would hit the sticky patch…

He was going to mop the floor as soon as he had a chance. He was going to make the boys pick up after themselves. He really *was* going to make lunches the night before, from here on out.

But first he had to find out why Crystal had thought she was dying.

Jenny refused his offer to sit. He introduced her to the boys as a friend of Crystal's. They hovered around the fringes of the room like groupies hanging out at the locker room after a game, looking everywhere but at Jenny and Crystal.

Mitch lounged against the counter, a deceptively casual pose. "Okay," he said quietly. "Why did you think you were dying, Crystal?"

She took another look at Jenny, who squeezed her shoulders.

In a small voice, she told about the football game of the day before.

"It was touch," Ryan said quickly, and Mitch

made a slicing motion with his hand to cut his son off before he could explain further.

"It was touch," Crystal agreed. "But they touched real hard. They made me bleed. Then they made me promise not to tell. But before dinner, my arm stopped bleeding. I sort of forgot I sent the e-mail. But before I went to bed I wanted Miss Jenny to come. I want Miss Jenny to come before I go to bed every night."

That guilt came again, along with pressure in his chest. She still wanted Jenny to come and take her away? Crystal called her every night, but Mitch hadn't known she went to sleep wanting anybody other than her mom, and he couldn't bring back Kathy.

He raked a hand through his hair again. Where was that absolute certainty that he was doing the right thing that had gripped him all the way to South Carolina, the sensation that had gotten him through his sister's funeral and the decisions that followed?

"Let me see your arm," Jenny said in her slow southern drawl, a drawl that by its very slowness seemed comforting. She sat Crystal in a chair and knelt beside her as she carefully pulled up the girl's sleeve.

"It's scratched," she said in the same tone he imagined she'd use for "It's broken."

He peered down.

"It bled and bled," Crystal said earnestly. "Or I wouldn't bother Miss Jenny."

Jenny gave her hand a quick squeeze. "Sweetheart, you're never bothering me."

Mitch looked the boys over real good. "Okay, which one of you had the lamebrained idea of playing football with a little girl?"

"It was touch," someone said again.

"Touch or not, which one of you came up with this one?"

Tommy pointed at Ryan, Ryan pointed at Tommy. Mitch sighed and said, "I thought I told you to be nice."

Tommy said, "We were nice. It's how we're nice. We play with the Squirt, we play with the kid."

Mitch quelled the urge to throttle him. Then Jenny got a tight-lipped look about her that irritated him. He'd just bet that Miss Jenny Litton didn't like his kids any more than she liked *him*. In a flash, he went from wanting to throttle his sons to wanting to defend them in front of this judgmental woman. If she walked across that sticky spot on his floor and dared to say anything—

"Dad? There goes the bus." Luke, who'd been silent up till now, pointed out the window.

Damn. "Luke, can you drive the boys? I'll take Crystal to the elementary school before I head for the store. I've got a meeting there, but I'll ask the guy to reschedule. I won't be long," he said to Jenny. "Then I can come back and we'll talk."

She seemed to perk up a little at that. He tried not to sigh. His experience with women was limited, but he remembered how Anne had always liked to talk about stuff like this. He went up to grab a sweater, deciding he'd have to shave when he got home. He swiped a hand across his chin and felt the stubble there. Great. He sure hated mornings.

When he got back downstairs, Jenny was helping Crystal into her coat. "Will you be here when I get home from school?" Crystal asked Jenny, her eyes bright with hope.

Jenny looked up at Mitch. He nodded.

"Sure. You bet I'll be here." Crystal threw her arms around Jenny's waist, and Jenny bent and hugged her tight, before releasing her to Mitch.

"Can you manage to get her to school in one piece, or would that be too much to ask?" she whispered as he was walking out the door.

"The boys were just playing." But he shut up after that. He understood that she was upset. The e-mail must have really scared her. "I'll be back in a few minutes. Oh, by the way, don't open the door to the laundry room. The dog's in there. He'll probably just go to sleep."

As he turned the key in the Jeep, he thought of how Jenny looked, pretty and fragile. But that was deceptive. She had a will and a mouth to follow up on that will. He was going to have to do some real smooth talking.

He frowned and looked in the rearview mirror at Crystal. She was sitting in the back seat, and she was smiling a little, looking out the window.

When had he last seen her smile? Not since she'd left South Carolina, he realized.

JENNY THOUGHT briefly about trying to create some order in this kitchen, but quickly changed her mind.

Cleaning up here would be…presumptuous, not that she guessed that would be a word they'd use in this house. Not that she'd bet Mitch would even notice. He hadn't even noticed that Crystal had cut herself playing football. Football! So what if he hadn't been home? He should have seen that Crystal was upset when he'd got back last night.

She looked around the kitchen. What had they had here, anyway? A food fight?

She was still fuming about Crystal, about the scare that had brought Jenny halfway across the country without much more than the clothes she wore. She picked up a sponge and squirted some soap on it, then began to attack the kitchen counter with short, vehement strokes. She was probably going to ruin her nails on his kitchen counter. *And* her stomach was doing the usual morning flip-flops.

And she couldn't stop thinking about a certain man's bare chest, those clearly defined muscles, the dark hair that glistened and curled, about the goose bumps on all that bare skin. He looked so…physical. *Male.*

Not her type, of course.

Her sponge knocked a piece of cereal off the counter. Glad for the diversion, she picked it up and threw it into the disposal.

Over the past two weeks, she'd tried to picture Mitch Oliver's house. He'd described it to Crystal. *An old farmhouse that's been added on to a lot.* She'd had her own mental picture of that house—white and meticulously cared for, a green roof and shutters, kind of like the houses rich people had in the Hamptons. Pretentiously unpretentious.

Jenny's mother had been a maid in a house that was pretentious, a little Tara, big white pillars and all. It was fake, just as these rambling farmhouses were fake in their own way.

Fake, she told herself. Fake.

She hadn't had a really good look at the outside of Mitch's house. She'd been too worried about Crystal, too afraid that she'd miss the turn, that the directions she'd got at the gas station were wrong.

But she'd got a bit of a look. The house was big, and it was white, and the green shutters were surely there. But there was something so *un*pretentious about it that it hadn't registered until now that Mitch's house appeared to be the genuine article— a big old farmhouse.

Okay, it wasn't pretentious. But it was a mess. Why would someone with all his money want to live like this? She forced herself to stop picking up bits of cereal. Let him clean his own kitchen.

She tossed the sponge into the sink and took a look around. It was very odd, being alone in a house of a man she hardly knew. There was a hush. The dog in the laundry room must be sleeping; she didn't hear so much as a sigh.

A few of Mitch's cabinet doors were open; she closed them. She wandered into the family room, tucking the breakfast-room curtain into place as she went.

The house had good bones. In the family room, there was a big stone fireplace that took up most of the end wall. Built-in bookshelves stood on either side of it, but there weren't many books there. Instead, there were photographs, and there were lots of trophies. The big hockey star was obviously proud of his trophies and not much of a reader. There was a big-screen television, some comfortable leather chairs, a set of barbells askew on the floor in front of the fireplace. The whole place needed a good dusting.

She saw open French doors to her left, and a lot of sunlight shining through them. She wandered over and stood in the doorway looking in. It was a huge room, modern and light, apparently new. Various exercise machines—expensive, professional-looking models, were arranged in front of floor-to-ceiling mirrors. There was a weight bench and even more weights. At the rear, a wall of sliding glass doors led to a deck and hot tub. Beyond the deck, a lawn, white with frost, sloped down to a pond, which was brilliant blue in the early-morning sunshine.

Well. Mitch's house might be messier than she'd expected, but it was expensively fitted just the same, and those trophies—and this room—showed plenty of ego.

Just because some judge put blood and money over love, Mitch had been given the opportunity to raise Crystal…and he was making a mess of it.

She heard an automatic garage door opening. Finally. She heard him open the outside door, then a friendly whine of the dog. When he opened the door to the kitchen, she was already walking back to meet him there.

He was leaning down, with a big hand on the collar of the dog...horse. The animal strained, whined again, looked at her. Mitch said, "I guess this is as good a time as any to meet Face-off." He nodded toward the dog.

"Okay." She stopped in her tracks, her gaze riveted on the dog. She swallowed. "I don't think I've ever seen a dog that big." *Crystal, you poor thing, having to deal with this beast, on top of everything else!*

Mitch's head was bowed. One hand still held the dog's collar, another scratched behind its ears. The dog quieted some, but still eyed her. "He's big, but he's gentle. He's never growled at the kids, let alone bitten anyone." The scratching continued, big, competent hands, blunt fingertips buried in the dog's glossy fur.

"Well, as long as he doesn't bite," she said uncertainly, taking a few cautious steps forward. "But if he doesn't bite, why do you have that death grip on his collar?"

She was almost upon him, so close she could smell the sharp cold that radiated off his leather jacket. He looked up, and she found herself staring into his eyes.

Brown eyes. She remembered those eyes. As deep and rich as dark, polished wood, set in that arresting face of strong features. She looked away quickly.

Mitch said, "Face-off doesn't bite, but he doesn't

seem to know how big he is, either. If he gets the chance, he'll knock you down and lick your face.''

She shuddered, and he gave her an odd look. ''You don't like dogs?''

''Well, I've never owned one.''

She was close now, and she could see the weave of Mitch's sweater, revealed in the open vee of his partially unzipped jacket, and her traitorous mind conjured that bare chest. Quickly, she bent toward the dog, put out her hand. The dog made her nervous. That's why her stomach was doing *double* flip-flops now.

Mitch said, ''Every kid should have a dog.''

''Oh, I don't know.'' She gave Face-off a tentative pat. At the contact, the dog quivered, sniffed. She forced herself to pat his head again. Her hand was close to Mitch's now. Oh, yes, the dog was making her nervous, all right. ''Dogs are so messy.''

''Messy is okay sometimes.''

I guess you'd know.

She continued to pat Face-off. Slowly, Mitch relaxed his grip. The dog started to surge; she jerked back. Mitch pulled him back in line.

Face-off submitted to the restraint. But he looked up at her with a droll expression on his face, as if ready to make friends in the only way he was permitted, given Mitch's hand on his collar. His tongue came out, pink and wet and soft-looking, and something in Jenny went suddenly, unexpectedly soft in response. The tongue looked twice as wide as his face; despite her unsettled stomach and the close proximity of a very large, attractive man, that lolling tongue was suddenly comical. She looked down into the dog's round, friendly eyes. "Is that dog..." She hesitated. "Is that dog *smiling* at me?"

Mitch looked up, obviously startled. "You see it, huh? It's the weirdest thing, a dog smiling, but he does. When we were looking around at the shelter for a pup, I didn't really want this one—I knew with those paws, he was going to be huge. But he smiled at the kids, and that was all it took for them to want him, so..." His eyes met hers, and he was suddenly grinning.

Oh, he had a great smile, sure and confident, with strong, square white teeth. It set off the regularity of his features, sent lines arcing from the corners of his eyes. Caught by that grin, she started to smile back. Another little skitter of nerves, of awareness of his closeness, brought her up short. "We need to talk about Crystal," she said quickly.

"Sure. Right." Mitch's smile disappeared. "Let me lock up Face-off again."

"If you don't mind." The animal might be smiling, but she didn't need paws on her good silk blouse.

He put the dog in the laundry room, and Jenny quickly recovered her composure.

He came back into the kitchen. "Okay, time to talk. Would you like to sit down? Would you like a cup of coffee? Hey, how about some breakfast? I bet you didn't have breakfast, and if the kids have left any cereal, or eggs, I could take a stab at frying a couple of eggs—"

Even the thought of something frying in the

morning was enough to send her looking for the bathroom. "Thank you, but I'm fine."

It occurred to her that Mitch might be nervous, too. But he had little reason to be. He had Crystal, and this incident, bad as it had been, would be hard to prove. The girl's e-mail had arrived at Kyle Development yesterday, a few hours before the door had been shut on orders of the bankruptcy court. Lord only knew where her computer had gone. Besides, she was pretty sure this one incident wouldn't be enough to get a judge to change custody.

"Would you like to sit here or in the family room?" Mitch asked now.

Was he stalling? "Here's fine," she replied.

"Oh, okay, now about that coffee..." His voice trailed off as he stood in the kitchen, looking around with a slightly bewildered expression on his face. "Did you clean up?"

"A little."

He frowned. "You didn't need to do that."

"Somebody needed to."

The frown got deeper. "I was going to handle it."

She felt her eyebrow rising.

He noticed. "Okay, we'll skip the coffee and get right to it." He came over to the table and took the chair opposite hers. "You've obviously got your back up about this. I understand you were upset, and I know the trip up here isn't easy—I just made it myself two weeks ago. I feel bad you felt you had to come, and I sure wish Tommy hadn't left the phone off the hook all night long, or you could've called, and a five-minute conversation would have taken care of everything.''

His voice picked up speed. ''The kitchen was a mess this morning. But we weren't expecting visitors.'' His back was straight, his broad chest rising above the table, his hands resting, palms down, on the surface.

She was very aware of him, but she forced herself to respond calmly. ''It's none of my business how you live, except that it has an impact on Crystal.'' Her own voice was crisper than his. His had had a sort of reasonable, aw-shucks quality to it, as if he was inviting her to make light of what was a very serious situation. ''This is a very serious situation,'' she told him. She sounded good and prim, just like her mother, but good and prim was called for in a…serious situation like this.

A line formed between his eyes.

''I don't think the kitchen was actually unsanitary, but added to the real problem here—''

''Crystal is okay,'' he said quickly.

''This time, but that's not the point. There are, as I see it, two points here. First, that the boys were too rough with her. Either they haven't been told what the rules are for playing with a little girl, or they disobeyed them.''

He started to speak, but she lifted a hand and cut him off. ''The other issue is more important. How is it Crystal got that upset and you didn't know about it? She's just lost her mother. She's scared and vulnerable. Are you talking to her?''

''I talk to her.''

"Then how come you didn't know that she was this upset? She was bleeding, she felt bad enough to send me an e-mail, of all things, and you didn't even know about it."

He got up abruptly. The chair skidded hard on the floor. He turned and walked a couple of paces toward the window. Instead of looking out, he turned to face her. She realized again just how tall he was.

"Look." He shoved a hand into the pocket of his jeans. "It happened after school yesterday. Like most people, I work in the afternoons. It's no different than if she got hurt after school and you were at work. It was such a nothing incident that she'd forgotten about it by the time I got home last night. She ate dinner, she did her homework, she didn't mention a thing. I'm not a mind reader."

"Was she quieter than usual?"

"Crystal's always quiet."

No, she wasn't. Crystal was a chatterer. She chatted about Barbie and books, about the sunshine and the smell of a hot screen door after a rain, about lightning bugs and princesses with diamond tiaras. "Oh, Mitch," Jenny said softly.

She saw him take in a breath before he turned quickly toward the window. In the little silence that followed, he noticed where she had replaced the drapery. His hand ran along the tieback in a gesture that seemed oddly vulnerable. And that vulnerability mixed her all up inside. One part of her wanted him uncaring, unfeeling, so that she'd have to find some way to take Crystal back with her.

She shook her head to clear her thoughts. Mitch

wasn't about to give up the child, so Jenny had to set him straight. "You've got to be talking with her. You've got to try to understand her, give her a chance to express herself. You work, but you've got to make time for her, you've got to make sure the boys aren't making so much noise that you can't check on her." Her voice started to shake. "You owe her that, after bringing her here and changing her life, and if you can't see that, or if you can't handle that—"

"I'll handle it. I *am* handling it." His grip tightened on the tieback. "This whole thing has been blown way out of proportion. The kids didn't mean anything. Crystal will adjust, she'll see that the kids just play a little rough."

She heard the conviction in his voice, and she was puzzled. He had everything money could buy, he had three teenagers and a younger son, a life that might be easy materially but was hard in other ways. Surely he didn't need a little girl.

What drove him to insist on claiming Crystal? Despite herself, she couldn't help admiring his unexpected commitment when it came to Crystal.

He turned from the window and shrugged, as if he hadn't been white-knuckled on that tieback after all. "If it would make you feel better, why don't you stay a few days?"

"If that would make *me* feel better."

"Yeah." He put a hand back in his pocket, a casual pose again. "I don't think this is a big deal. But you do, so why don't you stay a few days and look us over? Maybe you'll see we aren't that bad."

Everything about this place was that bad. Worst of all was that she was so conscious of him as a man. Conscious in a way she didn't remember feeling about Delane, or even about her first love as a teenager. That puzzled her, too. She'd always been attracted to the smoothly handsome type, the kind who knew how to dress and what wine to order. She had a feeling Mitch would be happiest with a beer.

He gave her a grin and said, "After all, we've got a dog that smiles, so how could we be that bad?"

He paused, but before she could speak, he added, "You could spend time with Crystal. I know she'd really like it if you stayed. I realize you have a job with a lot of responsibility, but maybe you could get a few days off, now that you're up here."

She decided she didn't want to tell him she was out of a job. "Sure. I could set things up. While I'm at it, if I could use your telephone, I could make reservations at the nearest hotel."

That would cut into her suddenly constricted budget, but Mitch was right; she should stay. Crystal had been traumatized, whether he wanted to admit it or not. The social worker was supposed to be submitting her report, but Jenny would just as soon see with her own eyes how things were really going in this household.

Mitch said, "You could stay here."

"Here? At your house?"

"Why not? It's big enough. And there's the whole guest wing, with Crystal using only one of the bedrooms."

Somehow, she couldn't imagine staying in his

house. And he certainly couldn't want her here, toting up stray Froot Loops in order to be able to tell the judge what pigs the Oliver men were. What was his game?

But he was looking right at her, straight and sincere, and she thought maybe it was no game, that he wanted her here for the reason he'd told her: for Crystal. She had to admit that staying here would be better for her finances. Besides, if she wanted to, she *could* tote up the Froot Loops, in case this custody issue wasn't really settled after all.

"Thank you. I'll stay, perhaps for a week or so if that's all right."

He nodded, one graceful nod from a handsome, athletic man. He let out another long breath, and she found herself doing the same, as an odd sort of prickle went up her spine.

A quick vision formed, of him rumpled and sleepy-eyed, in his sweatpants and nothing else, goose bumps highlighting muscles that were toned and...sexy.

Did he look that way every morning?

As he'd said, the house was big...but perhaps not big enough.

CHAPTER FOUR

THAT NIGHT Mitch brought home fried chicken and coleslaw, and discovered Jenny had set the table already. "Jason helped me, showed me where everything was," she explained. "Crystal helped, too."

"You didn't have to do this."

"Well, I figured you wouldn't mind."

Wouldn't mind? He sure didn't mind. When was the last time he'd come home to find the table set? Really set, with the napkins folded, with a fork on the left, and a knife and spoon on the right, and glasses that all matched? Not very many times since Anne had died. They went to restaurants for things like that.

Jason said, "It wasn't that hard. I remembered where everything went." When they sat down to eat, Mitch noticed that the boys had better table manners than usual.

It made him feel a bit warmer toward the cool blonde who sat across from him, eating her fried chicken.

When dinner was over and the twins were loading the dishwasher, Jenny waylaid him on his way to the study, where he was taking the paperwork he'd brought home.

"It occurs to me," she said quietly, "that we didn't resolve one point this morning."

Mentally, he groaned, but he made sure to smile at her. "What point was that?" *Ma'am.*

"Are you going to punish the boys for playing so rough with Crystal?"

He kept up the smile, though it was hard. He pressed his back to the hallway wall. The hallway seemed narrower than usual. Everything seemed a little odd, a little different with a woman in the house.

"I talked to them. I told them not to play so rough with Crystal."

"And that's all you did?"

He nodded.

"You aren't going to discipline them?"

Discipline wasn't his strong suit, and he certainly didn't see the need for it in this case. "I don't think so."

She pursed her lips as prissy as could be. "It was fortunate that Crystal wasn't badly hurt, but it could be a whole lot worse next time."

"I talked to them, okay?"

"But some sort of consequences—"

He lost patience. "When did *you* get to be an expert on parenting?" Wrong approach, because her lips got tighter than ever.

"I've spent a lot of time with Crystal—"

"But you don't have kids."

There was a kind of charged silence. He felt bad, then, and added, "I know that not having kids doesn't mean you can't have an opinion, but believe me, I've learned in the past four years that parenting day in and day out gives you a whole different perspective.''

She spoke finally. ''You're right, of course. They're your children, and I'm only visiting. You know best.''

He felt an urge to explain. To tell her that his kids had been through too much for him to be a heavy-handed parent. He could have said that it was easier, too, to ruffle their hair, to throw an arm over their shoulders, to just love them the way she did Crystal. But he didn't. If she was going to judge him, he didn't owe her anything.

Instead, he said, ''Well, okay, if we've got all that straight, I'm going to the rink. I promised Luke's coach that I'd help with the drills. Tommy's in charge of the kids tonight.''

''I'll be here.'' But she said it a little timidly. As if being left with the boys was more than she'd bargained for. He winced as he heard a loud crash from the kitchen.

He made good his escape then, to the hockey rink, where it was definitely a man's world.

THE ZAMBONI CAME OUT and started circling the rink as slowly as a street cleaner, smoothing the ice after a full practice session of the Northern Lights. Though it was nearly midnight, a youth league of smaller boys would be playing soon.

Mitch sat on the bench and shoved his hands in his pockets. It was cold out here so close to the rink. Once upon a time, it hadn't been cold around a hockey rink. Once, he'd been so warmed by each ninety-second session of play that his hair had been soaking wet, and he'd trickled sweat under his arms and on the inside of his palms in their gloves.

Once, sitting with the other first liners on a bench like this had been all he'd ever wanted out of life.

"Hey, guy, how's it going?" The Northern Lights coach, Buddy Campbell, put a hand on Mitch's shoulder and squeezed lightly before flopping into the seat beside him. A little puff of air escaped him as he sat.

"It's going," Mitch said briefly. The Zamboni was finishing now, lumbering almost silently off the ice. Some of the younger boys—kids Jason's age, began to take the ice for their session.

"Can you sign this?" Mitch looked up. Most of the kids were used to seeing him here, but this one was new. A boy of about twelve was holding out his sleeve and a marker.

"Sure thing," Mitch said, signing his name on the kid's sleeve—the kid turned bright red and breathed *Wow*—and giving him a thwack on the shoulder.

The boy blushed again. "Thanks." He took off, over the boards instead of through the doorway, hitting the ice with a burst of speed that ended in an ice-churning dead stop.

"They never ask me for my autograph," Buddy grumbled good-naturedly. "I'm too damn old. Finished my career before most of these kids were born."

"Sooner or later we'll all be too old for these

young guys to remember." Regret pierced him. Five years ago he'd been well on his way to becoming a hockey legend. Then he would've been remembered.

That was the same time they'd discovered Anne's cancer, and there'd been no question about playing hockey. His family had needed him home. There had been a hardship clause in his contract. The team owners had argued, but legally he'd been able to leave.

After Anne's death, he'd longed to bury himself in the sport, pounding out his grief on the ice, numbing his sharp sadness with a fierce concentration on hockey, hockey, hockey. But there had been the boys to consider. He'd known the day she died that he wasn't returning.

If only he didn't miss the game so damn much! If only he hadn't lost them both.

"Dad?"

It was Luke, with his friend, David Chandler. Luke was the star shooter for the Lights; David was a talented defenseman. They'd grown up together playing on the ice on Mitch's pond. "Ready to go?" Mitch asked.

"Yeah, I guess," Luke said. He wandered over to the boards, watched the kids.

Mitch looked at his son's broad back, watched him concentrating on the practice. Mitch recognized the single-minded approach. Like father, like son. *Hope you never have to give up something you love, son.*

Abruptly, he stood. This was nuts. He had a good

life. He went with the flow. He had the kids. He had the store. It wasn't like him to question things so much; he'd done with that long ago. Somehow, though, the table Jenny had set tonight had conjured too many memories. She was very different from Anne, with her curvy body, her slow drawl…and her definite point of view. But she was a woman— definitely a woman—and that had him remembering.

He grabbed Luke's bag. "David! Luke!" he shouted. Luke turned from the boards, but David was over near the locker-room door, talking to a couple of young women who had turned out to watch practice. "You hungry? You want a burger?"

"Great."

"Sure."

Like big puppies they bounded over to him. They were always hungry. "Coach, want to come along?" Luke asked Buddy.

Buddy declined. About fifteen minutes later, Mitch and the boys were seated at a diner about halfway between the rink and the farm. It wasn't one of their usual places, but the waitress obviously recognized Mitch. She smiled shyly as she took their order, and even engaged in a bit of nervous flirting.

He noticed the flirting, though he pretended not to. As it was, the boys teased him when the waitress had gone back to the kitchen. "Whoo-ee, she likes you," David said in a stage whisper.

"Yeah, the over-fifty set really goes for Dad." Luke started to laugh, then to sputter on a mouthful of milk shake. David pounded him on the shoulder.

"Ain't hockey great?" David leaned back in the

booth. "Twelve on twelve saves at goal during practice and every wench you meet dying to get in
your…" He trailed off and winked at Luke.

A finger of alarm went up Mitch's spine. "I've
told you guys how to handle that."

Luke gave him a glance. "We know, Dad. 'The
fans. They only want one thing.'" He took a bite
of his burger.

Mitch leaned forward. "I'm not talking about fans
here. I'm talking about groupies. Those girls who
hang out after the games." Since it had become
known that Luke and David had been signed to
teams in the National Hockey League, there were
almost always young women at the rink. "You can
recognize them by the way they dress, the way they
act."

David popped a French fry into his mouth and
said, "This is the part where you tell how one time
a woman sent you a fax with a picture of her pant-
ies."

Guess he'd told that story one too many times.
"You've heard it before, but do you listen to it?"

Luke shot an amused glance at David. "I don't
need the lecture, but *he* does, don't you, pal? I mean,
Robin's got the hots for you, big time, Davey, and
I don't see you exactly resisting."

Mitch put down his cup. He'd seen Robin Donovan around the rink. She also worked for Mitch at
the store after school. She was a year younger than
David's nineteen, still in high school, but there
wasn't much girlish about her. She was moody and
starstruck, and he hadn't missed the tightness of the

clothes she wore to the rink. Or her attentions to David. The pats on the rear, the curling, possessive arm around his waist, the fact that when the guys hung out she always seemed to be there.

"Be careful," he said to David, his eyes including Luke.

David wouldn't quite meet his eyes. "If you use something, you're being careful."

"Only if you use it *every* time. Let's face it, to some of these women, the life-style looks glamorous. And they know that if you have a career in the NHL, you'll earn good money." He looked at both boys. "If you're old enough to get involved, you're old enough to know the real score."

Mitch's eye caught the giant ring on his finger. It was his ring from when his NHL team—the Great Chicago Fire—had won the Stanley Cup six years ago. The ring was so huge it got in his way, but it was good for business. He'd forgotten to take it off tonight.

The big ring glinted. Of course, someday Luke or David might have one, and for all he knew—suspected, in fact—the ring was what attracted Robin Donovan. "David—you, too, Luke—you've got plenty of time. You haven't even been called up to the NHL yet, and believe me, your lives will change when you are. You'll practice more, travel more and the stakes will get higher than hell real fast."

Both kids were looking at him respectfully now. They always looked that way when he seemed to be warming up to tell Real Stories of His Days in Hockey.

But after David motioned the waitress over and asked for pie, he said, "Bet there are real babes in the NHL."

Luke punched David in the arm, and David laughed, a small, uneasy laugh. Despite their cockiness, the boys were just that—boys.

The waitress came by with the check. Blushing, she handed it to Mitch. "Mr. Oliver?" she asked tentatively. "Could you please sign this?" She handed him a paper napkin and a pen. "It's for my grandson."

"Sure." Mitch gave her a smile and held the pen poised. He asked for the name of her grandson, then wrote.

"Oh, thank you." She clutched the napkin to her chest. Her fingernails were bitten to the quick; her knuckles slightly swollen and damp; a chip of a diamond adorned her ring finger. "My Larry just loves to play."

"Does he play in a league?" Mitch inquired politely.

"Oh, no." Her fingers gripped the napkin harder. "He plays street hockey. I know that's not real hockey but—"

"The skills are the same," Luke cut in. Mitch knew that his oldest son—the most sensitive of his children—had picked up on what the woman really meant: hockey was a very expensive sport, and the family couldn't afford to have Larry play on a league.

"The skills are the same?" She looked at Mitch for confirmation. When he nodded, she said, "I'll tell him that. Thank you again, Mr. Oliver.'' She hurried off, and Mitch lost sight of her as she went around the counter.

There were fans and there were fans, and she was one of the ones who made being a hockey star pleasant indeed. All Mitch could do was hope that both the boys understood the difference between a fan and a groupie.

''HERE, LIKE THIS. Just a spoonful. Good. Drop it next to the other one,'' Jenny instructed Jason and Crystal, who had pulled up stools to the counter and were helping her cook. The job had taken twice as long today...and been twice as much fun.

Now Jenny watched as Jason and Crystal each scooped up about a tablespoon of mashed potatoes. Two heads bent over a casserole dish, and two freshly washed hands carefully eased a mound of mashed potatoes from the spoon to the proper place near the perimeter of the dish. They looked up, smiling.

Jenny beamed back. ''Y'all are going to make the best shepherd's pie from here to Savannah.'' She loved to cook, and over the course of the last three days had taken on the task of preparing the evening meal. If she didn't want pizza or take-out chicken every night, it was in her own interest to cook.

Besides, Crystal and Jason enjoyed helping her, and the twins wolfed down whatever she made with gratifying speed and in an even more gratifying quantity. She'd learned to triple each recipe.

Mitch often arrived home late and looking harried, and he was obviously pleased by her efforts. She'd gathered that he was trying to make his one store into a chain of sports superstores, but he was often bogged down in details. She wondered why a guy who was as rich as he must be would be working so hard. It didn't make sense.

The man was big; and he, too, liked to eat. But she wasn't cooking for him. Never mind that she couldn't help smiling whenever she saw him pile his plate or go back for seconds. Never mind that under the softly lit chandelier his dark hair glowed with inner fire, and that there were intriguing shadows under his bottom lip, and that his hands worked his silverware with a masculine deftness that always drew her eye. He made her nervous, but she couldn't help watching him, being aware of his every movement, his every word.

She wasn't cooking for him!

She took the empty pot of mashed potatoes from the kids. "My momma always said the way to a man's—a *person's* heart is through his stomach."

"What's that mean?" Crystal asked.

"It means," Jason said, "that if you want people to like you, you make them good stuff. Isn't that right, Miss Jenny?" He'd adopted Crystal's form of address.

"Sure is."

"I bet your mom was a good cook," Jason said.

"Yes, she was. She made the lightest biscuits in Crawford County, and the best sweet tea with mint. Mr. Talbot always said so."

"Who was he?"

"He was her employer. She was his maid."

"No kidding." Jason was looking at her with interest. "My dad is always looking for a maid. He can never find one, or if he finds one they hate Ryan or Tommy and quit. Dad says maids are a vanishing species."

"That's because nobody wants to do that kind of work anymore." A little tightness had begun to take hold in her throat. "They don't want to clean other people's houses and do their cooking. They want something better for themselves, to get ahead."

"But people do cook for other people. You make dinner for us," Jason pointed out.

Crystal took the spoon from him. "That's because she wants to, right, Miss Jenny?"

"Right, sweetheart. I do it because I want to." And in that instant, the tightness was gone.

Jason hung his head in a sudden and unaccustomed shyness. "My mom liked to cook for us, too."

"Did she?" Jenny asked gently. "I bet she was good at it like my momma."

"Well, she was real good, but she didn't make any herder's pie. But she made roast beef and pigs in a blanket. And she put mashed potatoes on the side of those instead of on top."

Jenny put out her hand, touched Jason's arm. "Would you like roast beef sometime or is that something you want to remember only your mother making?"

He hesitated. "It would be okay." He gave her a

smile. "If you made it, I could eat it and remember her."

"Good. We'll do it as soon as I can go to the market." He kept smiling at her, and there was a wistfulness there that tugged at her heart.

Crystal said, "My momma used to have Miss Jenny over to cook."

Jenny went to the sink and ran water into a mixing bowl. "That's not quite right. Your momma had me over, and I wanted to help. Sometimes you came over to my house. Your momma didn't have much time, and I never liked making a meal for only one person. Anyway, Jason, I met Crystal's momma because she lived in the same building I did, and we got to talking and she mentioned she didn't like to cook."

Jason said to Crystal, "Your mom didn't like to cook? How weird."

"Not everybody likes it," Jenny said quickly as she saw a little frown growing on Crystal's face.

"Yeah," Crystal said. "She didn't like to cook, but she liked to eat. On Saturdays when it was her turn, she bought a big pizza with extra pepperoni on it, and we watched videos."

"Cool," Jason said, and all was forgiven.

Jenny washed up, her mind on her own mother. Momma had had a hard life, but she'd done the best she could with her only child. "Learn to cook," she'd say. "Learn everything you can, whenever you get the chance. You always want to learn and do for yourself, even if we manage to get you to college."

It was a bold ambition, their shared drive to get Jenny to college. Sweetspring, South Carolina, was miles from any university, and no Litton in that town had ever even finished high school. So when Jenny had won a scholarship, no one had been happier than Momma. The scholarship hadn't covered everything. Both had worked and saved…and dreamed.

Jenny's eyes pricked with sudden tears. *Oh, Momma, would you have been proud if you could have seen me graduate from college.*

After college, she'd thought the bad years were behind her. Yet now she was out of a job, pregnant and staying at a hockey player's house in Ohio, of all places.

Life had thrown her a curve, but she was going to handle it. After all, getting out of Sweetspring and going to college was much harder than being a single mother. Momma wouldn't have liked the baby part, but then again, her momma would have figured out Delane Kyle with one shrewd glance; her eye for trash had been finely honed over the years.

By the time she'd met Delane, Jenny had had to rely on her own judgment, and she knew now that her longing for a child like Crystal had impaired that judgment. Well, Kathy had been a single mother, and she had coped, as Jenny would.

But Kathy had had a job.

The door from the laundry room crashed open and Tommy—no, Ryan—came in, followed by his twin, Face-off at their heels. They swept through the kitchen like blowing leaves, shedding as they went.

A coat on the chair, a dirty football on the buffet, a sweatshirt wadded up on the counter.

Jenny said, "Pick up the sweatshirt, please."

Tommy said, "Huh?" and bent to pick up the garment.

Ryan dipped a finger into her casserole and licked. "Wow, that's good."

"Thank you." Her back got straight. Ryan had complimented her, and the boys meant no harm, but they were always doing things like poking their fingers in her food. "I don't suppose you washed that hand."

"It's dirty?" Ryan ran an assessing gaze over his finger. "Yeah, I guess it's got gravy on it."

"My guess is that it was dirty before you stuck it in my casserole. You were playing football. From the condition of that ball—" She looked pointedly over at it "—I'm sure your hands could do with a wash." She couldn't help her sharpness. She liked kids. But did these two have to stomp all over like mules, and act as dumb as stumps about her efforts to get them to clean up?

Ryan and Tommy obviously caught her tone, which was a first. They stilled in their constant motion. They looked at her. From over by the table, Jason said, "You dork. Everybody knows you gotta wash up before you mess with food. Mom always made me."

"Is that so?" Defiantly, Ryan stuck his finger in her casserole again.

Jenny's temperature went from warm to simmer.

"What do you call this?" Ryan licked his finger again.

Crystal frowned at him. "It's shepherd's pie."

"Shepherd. What's it got in it? Sheep meat?"

"Lamb," Jenny said. "But in fact, this particular pie has beef in it."

Ryan said, "Oh, a little lamb died to make this casserole. A tiny, soft lambkins croaked so that we could eat."

"It's beef!" Jason said, slamming a knife down on the table.

"A lamb died?" Crystal looked alarmed.

"It's beef," Jenny said quickly.

"A cow then. That's what beef is, isn't it? Cow meat. Elsie the Cow had to die to make this dinner." Ryan looked right at Crystal.

Jenny's temperature abruptly went to boil. "You boys are going to stop it right now or you won't be eating this dinner!"

Ryan and Tommy gave her a *say what?* look. "I mean it. One more word and it won't be served to you. I may be a guest, but I made this and I guess I can say who gets to eat it!" Her hands were trembling.

There was a long, charged silence. Finally, Ryan said, "Hey, take a chill pill. We were only teasing."

"You're always teasing."

"Yeah." And so? he seemed to imply. He turned away without apology, a dislike of her evident in his retreating back.

The boys crashed and banged their way upstairs. Jason and Crystal finished setting the table and took off. The twins had spoiled the good mood in the kitchen. Jenny was going to have to talk to Mitch. He'd let things slide when the boys had hurt Crystal. But he couldn't do that forever; the kids needed some discipline.

It wasn't her business. She didn't need to get any more involved in this family. With his kids.

But Crystal was her business, wasn't she? Yes, Jenny would talk to Mitch tonight.

CHAPTER FIVE

THE HOUSE WAS finally quiet. All the kids except Luke were in bed, and Luke had come home from an early practice session and headed to his room. Mitch had the television down low and was sitting in his comfy recliner reading the business section of the newspaper.

Well, he was pretending to read.

But he was watching Jenny, who was reading a paperback in the chair across from him.

She'd been here four days, and this was the first time she'd joined him. Usually, she played with Crystal after dinner or helped with homework. Often Jason got help from her as well.

But as soon as the younger ones were in bed, she'd go to her room. In fact, she didn't pay much attention to him at all. He wasn't used to that from women, and it kept him off his game. He, in turn, didn't seem to know how to make conversation with her.

Yet tonight, instead of heading for her room at nine o'clock, she'd hung around.

He hadn't been able to read the newspaper. Hell, he hadn't been able to concentrate on TV, even the hockey scores. Instead, he'd watched her, her head bent over her book. He could see the sheen of her hair, the pristine line of white where it was parted. If he looked lower—well, her blouse was modest, but she was a well-built woman.

Her sense of...femaleness pervaded the room. He imagined he could smell her shampoo. She always wore earrings, he'd noticed. Little gold ones that glinted at her ears. He'd never thought of himself as the kind of guy who was big on earrings. But now he found himself irresistibly drawn to earrings.

It was pleasant to sit here like this. It was nice to have another adult around.

Hell, who was he kidding? It was nice to have a *female* around. It was nice to have *Jenny* around. And *nice* wasn't exactly the word for it, either.

Now she glanced up from her book and blushed when she caught him looking at her. She swallowed quickly and said, "I think we need to talk." The woman had cheeks as pink as cotton candy, a voice like honey and an expression like an old-lady schoolteacher.

Mentally, he groaned. "Talk. Well, okay, but I thought the quiet around here was rare and peaceful."

She held her book in her lap. "Yes, it was, but—" She bit her lip. "It's the boys."

His back tensed, and he sat up a little straighter. "What's up?"

"They—Tommy and Ryan, I mean, and especially Ryan—upset us all today after school."

"What happened?"

She told him about dirty footballs and dirty fingers, about the twins teasing Jason and Crystal. It didn't sound like too much, not from Ryan and Tommy. He said that.

Surprisingly, she agreed. ''I'm trying to get used to the teasing. I know they're just boys. But their meanness was inexcusable.''

He chuckled at that. ''All teasing is mean, when you think about it. Don't you remember kids teasing while you were growing up?''

''I hated it when—well, sure. I know it doesn't mean much.''

''Jason can give as good as he gets, and I bet even Crystal has been known to dish it out.''

She drew up her knees and folded her arms around them. She had a dainty gold watch on. There was something about her stillness that bothered him. ''Ryan and Tommy weren't rude to you, were they?'' he asked. Teasing the other kids was one thing, but he didn't want them upsetting Jenny.

If she got upset enough, she'd be out of here and on a plane to South Carolina, and for reasons he didn't care to examine, he didn't want her to go yet. She hadn't said exactly how long she'd be staying, and he'd been careful not to ask.

When she didn't answer, he stood. ''Jenny? Are the twins okay to you?''

''Sure. I can handle them.'' She bit her lip again, then stood, too. ''It's just the mess, Mitch. I'm not used to so much mess.''

''I'll try to hire a housekeeper again. I'll put another ad in the paper tomorrow.'' His eyes scanned the room, and he realized that it *was* messier than he'd realized.

She laid a hand on the back of her chair. "That's really only a partial solution, you know. Even a housekeeper can't clean unless people pick up first." She added, "Really, if you'd just have some rules—"

"I have rules."

"Well then, rules you actually enforce."

There wasn't much arguing with that, and Mitch knew it, so he focused on her tone. "You sure sound prissy when you talk like that."

He'd meant the comment to be teasing, to cajole her into lightening up, but it hadn't come out that way. Oh, hell, he'd hurt her. He could see it in her eyes. But she'd hurt *him* by being so critical of his kids. Besides, she *was* prissy.

"If you could just go with the flow sometimes," he suggested helpfully. "It works pretty well."

She still looked hurt. "That sounds like a lazy way to get through life."

"Yeah, well, it works when we don't have a housekeeper."

Even hurt and a little angry, she was pretty. He remembered how once in a while he and Anne would argue. Then they'd make up…and make love.

A spurt of something purely sexual went through him. He concentrated on quelling it.

"I'll talk to the boys," he promised.

She must've picked up on the reluctance in his tone, but instead of getting her back up, her voice softened. "It's just that I can't stay here forever.

Crystal is a feminine little girl, in the traditional sense, and I realize how she feels because I'm that kind of woman—''

He couldn't help it; he took a step toward her. *Feminine* was that most foreign of words, and it sounded…sexy. He stopped close to her chair, right in front of her, as a matter of fact. To cover the fact that he was nearly across the room—and had no idea why—he made a great show of fiddling with the TV and then shutting it off.

The room went quiet. He imagined he could hear her breathing. He looked down onto the top of her head.

He put his hands safely in his pockets. ''We're opposites, you know.'' *Opposites in more ways than one.*

She looked up at him. Her lips parted. ''I guess we are,'' she said. Was that a little breathlessness he heard in that sweet, so-southern voice?

''Opposites attract.'' *Whoa.* He hadn't meant to say that. He knew how to flirt, but he wasn't *flirting,* was he? Her eyes got round.

He quickly adopted a forced pose of ease, the kind of pose that had enabled him to give a good television interview. ''Sure. Opposites attract, but that hasn't happened in our case, has it? In fact, when you think about it, we don't really even get along.'' *Yeah, like getting along has anything to do with wanting to lean over and kiss her right on the lips. You want to kiss a woman who would like to take your niece away, a woman who doesn't even like your kids.*

He focused for a second on the blank television screen, telling himself he was acting worse than Luke and David around the groupies. That helped him get back his equilibrium.

"What you really need to do is learn more about us, what it means to be a guy, and then you'll understand that we don't mean any harm to Crystal." There. Safe ground again.

She gave a little nervous laugh. "I'm not sure I really want to understand all of you."

"It would be better if you did, then you could help Crystal—"

"I know, go with the flow."

"Right." He paused, thinking. "Hockey," he said decisively.

"What?"

"Hockey. You need to see a hockey game. You need to hang out with us, with the kids, and see a hockey game. It'll help you see what we're like, that we're just sports-minded, not a bunch of animals."

There were a few faint freckles scattered over the delicate skin under her eyes. Otherwise, her skin was flawless.

Don't look.

"Isn't hockey rough? You think a *hockey game* is going to make me understand you better?"

Her tone might have pissed him off. In fact, it did a little, but he found himself grinning at the thought of taking her to a hockey game, sitting beside her in the stands, explaining the plays. Hockey was the perfect sport, the perfect blending of head and muscle and heart.

And if she didn't like it, well, that'd take care of any attraction. He couldn't imagine being attracted to a woman who didn't like hockey.

JENNY COULDN'T SLEEP. She finally gave up. The floor was carpeted, but it was faintly chilly as she walked to the window and cracked the blinds.

Frost coated the outside edges of the window, and a cold draft sifted in around the old panes. A half-moon shone over the pond and fields. Haze hung close to the pond. The scene was black-and-white, indistinct and grainy, like an old movie. It looked cold out there. It *was* cold in here by the window. She shivered and hugged her arms.

Another good reason that she ought to go back to South Carolina.

It had been two hours since she'd sat downstairs with Mitch. Why had she done that, when she'd been careful to avoid being alone with him up until now?

She knew why. She was turned on by the man, and that was the long and short of it. Turned on by—of all things—muscles. Other women went for things like that. She herself looked beyond the physical, was attracted to men who liked books and stimulating conversation. Or used to be.

She was nearly two months pregnant. A baby machine, not a sexy woman. In fact, before coming to Ohio, she hadn't thought that much about sex at all.

And now she eyed biceps and forearms, remembered a big chest scattered with the darkest hair, and went dry in the mouth and damp in the palm. Mitch used the space around him so well. He was oddly graceful for such an athletic man, and that economy of movement, that was...well, sexy.

He, of course, thought she was prissy. Prissy! A guy word, if there ever was one. He thought of her as prissy, and she thought of him as sexy. The *S* word again!

It was hormones, she decided. By making a baby, her body had got a taste of what it could do, and now her hormones had turned her into the kind of woman who swooned over sports stars.

What she needed to do was concentrate on her baby.

She felt her belly, but there was nothing there yet. No gentle swelling, no swimming baby to give her a swift kick when she needed one. The baby didn't feel very real just yet, except when its mother was having the heaves in the morning. Except when her breasts got heavy and tender. Except when she was tired even though she'd done virtually nothing strenuous all day.

Except when she closed her eyes and dreamed, and once in a while got the most tantalizing glimpse of a baby girl.

She pressed a hand to her stomach again, and told her little girl that she would grow up strong and independent and happy.

If the baby's mother had the good sense to do what her own momma had taught her: rely on herself, and herself alone.

IT WAS CHILLY at the rink, especially since Mitch's tickets were for seats so close to the ice. Jenny juggled a wand of cotton candy in one hand—Crystal had asked her to hold it—and an icy paper cup of Coke in the other. Jason was on the other side of Crystal.

The twins had seen some girls they knew from school and taken off. Jenny was relieved. Since the incident in the kitchen, Ryan seldom missed a chance to be sarcastic, make fun of her accent or just make life a little bit harder for her.

Mitch was to her left. He was so big that her arm kept brushing his leather jacket, and even through her sweater the leather felt warm. She kept trying to pull away, but he kept shifting, something she'd never seen him do. Apparently he was having difficulty getting comfortable in these seats.

Before the game, Mitch had taken Crystal, Jason and Jenny to meet a few of the Northern Lights players. She'd been led past a group of envious-looking teenage girls into that most masculine of sanctums— the locker room. There Mitch had introduced her to Luke's friend, David Chandler. Both Luke and David had been giving interviews to the sports editor of the local paper. Afterward, Mitch took Luke aside for a short, quiet, intense conversation. Then Mitch, at the request of the coach, gave a short talk to the team about strategy.

Crystal and Jason had gotten bored and fidgeted, but Jenny found herself concentrating. She knew nothing about hockey, and the talk was too technical to follow, so she really wasn't thinking about the words. Instead, she'd found herself captivated by the man. He was brief, focused, obviously in his element. She was impressed by the way he kept the team's attention. She couldn't help watching his mouth as he spoke.

Now they were in the stands, and Mitch was trying—again—to explain the complexities of the game to her. All around her were fans. Guys with paper cups of beer, yelling, even though there was nothing yet to yell about. Eager teenage girls decked out in Lights colors, navy and white, with stars stenciled on their cheeks.

It wasn't that Jenny knew nothing about sports. She'd followed golf for a while. Delane had liked to play, and he'd taken her to the Family Circle Open when it had been held in Harbor Town. There it had been quiet and hushed and green and hot, and here it was navy and white and cold and anything but quiet.

And the thing that confused her, the thing that sent something scary shimmying down her spine, was the realization that—tonight at least—she liked noisy and cold better, and she feared it had something to do with the man beside her.

His voice was low and husky as he bent to say, "The other team will try to bully up on Luke, put at least two defensemen in his path, to stop him from scoring."

She nodded. He shifted, and his arm brushed hers again. She pulled away quickly.

Too quickly perhaps, because he stiffened a little. Now she was embarrassed. "I'm sorry. It's just that you're so big.'' Ouch, she hadn't meant to say that out loud.

He didn't answer, but scrunched up in the seat. He looked so uncomfortable that she felt worse. The arena was huge; couldn't they have given people a few more inches when they'd designed the seats? She tried to explain. ''It's just that the seats are so small, and you're so—'' Abruptly, she shut up, her cheeks heating.

After a few awkward moments of silence, Crystal asked for her cotton candy, and Jenny turned gratefully to the child with cheerful comments about the game, the arena, the excitement of the crowd. The distraction didn't help—she was more aware of the man beside her than the noise all around her.

Then a shout went up and people surged to their feet as one. The Northern Lights were coming out of the locker room and taking their places on the bench.

''I can't see! I can't see! Where's Luke?'' Crystal stood up on her chair and craned her neck. ''Oh, I see him. Number thirty-three. That's Luke!''

Jenny smiled at the girl's excitement. Crystal really liked Luke. Jenny herself liked the thoughtful young man, who seemed to go out of his way to be kind to Crystal.

Then the two teams were on the ice and Luke and the other team's forward got their sticks ready for a face-off. A blare of a siren, and the game had begun.

''Yes! He's got it!'' Next to her, Mitch surged to his feet and virtually carried Jenny with him.

She stood up next to him. "Where's the ball—the puck? I can't see it."

"Luke's got it, there he goes, oh yes, go for it son." Mitch's hands were clenched.

The crowd made noise, a low roar of anticipation.

Jenny finally spotted the puck, on the end of Luke's stick as he skated down the ice, faster and faster.

From out of nowhere, a defenseman blocked his path, and Luke sailed into him at about a hundred miles an hour. Both bodies slammed into the boards that lined the perimeter of the ice.

"Damn," Mitch muttered.

"Oh, my goodness," Jenny said. When the bodies untangled and Luke skated away, apparently unhurt, she let out a breath.

"He has pads on, Miss Jenny," Crystal said. "That's why he doesn't get hurt."

Jenny shot a look at Crystal. In her navy-and-white sweatshirt, with a wisp of cotton candy on her lip, the child looked happy.

Jenny started to relax, and found herself enjoying a few minutes of the game as Mitch explained strategy.

She tensed again when a fistfight broke out among the players on the ice. "Oh, my Lord." She held her hands to her cheeks as all around her the crowd cheered and called for blood.

"It's just intimidation," Mitch explained. "Number seventeen tried to muscle David out of the way, and the Lights have got to show they aren't going to be shoved around."

"Oh," she said weakly, not looking at the melee on the ice.

If horse racing was the sport of kings, she thought, hockey was the sport of cavemen.

But she had to admit it *was* fast and exciting, and after two rounds of pushing had been broken up by the referees—with no blood spilled after all—Jenny started to understand enough of the game to realize where the puck was most of the time. And once she did so, she found herself increasingly interested in what was happening on the ice. By the beginning of the second period, she was watching the game in earnest.

Luke was amazing. He was so graceful and so fast. He frequently had the other team scrambling to keep up. When he did a quick pivot around a threatening defenseman and put the puck between the goalie's legs to score his first goal, Jenny raised a fist and let out a cheer.

Mitch turned to look at her in surprise.

She'd been having fun. For the first time in a long time, she'd forgotten her troubles and her plans, and just had fun. Sheepishly she said, "Well, Luke did score a goal."

He grinned, a kind of boyish smile that flipped her insides. "Yeah, he did. That's good, but we've got to get more as insurance. Hockey's fast. You can have goals scored in a matter of seconds. This game's not over yet."

"Of course not."

She settled back down next to him. But her shout and his grin had changed something. He didn't seem to try so hard to squeeze into his seat. His arm brushed hers more often.

And she didn't pull away. She didn't shrink into her seat, either, or try to make conversation with Crystal on her other side.

Instead, she watched Mitch's son, and in full uniform and helmet, it wasn't hard to imagine that it was Mitch, himself, out there. She knew he'd been a major star, a great player. Now as she watched Luke dodge and pivot, she thought of Mitch's grace that seemed odd in so large a man. And when Luke came back to the bench and pulled off his helmet, she pictured another dark head…

Mitch's arm came out, rested casually on the back of her chair.

Oh, my Lord.

She found herself suddenly less interested in the game—though the score was now tied at two to two.

She told herself he wasn't putting his arm around her shoulders, only resting it on the back of the chair because his seat was so uncomfortable. He certainly would have no way of knowing her thoughts. She turned to look at Crystal and caught sight of his fingertips resting on the chair back.

She was drawn back to the game when a shout erupted from the stands. David smashed into the opposing team's player, and both went flying. The referee blew a whistle, and all play stopped. The loudspeakers blared with some rock tune as they waited. It was noisy, and Mitch had to lean toward her to explain what was happening.

He gestured with the hand resting on the back of

her seat. As he pointed, his arm came around her shoulders.

And stayed there.

She stole a glance his way. He was watching the ice. But the way he *didn't* look at her made her realize his nonchalance was fake. She was puzzled. Mitch was a celebrity, she'd seen the way people—*women*—looked at him. Any one of them would be thrilled to have Mitch Oliver's arm around her. So why was he acting so unsure of himself?

Jenny forced the thought away. She liked having his arm across her shoulders, so heavy and warm, so she made no effort to pull away, even though she knew she should.

They sat that way until the game was almost over. Until there were only twenty-three seconds to go and the score was still tied. Until Luke got a breakaway and he was skating, skating, all alone, and the crowd was on its feet, and it was roaring…

Luke slammed the puck into the net, raised his stick in triumph and the horn sounded the end of the game.

Jenny was on her feet before she knew it. Popcorn spilled and beer sloshed as people yelled and high-fived each other. Crystal jumped up and down and cheered and splatted Jenny with a wad of cotton candy. "Luke! Luke!" the little girl yelled.

Mitch grabbed Jenny and pulled her into his arms. Her face landed against the front of his leather jacket, and she got the sharp, cool smell of it in her nostrils, felt the cold of the zipper on her cheek and a sense of the rock-hard chest behind it. Something deep inside her clenched.

Stunned by the strength of the sensation, she lifted her head. His eyes were dark, intent, looking directly into hers. Under that intense scrutiny, the sounds of the crowd got less distinct, became a buzz. The spotlights around the arena seemed to focus on Mitch. His mouth firmed, and he bent his head... She rose on tiptoe, helpless to resist...

Then abruptly he let her go.

He shoved his hands in his pockets. "Luke had a pretty good game. That last goal was a beauty."

Jenny swallowed hard. "Right. That's super for Luke." She quickly busied herself gathering Crystal's mittens and the purse the girl had insisted on bringing with her.

Mitch had been caught up in the excitement, that was all. He hadn't ever intended to kiss her; that part was her overactive imagination. As for that hard hug... That hug meant nothing. After all, four thousand screaming fans had been doing the same thing.

She lifted her head, scanning the crowd, reassuring herself that everyone had gone a little crazy there for a few moments. People were milling around, smiling, happily yelling about the game as they were filing out of the area.

Her eye caught Ryan and Tommy. They were down by the boards, to the right, about thirty feet away. She started to point them out to Mitch, to tell him to wait until the twins could find a way through the crowd to join them.

Then she realized Ryan was scowling at her. His

body was still for a long moment, and even Tommy pulling on his elbow didn't get him moving.

Jenny frowned. Had he seen Mitch's arms around her? Was he showing his disapproval? The teenager had made no secret of his dislike of her.

Well, that wasn't going to be a problem for long. Because no matter how much she'd enjoyed the evening, that hug had changed everything.

She'd liked it too much.

It was time for her to go home.

CHAPTER SIX

"I WISH YOU COULD STAY forever."

"Well, in a way, I wish so, too. What I wish is that we could be together. But my home is in Hilton Head, and I've been away more than a week."

"It's my home, too. Sort of. Though here is home, sort of, only I sort of wish it wasn't. Sort of." Crystal's nose wrinkled thoughtfully as she colored in her coloring book. Her kitten sat beside her vigorously licking the tip of one paw. Jenny was relieved that the girl wasn't more upset. The first time Jenny had mentioned returning home, the day after the hockey game, Crystal had cried, and Jenny hadn't been able to bring herself to make plane reservations.

She sighed. This decision was a really tough one. She knew that putting off her departure would only postpone Crystal's—and Jason's—distress. The two of them were coming to rely too much on a situation that was temporary.

Crystal looked up. "But I want to be here to see it snow. Jason says it snows in Ohio every winter. Do you think that's true?"

"I do." Jenny put aside the résumé she'd supposedly been working on.

Crystal outlined a leaf with a purple crayon before filling it in with hot pink. "You can't always believe Jason because he's just a boy. So I didn't know if I should believe him about the snow. But I knew if I asked you, you'd tell me the truth." She held up her coloring book. "Don't you like pink leaves?"

"I surely do." Jenny swallowed. She added, "When you don't think the boys are telling the truth about something, you could always ask your uncle Mitch."

Crystal put the coloring book down. "He's a boy, too. I mean, he's a man, but before he grew up he was a boy."

Jenny's heart contracted. She loved this child so much. How could she ever leave her? "Lying isn't gender specific, sweetheart," she heard herself say. Then despite everything, she chuckled. "What I mean is, not all boys lie and not all girls tell the truth. It depends on the person."

"Oh, I know. It's just that here the boys might lie if they think it's funny."

"Right. But Uncle Mitch won't."

"He teases the boys. But he doesn't tease me too much. Teasing is how Uncle Mitch tells the boys he loves them."

Jenny had told her that. "He loves you, though."

Crystal was quiet, thinking. Finally she said, "Maybe someday he will."

Jenny forced her tears back. She wouldn't cry in front of Crystal. But she wished she could tell the child she'd stay in Ohio for as long as it took for Mitch to learn how to cope with his niece.

A door slammed. Jason came in, shedding his coat.

Crystal perked right up. "Where have you been? This morning, you said I could feed Nosy right after school. Let's go."

Jason said, "Now? I was just gonna get a cookie and call one of my friends."

"You promised. You have to keep your promise or you're a liar."

Jason didn't say anything for a second, and then he said, "Well, it's no skin off my nose if you feed my hamster. Take some chores off'a me."

In a minute, they were headed up the stairs, Jason in the lead and Crystal following like a puppy. Despite her melancholy thoughts, Jenny couldn't help smiling. This eleven-year-old boy was turning out to be a treasure. In time, Crystal would do all right here.

She heard a car pull into the driveway and a few moments later the doorbell rang.

A young woman—not much more than a girl, really—stood on the doorstep. She looked taken aback by Jenny's presence.

As was Jenny. The woman's coat was open, revealing a tight sweater, and a person could see as plain as day that she wasn't wearing a bra under it. She woman had long black hair and lipstick in a shade so dark it was almost purple.

The visitor spoke. "Oh, no, did you get it already?

"Excuse me?"

"The job. The housekeeper's job. Are you the housekeeper?"

"Well, no."

The young woman brightened. "Oh, good. I'm Stacey. Stacey Jones. Is Mr. Oliver here?" She peered around Jenny to look inside the house.

"Mitch—Mr. Oliver is at work."

"Maybe Luke's here?"

"No—"

"I'll just wait then." With a cheerful smile, she swept right by Jenny and into the front hall.

Taken aback, Jenny trailed her down the hall toward the kitchen. Perfume wafted back, some overpowering scent.

Once in the kitchen, Jenny's innate sense of southern hospitality actually had her offering a cup of coffee. Stacey asked for a Coke, instead. When Jenny handed her a can of soda and a glass filled with ice, she popped the top in one quick motion of her long, long airbrushed nails. Then she sat down on one of the stools by the counter. "I'm here to apply for this housekeeper job."

"Oh. Well, that's already been filled," Jenny heard herself say. No way was she going to let this girl within twenty miles of Crystal or Jason.

"Too bad," Stacey said, looking disappointed. "Oh well, maybe I'll still wait for Luke to come home. Catch up on old times." She tapped her navy-and-white nail on the soda can.

"You know Luke?"

"We went to high school together. He's a real hunk. I was a year older, and usually the guys go for older women, but not Luke. He hardly knew I was alive.''

She gave Jenny a knowing smile. "I had the hots for that guy. Still have. I figured I'd start hanging at the rink. You know, to learn about hockey." She twisted a lock of hair around her finger, looking pleased with herself. "He passed me on the way to the locker room last week and said hi. That's a good sign, don't you think?"

Jenny tried not to stare at her.

"So, then I was in the store—you know, Mr. Oliver's store, Serious Gear? And I heard the Olivers were looking for a housekeeper and I thought, hey, I could be a housekeeper. I mean, how hard could it be?"

"Harder than it might seem," Jenny murmured.

"Huh?"

"Well, if you're done with that Coke, I'm sure you're really busy, what with job hunting—"

"No, I'll just stay and wait for Luke."

"Miss Jones, he's at practice. He won't be home until dinner, and maybe not even then."

The girl shifted in her chair, and threw back her shoulders. Her breasts—though it did not seem possible—became even more prominent as they bobbed. "I'll just wait for Mr. Oliver."

Jenny gave up on manners and just stared.

Stacey must have caught the expression on her face. "Hey, I'm sorry. You're not his girlfriend, are you?"

"No."

"Good." The woman didn't even look curious as to what Jenny's role actually was in the household.

"Mr. Oliver isn't too bad," Stacey went on. "This house is awesome and there's not a bit of flab on him, is there? I met him at the rink and he also said hi to me."

Lord, Mitch couldn't be interested in this girl, could he?

It wasn't any of her business what kind of woman he liked, Jenny reminded herself. She was only concerned that Crystal's home life be happy and secure.

Somehow, Jenny managed to hustle Stacey out of the house. As the woman fished in her pockets for her car keys, she said, "Well, it was nice talking to you. You know, about the guys. Maybe I'll see you at the rink."

Jenny managed to smile and say a polite goodbye. Her momma's upbringing was designed for just such situations.

That night after the kids were in bed, she went in search of Mitch. He'd come home late and missed dinner.

The light was on in the exercise room. She paused in the doorway. He was seated on a bench, using the weights. Though he wore a T-shirt with a pair of sweatpants, she could see the flex and bunch of well-toned muscles as he lifted the large dumbbells to his shoulders. Under the high light of the fluorescent fixtures his dark hair gleamed. His skin was shiny with sweat. Against the modern, hard surfaces, he looked real, vital. He caught sight of her in the doorway and smiled.

A smile that went right to her insides. "Hi," he said softly.

"Hi." A little more warmth bloomed in her.

The dumbbells came down, rested on his powerful thighs. "Guess what I did today? I tried that new inventory system you suggested." The night before, Mitch had complained about an accounting problem at the store, and Jenny had suggested he try some software that he had on his computer but had never used. "Looks like it's going to work. Of course, getting the data put in is time-consuming, that's what made me late again today, but—"

"It needs to be done," she said quickly. That was another difference between them. Mitch loved to look at the big picture, talk about the possibilities for the store. But he hated the details of running the business, the details that, when organized properly, gave her such satisfaction.

"Yeah, I know." He was still smiling at her, and it occurred to her that somehow the two of them had become...friends. Going to the hockey game had done that to them.

It didn't feel like "friends" when he put his arms around you.

He added, "Sorry I missed dinner."

"That's okay."

"No, I mean it. I really *am* sorry, because a fast-food burger just doesn't cut it anymore."

"Oh. Thanks." She felt suddenly absurdly awkward. You weren't supposed to feel awkward around friends. "Now that things are going so well, I'm thinking it's time to go home," she blurted.

There was a long pause. "Crystal has been doing better since you came here."

She nodded. "I know, but I think she'll be fine after I'm gone. Though I'll surely miss her. If you'll just remember to talk to her. Tell her about her momma, stories from when you and Kathy were growing up. Make her feel special and wanted." Sudden tears seemed to start in the corners of her eyes. She quelled them. She was so emotional these days.

The dumbbells never moved. "Jason's going to miss you, too."

"Yes, he likes to cook, and I like to spend time with him." There was a short pause. He didn't mention the twins, because he must know Ryan, at least, wouldn't miss her. He didn't mention himself. She finally added, "I wish you'd managed to get a housekeeper before I had to leave."

"I've about used them up," he said ruefully. "The ones from the employment agencies know us. Even more money doesn't get them out anymore. I'm lucky to be able to get the laundry done." He stood, put down the weights and picked up a terry-cloth towel. He wiped his face and slung the towel around his neck.

"A woman came out to interview today," she said. There was a curious tension in her back.

"How was she? Did the kids like her?"

"We never got that far." She laughed a little nervously. "She…wasn't appropriate. She was dressed in very tight clothes and…she didn't wear a bra."

His eyes flashed to her chest. She flushed. Her

breasts had grown bigger with her pregnancy, more tender. She resisted the urge to fold her arms over her chest. "She didn't seem to care about the kids. Except for Luke." Jenny explained how Stacey knew him. "Or she could care about you."

Now his eyes met hers. "Me."

"You." She paused. "Luke or you, she didn't seem to care."

He said in disgust, "Another groupie." At her questioning look, he added, "You noticed them at the game, didn't you? They hang out. They wait until you're vulnerable, until you're drunk on victory and high on your own plays, or until you've been skunked in the playoffs and are low, or until you've had a fight with your wife—by phone, because you haven't been home for a month—and you're so lonely and missing her that you end up—" He cut himself off.

Her mouth felt dry, her back so, so tense. "Did you...?"

He didn't pretend not to know what she was talking about. "Never."

A dizzying kind of relief swept over her. Her mind flashed to Delane, to their breakup. *Jenny, I like my freedom, you know that.* Somehow, she'd known they were talking about more than him being tied down by a baby. She'd said, *"We were engaged. You weren't free..."* He'd turned away, and she'd known. She'd *known.*

How good it was to hear Mitch say one word: never.

He was looking out the window now, at his reflection probably, because with the light on, you could see nothing of the outside.

She remembered something then, and a chill washed over her.

Delane had told her he loved her. There had been a big engagement party, and he'd told all the guests how much he cared for her. He'd also told the employees at Kyle Development they were going to have their best year ever, a month before the bankruptcy court shut the place down. He'd been lying.

She didn't want Mitch to be lying. She studied him. His back was straight, a little proud. His eyes had met hers directly as he'd said "never."

She said, testing him, "That must have been hard, to turn down those women, when, like you say—"

"I'd think about what I had and didn't want to lose. If you'd known Anne, you'd know that there wasn't anything a groupie could do to attract me. Anne was my life. And she was beautiful without any makeup or jewelry."

Jenny felt herself blushing again, because there wasn't a day that she didn't put on both.

He must have seen the color, because he said, "Hey, no, I didn't mean—ah, hell."

"That's all right." She still felt the heat on her cheeks.

"Come here," he said softly, motioning her to the long weight bench. He sat down on one end. "Come on, I'll explain why you could never be a groupie."

She came into the room, drawn as if by an unseen

thread, and sat down primly at the other end of the bench, leaving a few inches of space between them.

"A groupie pretends to be a fan," Mitch said. "But all she really wants is to snag one of the players. In any way possible."

"But, if the player isn't interested, how can she get him to marry her?"

He gave a short bark of laughter. "Who said anything about marriage? How long do you think it takes to make a baby? Five minutes? Ten on a good night?"

Shock ran through her. She pressed a quick hand to her stomach, to shield her little girl from such bitterness. She remembered Delane Kyle: *It's your fault. You said it was the wrong time of the month to get pregnant.* She'd been furious at that comment—he'd used a condom every time except the last time, when they were staying at the family home and he'd forgotten. He'd pressed her, he'd said he loved her, and she'd thought, it probably won't happen, and if it does, so what? We're going to be married and we love each other.

Now she looked over at Mitch and said exactly what she'd said to her ex-fiancé. "It takes two people to make a baby."

He heaved himself to his feet. "Sure it does, but isn't it supposed to be about something more than lies and manipulation?"

She stayed on the bench, her arms folded across her chest. "Yes, of course. But manipulation is sometimes in the eyes of the beholder."

He stared at her. "Let me tell you a story. I had

a friend, Denny Marr, who played defense for the D.C. Stars and Stripes. He was followed all the time by the groupies, like we all were. He had a wife at home, they'd been married about a year. He'd been having a rough season, but he still had a year to go on his contract. One night, his coach let slip that the team might not renew his contract.

"He was blown away, devastated. His wife was three thousand miles away, and when he called her, she wasn't feeling well and she snapped at him to get his act together. So along comes this pretty woman, full of sympathy. He has a one-night stand. She gets pregnant. She doesn't even try to get him to marry her. Turns out, all she wants from him is child support. Big child support." He turned to face her. "Okay, he messed up, but she was the one right there, taking advantage of the opportunity."

She saw the sorrow on his face. "What happened?" she whispered.

"About what you think. Denny was terrified, not thinking straight. He offered the woman money to keep the secret from his wife. The woman accepted, he paid, and then he got a guilty conscience and told his wife, after all. Kay couldn't forgive him, and she split. He's been so damn lonely ever since." He shook his head. "One lousy night, one stupid mistake."

"And a baby who probably never gets to see its father."

He put a hand on a pipe of shiny chrome that wrapped around a treadmill. "Right. Those women wreck lives. Everybody's lives."

She paused. "But if he'd used something—"

"He did. She sabotaged it."

Jenny gasped.

"It's true. She admitted it."

He sat down again, shaking his head. "I can see you're appalled. Good. It is appalling."

For a long moment, they just sat there, on either side of the bench.

Then Mitch said, "I worry about Luke."

"Oh, Lord. I hadn't thought of that." Jenny pictured Luke. So good-looking and thoughtful. So young. She thought of Stacey Jones and shuddered.

"He loves the game. I could no more keep Luke from hockey than, well, than my parents could have kept me from it at his age. I've talked to Luke, now I've got to trust him to know what can happen. I talked to David, too, but it doesn't seem to do any good."

"David is...hanging with groupies?" She deliberately used Mitch's language. But her drawl must have done something to the word *groupie,* because a faint smile came and went on Mitch's face.

"*One* groupie, Robin Donovan. She works at the store, but sometimes I think she wanted the job only because she thinks being close to me gets her closer to Luke and then to David. If you saw her, with her arm around David's waist—"

"They're dating?"

"Dating. Yeah, sure. But she's just there, all the time."

"Mitch." She hesitated. "If he's dating her, well,

then we aren't talking about a one-night stand. Maybe they really care about each other.''

He made a dismissive sound in his throat, one note. ''He's only nineteen. He's not even had a season in the NHL yet.''

This wasn't her issue. She had no business sticking up for a woman she didn't even know. But the thought of her own baby, the thought of the whispers she'd heard growing up in her own small, southern town when a baby was born six months after the wedding, made her say, ''How old were you when you met Anne?''

There was a long, uncomfortable pause. ''Not fair,'' he finally said quietly.

Jenny said, ''Tell me about her.'' She looked at Mitch's profile now, at the tenseness in his jaw as he hesitated. ''Really, I'd like to know,'' she said softly.

He got up, said, ''Come here.''

She knew where he was taking her. To the family room and its shelves of pictures and trophies. She'd already studied both. And been a little embarrassed to find that the trophies were not Mitch's, but his kids'.

They stopped before one shelf. At eye level, there was a big studio portrait of the family. The boys were a lot younger; Jason only a toddler. On the same shelf, there were a lot of candid shots, small photos, several in frames that the kids must have made in art class.

''Everything you see in these pictures is what she was,'' Mitch said quietly.

Jenny studied the photos again, and after a second, she realized what Mitch meant. "A woman who loved her family."

He nodded, and his mouth got a little soft.

Emotions pierced her. Mitch had loved Anne, a love Jenny herself would apparently never inspire in a man. She was sorry for his loss. At the same time, she was...jealous of everything this dead woman had had.

He reached out, took a small photo from the shelf. "This is my favorite. Anne liked to go camping. She loved the outdoors."

A smiling woman sat on a large boulder, a backpack at her feet. Mitch's arm was around her. Her smile was genuine and true. But Anne wasn't beautiful in the conventional way. Her wavy hair was long and shiny, but it was pulled back in an unceremonious ponytail. Her features were pleasant and functional, nothing more. Her breasts were small, and her legs too short.

"She was so pretty," Mitch said.

It occurred to Jenny that Delane would not have been attracted to a woman like Anne, and that seemed significant. She studied the woman's smile again, and was ashamed of her judgment. She said sincerely, "Yes, she was."

He set the picture back on the shelf, but his hand lingered there for a moment. Then he said, "We met in high school. All Anne wanted for me was to play hockey, to excel. She never complained about practice, the way some of the other guys' girlfriends would. After we were married, there was no pressure for me to get home more than I could manage." He turned to Jenny and gave her a small, self-deprecating smile. "She was organized, but she could take things in stride. The house wasn't messy before she got sick. The kids got to school on time every day."

"And then she got sick."

"Yes. I found out in the middle of the season. At first, she tried to tell me it was nothing, that I didn't have to come home. So I played another couple of games, then got the notion to call her doctor myself. When the doctor told me how serious it was, I came home. As soon as I saw her, I realized she was too sick for me to go back. Ten months later, she was gone."

The lingering sorrow in his voice made tears prick her own eyes.

"Now you know why I never flirted with other women. I never wanted Anne to pick up a tabloid and find lies about me in it. I never wanted her to worry about what I was doing on the road."

"But you do sort of flirt sometimes to get what you want." At his look of surprise, she said, "Mrs. Winters, for example. The social worker in Hilton Head. You had her eating out of your hand." She tried not to let a bitter note of her own creep into her voice.

He put a hand in his pocket and looked briefly abashed. "I guess so. I guess I know *how* to do it, but I never did anything to hurt Anne."

"I believe you. You loved her." She hesitated, not wanting to say it. "You still love her."

The silence got a little long after that. She heard the sound of pounding feet upstairs, running water in the bathroom. She heard the furnace come on, watched the warm air stir the drapes that framed the French doors.

He didn't look directly at her. "Maybe a part of me will always love her. When she died I was sure I'd never be interested in meeting anyone else, or dating. I got good at ignoring anything I felt. Then, when I started thinking about having a life again, I realized my chances to meet women weren't very good. There are the Staceys of the world, and women a lot more subtle, but how would I ever be sure that the person I was with didn't want the money, or the celebrity? I couldn't take a chance. Even if I was only dating, I had the kids' feelings to consider."

"I understand."

He turned quickly to her, looked down at her. She met his eyes. "Do you?" he asked.

She took a sharp, indrawn breath. He couldn't be saying—

"I know you have nothing in common with women like that. Your commitment to Crystal is proof. I thought you were reserved, and you are. But you're also warm and caring. I hear you laugh with Jason, I saw you put your fist in the air to cheer Luke on." His eyes still held hers.

A long pause. She couldn't move. She remembered the feel of his arms around her, the cool, buttery softness of leather on her cheek. She fancied she could hear her own heartbeat, and suddenly, under his scrutiny, she was delightedly aware of every cell in her body. She fought the sensation. "Well, that doesn't mean—"

He kissed her. He pulled her to him and tipped her chin up and he kissed her.

Oh, how he kissed her. His mouth, his perfect, well-made mouth was soft and moving on hers. It coaxed her lips, molded them, tried gently to part them. His arms went around her, and he drew her even closer. Gentleness and power.

She forgot resistance, reserve, her careful plans. Her breasts were pressed against his chest, and their constant, heavy tenderness seemed to heighten her excitement. She had to resist pushing against his T-shirt, trying to get closer to his warm skin and the muscles beneath.

She sensed the breadth of his shoulders and chest, the sheer masculinity of him. She breathed in a clean sweat from his workout, underlined with the spicy scent of the cologne he must have put on this morning. *Man,* that scent said. And everything about her hormone-driven body shrieked, *woman.* Helplessly, she brought her hands up, into his crisp, thick hair.

Abruptly, he tightened his hold and made a small, deep sound in his throat. His lips had coaxed; now they demanded. He gave her another hint of the strength in him, and she wanted more. He pressed and moved his mouth until her lips opened.

The entry of his tongue sent a shock wave of pleasure through her body. Her thighs trembled as his tongue began to stroke hers.

"Dad! Dad! Ryan won't give me my fish food."

A pounding of feet on the stairs and through the front hall.

Abruptly, Mitch broke the kiss. He was breathing hard.

"Dad!"

He said in a low voice, "Stay there." He took a few long strides to the kitchen doorway. "Ryan, give Jason his fish food. Now." His voice was hoarse, and he cleared his throat.

Some voices, a little indistinct. Mitch, sounding as annoyed as she'd ever heard him. "Just give him the fish food. Can't you let me have a minute here before I have to referee your battles?"

Jenny smoothed down her blouse, which had worked its way out of her slacks. Her hands were shaking. Good thing the kids had come down.

A very good thing, because if Mitch meant what she thought he meant—

He doesn't want to marry you, for heaven's sake. He's talking about starting a relationship. As in a date.

And sex. She licked her lips, her body on fire for just that.

She couldn't date the man, even if she wanted to. What Mitch didn't realize was that he was kissing a woman who was carrying another man's baby.

She fled. She caught sight of him in the kitchen with Ryan and Jason. She had a sense of his—of the boys'—surprise, of Ryan giving her a scowl as her hurried footsteps became almost a run. She didn't stop until she reached her room.

Once there, she shut the door and paced. She

could still feel the tenderness of her lips where he'd kissed her, and she licked them, trying to rid them of the sensation…or to get more of it. Her body felt shaky, needy. She was terrified by her own response, by the way it lingered, how some part of her longed to feel his warmth again.

She reached the wall, turned, paced again. Okay, so Mitch seemed different from Delane. But those differences might not be as great as she thought. For all she knew, Mitch would use her, too.

Well, it wasn't going to be a problem. He wouldn't kiss her if he knew about her baby. It hadn't seemed necessary to tell him. She didn't owe him that kind of explanation just because she was spending a few days as a guest in his home.

In truth, she couldn't bear to tell him about the baby, because she knew what he'd think. She wanted this baby desperately, but to Mitch it might look as if she'd tried to snare Delane. *How long do you think it takes to make a baby? Five minutes? Ten on a good night?*

After a long time, the house quieted. Jenny opened the door and went to the desk in the hallway. She picked up the phone book, took it back to her room and shut the door.

She found the number and dialed. There was a flight leaving the next day for Savannah and then on to Hilton Head. She almost booked it, and only the belated realization of how Crystal would feel about it stopped her.

She did the next best thing. She got a ticket for the following Tuesday, four days away.

It was long past time to go home.

CHAPTER SEVEN

MITCH WAS HOME the next morning, though he often worked at the store on Saturdays. Now he was making toast next to the silent woman who was stirring orange juice in a pitcher, and wondering what to say to her.

He couldn't believe he was thinking what he was thinking. That they needed to talk. Every guy in the world knew that you never won when you sat down with a woman to talk.

He swiped the knife across a piece of toast and ended up buttering his finger. He kept looking at her. She seemed awfully careful not to look back.

Okay, so my technique was a little rusty. Maybe he'd pushed her too hard; what did he know about making love to a woman nowadays? But, hell, it was just a kiss.

She must've sensed how much he'd wanted her, that his control had been on a thin leash. Maybe she even knew that every time he came home and saw her laughing with the kids in the warm, bright kitchen, he wanted to kiss her. He wanted some of that laughter and light for himself. Every time he picked up his briefcase at the store and realized how much he wanted to come home, he thought about kissing her.

Okay, so he'd kissed her finally. He'd been careful not to press his erection against her. He'd only planned to kiss her, not drag her off to his cave and have her. But she'd obviously realized how very horny he'd been.

It had been four years. Four years was a long time for a healthy man.

Now the switch had been flipped. In fact, if he focused on how warm her lips were, dwelled on those round, soft breasts flattened against his chest, he was going to have a hard-on right here in his kitchen, right here among his kids.

The kids—all except Luke, who had gone to the rink already—had gathered at the breakfast table. Jason had set it, and the forks and napkins were in the right places again. Ryan was spooning scrambled eggs onto the plates, making a bit of a mess of the job, and Tommy was shaking the ketchup bottle so vigorously Mitch wondered how long it would be before the top blew off.

As Mitch sliced the last piece of toast in half, he saw Jason pull Crystal's hair.

"Ow!"

"Cut it out," Mitch said.

Jenny said nothing, which was pretty surprising.

Jason pulled again. "Ow," Crystal said again. Jason chuckled, and then Crystal said, clearly and deliberately, "Cut the crap."

Mitch looked at the little girl, stunned. Jason

must've been surprised, too, because he left off the kid's hair.

Mitch went over to the table and set down the plate of toast, waiting for Jenny to correct either kid. The fact she did not disturbed him.

It had been only a kiss.

She paid him no attention while he waited for her to take her seat. Then she noticed that he was waiting, and she flushed as she sat down.

As they started to eat, the kids kept up their usual chatter. Finally, Jenny put down her fork. Mitch noticed she hadn't eaten more than a bite of egg. He got a bad feeling just before she spoke. She said quietly, "I've booked a flight out. I wanted to tell y'all that I'm going home on Tuesday."

Her words hit him like a hockey stick to the gut.

The clatter of silverware on plates stopped.

Ryan smiled.

Jason and Crystal said as one, "No!"

From across the table Mitch saw Jenny put out her hand and cover the little girl's. "Sweetheart, I told you I could only stay a few more days. You knew this time was coming. We've talked about it."

Crystal's bottom lip trembled.

When Jenny spoke again, her voice was tight, her drawl hurried. "I waited until I thought you were comfortable here. Until you got used to how things were done in this house, until you realized you could talk to your uncle Mitch. Until you could handle the boys." A faint, sad smile played around her mouth. "I got my proof you could surely handle things just now, when you said 'Cut the crap' to Jason."

"*Crap* is a bad word," she said in a small voice.

"Yes, you're right, and you should find ways to say what you need to say without having to use bad words. What I meant was that you were sticking up for yourself, and that's really good. Every girl—every *person*—needs to learn to stick up for themselves, and you're doing great."

"But you could stay longer and watch me do great."

"Sweetheart, I don't live here, and this is your home now. You'll like it here. In a few months, you won't—" her voice faltered, then picked up speed "—you won't miss me so much. But I'll miss you, so I hope we can talk on the telephone every night. I bet this summer when school's out, Uncle Mitch will let you visit me in Hilton Head." Tears had gathered in her eyes. "There's no choice, Crystal. I need to earn a living."

In a tone that managed to sound forlorn and disgusted at the same time, Tommy said, "We'll be back to pizza every night if you go."

There was a small silence. Ryan sat with his head bowed, shoveling scrambled eggs into his mouth. Nobody else seemed hungry.

Then Jason brightened. "Hey, you could stay and be our cook! Our chef, I mean. That's a job, right, Dad?"

Jenny shook her head, as if speaking was too hard.

Something was breaking inside him at the rather desperate eagerness on his youngest son's face. At Crystal's obvious distress.

Crystal said, "But I don't want you to go."

A squeeze of Jenny's hand. "You can come visit."

"Then I'm going to think about the beach. I'm going to think about the beach every day, even on the first day of snow."

Oh, hell. Mitch was going to have to fix this somehow. But what was he supposed to do? From the beginning, Jenny had told him—she'd told them all—that she couldn't stay much more than a week.

He could talk to her, but her logic was irrefutable. Maybe that's all it was—time for her to go home and resume her job. After all, she was the manager of the whole office at that real estate place she worked. They probably couldn't operate too long without her. He didn't have to feel guilty. *Maybe last night's kiss wasn't the motivation.*

Yeah, right. Somehow, he'd got the notion that her prissiness—her prickliness—was a front, that she was warm and willing and wanting to kiss him. Well, somehow he'd got it wrong, and he'd scared her or something.

His niece had started to cry now. A few fat, silent tears rolled down her cheeks and made him feel worse than if she'd howled. Jason got up and took his plate to the sink—Jenny's influence—but ended up slamming it on the counter.

Guilt washed over him. For four years, he'd been paying for his lapses as a husband, as a father, in the best way he knew how. Now he realized he'd done something again to hurt the children he loved.

Think! How can you make this better for the kids?

Mitch glanced at the tank of tropical fish in the corner and got a sudden inspiration. "Well, if Jenny is going back on Tuesday, that doesn't give us much time for her to help us pick out a dog. We'd better get going."

Crystal looked up quickly. "A dog? For me?"

Jason said eagerly, "Another dog?"

"Another dog?" Tommy repeated. He punched Ryan on the arm. "All right."

Mitch said, "Crystal, didn't I promise you a dog when you first came here?"

"I thought you forgot." There was a little quaver in her voice.

"I don't forget my promises." But he had hoped *she'd* forget, or that she'd decide that two ponies, a tank of fish, a hamster, and Jules—not to mention Face-off—were enough.

"A dog just for me?"

"Well, yes, but maybe you'd let the other kids—"

"Oh, they can play with her. Especially Jason. He lets me feed Nosy, so I guess he can feed my dog. And she can be friends with Face-off and share the bed in the laundry room. She can be friends with Jewels, too, even though in cartoons cats and dogs aren't friends."

"Well, I'd rather have Miss Jenny," Jason said stubbornly from the sink, but the anger was gone from his voice.

"So would I," Crystal said, her head bobbing with emphasis. "But she's here until Tuesday, so she can help me pick out my dog. I know! We'll call my dog Miss Jenny.''

A sputter of milk from Ryan. A guffaw, quickly squelched in a napkin at a sign from Mitch.

''I don't think that's a good idea, Crystal,'' Mitch said. ''You don't want to get confused when you think about Miss Jenny.''

''I was just thinking, every time I thought of my dog, I could remember Miss Jenny.''

Mitch got up from the table to make a phone call to the breeder. Crystal and Jason went upstairs with Jenny to get ready to go. All the kids wanted to go. They liked animals in this house. But a few minutes later, Mitch heard the twins in the kitchen, talking about girls. ''She's a real dog,'' Ryan said. ''Bowwow!'' Suddenly angry at his sons' attitude, he told the twins they couldn't go along.

''What's the big deal?'' Ryan wanted to know. ''No girl's gonna know I called her a dog.''

''The big deal is I want Crystal's choosing a dog to be a happy memory. She's probably going to be crying in her sleep because Jenny is going home. I'm trying to give her something of her own to love. Is that so hard for you to understand? Does everything have to be a joke to you two?'' His tone was unusually fierce.

Ryan looked away. ''Well, we didn't want to go anyway.''

Tommy said, ''Well, maybe *I* did, and you screwed it up for me, you dork. You know, maybe if you didn't make fun of girls so much, Colleen would like you better.''

Ryan turned beet red. Without a word, he left the kitchen.

Mitch said, "Who's Colleen?"

"Colleen Hart. Just some girl at school. She's a fox but she doesn't know it. She reads all the time, and she turns up her nose, big time, at Ryan, and he's in *love* with her so bad it makes me want to puke to watch him standing by her locker, looking at his feet and trying to talk to her. He's a jock, and most girls like jocks, right? Just not Colleen." He shook his head as he followed Ryan out of the kitchen.

Mitch was bemused at this turn of events. This was the first time Ryan had expressed serious interest in any girl beyond the latest *Playboy* playmate.

But he put the incident out of his mind. He tried to put Jenny's leaving out of his mind, too, in order to make Crystal's day a good one. They drove to the breeder's house, which turned out to be a small home in the country. Since they were looking at toy poodles, Mitch had some notion that the breeder—who he'd been told won many of the local dog-show ribbons—would be some pink-haired lady who wore too much face powder, who fed her dogs white meat of chicken and…crumpets, who put rhinestone collars on every last dog.

He was wrong. Pam Stewart was a thirty-something woman who wore chic country wear straight out of L. L. Bean, and ran her kennel as if it was IBM. There was a computer set up, and a screen that showed how she was tracking her breeding lines. The kennel itself was immaculate, some of the runs brand-new and almost hospital-clean. She took them down the rows to where she had the puppies.

Two tiny white poodles, hardly bigger than Jules, cavorted behind one of the stalls. Crystal barreled in there, and both backed up, quivering in the nervous way he'd always associated with small dogs. One of them let out a high-pitched bark that sounded more like a squeak.

He grimaced. Great.

Jenny had been very quiet and serious on the ride to the kennel. Now he glanced at her and saw a little smile playing around her mouth.

He relaxed then.

Jason had joined Crystal, and they knelt in the pen and tried to coax the dogs to them. Tentatively, one came over, sniffing.

Mitch, Pam and Jenny watched the children over the gate.

"Why do those puppies look so fuzzy all over?" Mitch asked after a moment. "Why don't they have that knot of hair on their heads and ankles?" Actually, he liked this kind of coat better, but Crystal had mentioned "balls of fur on their heads."

Pam laughed and said, "I've given them a puppy cut. It's more informal." She hesitated. "Look, I'd like to make a sale, but I want to make sure you're happy with any dog you choose."

Before Mitch could answer, Crystal piped up. "Oh, I love you." One of the dogs had crawled into her lap. She was cuddling it and making little crooning sounds in her throat. Jason had sat down beside her and was scratching the top of the puppy's head.

"I'll choose whichever one she wants."

Pam nodded and smiled broadly. She explained to Mitch that these two puppies were the only ones left after the rest of the litter had been sold. "They're perfectly healthy. It's just that they aren't show quality, but they'll make fine pets."

"This one's a girl, right?" Crystal asked.

Pam said, "No, it's a male. They're both males."

Crystal looked crushed for a split second. Then she said thoughtfully, "Well, I guess sometimes you gotta take a boy."

Jason said, "Face-off is a boy, and he's a great dog. This dog can be great like Face-off."

Crystal looked at Jenny and made a face.

"Yeah, sometimes boys aren't as bad as they seem," Mitch said quietly to Jenny, and saw her stiffen. He'd meant the comment to be teasing, but a little sexual innuendo had crept in. He couldn't help it. He had the hots for her, and it was getting hard not to let it show.

Crystal picked up the puppy and brought him over to the gate. She had Jenny and then Mitch pet him in turn.

"He's weaned, but he's going to miss his brother," Pam said. "Put an old-fashioned alarm clock in his bed. One that ticks. He will think he's hearing the other dog's heartbeat. Otherwise, you're liable to be awakened *very* early tomorrow morning."

Mitch and Jenny exchanged glances, one moment

of shared camaraderie before she looked down again at the dog. Mitch had already discovered that Jenny liked mornings even less than he did.

"This puppy won't be lonely. He has Jewels. He has Face-off if Face-off can learn to be nice." Crystal wrinkled her nose. "I don't have any names picked out for boy dogs."

"Well," Mitch said, "that shouldn't be a big problem. You already have a boy name for a girl cat." Jenny and Crystal looked at him quizzically. "Well, you do. 'Jules' is a boy name and she's a girl cat."

There was a moment's pause. Then Jenny said softly, "It's 'Jewels.' Jew-els. Because she's Crystal, her momma suggested the name Jewels. It was sort of a word game they played."

He felt so foolish suddenly. He should have understood the name—and its significance—right away.

He was quiet on the way back to the farm. Crystal held the quivering new puppy in her lap until the dog peed on her, then she finally consented to let it ride in the cardboard box they'd brought along. Then the puppy cried. All the way home.

Well, buying a dog had seemed like a good idea this morning.

When they got home, the puppy played a little with the boys, sniffed at the laundry-room door, cried and jerked when Face-off—on the other side—whined. Jules—*Jewels*—spat at the newcomer. The pup seemed overwhelmed and shy with all the commotion.

Just like his niece.

Crystal asked Jenny if she thought Silver was a boy's name, and Jenny assured her solemnly it was. Mitch reached down to pat the dog, which was lying, exhausted now, in Crystal's lap. The dog raised his eyes, but hardly moved at the contact. The bones of his skull felt fragile. Mitch crouched to his niece's level.

"Crystal and Jewels and Silver. I get it."

She smiled at him, and the smile reached her eyes. "Thank you for my dog," she whispered.

Something pinched him in the chest. He said, "I'm trying to make you happy here. If I yell at you, it only means I talk loud. It doesn't mean any more than that."

She nodded thoughtfully.

He straightened, and caught Jenny looking at him. A weird, soft expression was in her eyes. That look sent something warm through him, something sexual and...even more. Whoa, the something more scared him.

He looked more closely, and he decided the expression was for Crystal, not him.

What difference did it make, anyway? Jenny Litton, with her perfect southern belle skin and her curvy, feminine body, couldn't wait to get away from him.

He forced himself to look away. Instead, he watched his niece stroke Silver to sleep, listened to her sing songs, breathy, piping songs, and he suddenly remembered Kathy. What a feminine child she'd been, just like this one. He resolved again to do right by Crystal. He could still use Jenny's help, but it seemed he'd be on his own here very soon.

And lonely as hell in a houseful of people...and animals.

JENNY WAS COOKING a ham. She had it in a Dutch oven on the stove, with a little liquid, and she'd been cooking it a long time. Everybody south of the Mason-Dixon Line knew you cooked ham until it fell off the bone. Crystal's favorite meal was ham prepared with green beans and potatoes, and Jenny was fixing that for dinner because it was her last night here.

Fortunately, Crystal also liked pizza, because soon that was all she was likely to get in this house.

She nudged the tip of Jewels's tail aside—the kitten was watching her from a perch in a patch of sunlight on the kitchen windowsill—and tried not to think about leaving. She tried not to think about Crystal and Jason, and how much she'd miss them. And Luke, too. Heck, sometimes she even thought the twins' antics were amusing.

Most of all, she tried not to think about one very good-looking, athletic man. The man she dreamed about kissing again with every fiber of her hormone-rife body. The man who had displayed a surprising—and appealing—sensitivity in letting Crystal choose a puppy. It was a gesture that surely would never have occurred to Delane.

She checked the pot and added more water.

Instead of thinking about everything here, she needed to think about the future. She'd scheduled a job interview in Hilton Head. If she got the position with the small company, she planned to do a good job and work right through her pregnancy. She was looking forward to making a life for herself and her little girl.

So why was she so miserable?

Now, even though it was early—the kids weren't home from school yet, in fact—she was snapping beans. Everybody knew you cooked beans to death when you fixed them with a ham.

She was almost glad when, a few minutes later, she heard the twins get off the bus and bang their way through the garage.

"Hey," Tommy greeted her as he came in and slung his backpack onto the kitchen table. "Wow, that smells good."

She smiled her thanks. She was starting to realize that the teenager's only problem was an excess of energy, what her momma would have called "high spirits."

"You must have Confederate blood in you," she said. "Nobody but a southerner could like biscuits and gravy as much as you. Maybe next time I'll try you on grits—" She stopped as she realized again that there wasn't going to be a next time.

Tommy, who was lifting the lid on the pot and taking an exaggerated sniff of the contents, didn't seem to hear her.

Ryan came in now, too, with Face-off right behind him. Ryan stopped short when he saw her in the kitchen. "We need the kitchen. We have to film a commercial for our Popular Culture class. We're doing a commercial for some bogus cooking school. We told you that.''

They'd said no such thing, but Jenny decided to let it pass. She studied his face. With his sandy hair and freckles, his slightly too-big nose, he wasn't as handsome as his father or Luke, but he was a nice-looking boy. He had a rough but fun sense of humor…around everybody but her.

''Can't you work around me?'' she asked.

''Sure we can,'' Tommy said.

''We could if you could stand a little mess.'' Ryan gave her a look that was outright challenging.

''I can stand a little mess. Just stay out of the path of my cooking, please.''

While the twins were going for the camera and setting up their commercial, Jason and Crystal came in. Silver ran around in circles, so happy to see the little girl.

When the twins came back, Jenny was suddenly glad for their presence in the kitchen. Everything around the boys moved at high octane. There wasn't a chance Crystal and Jason could brood about her last night here.

Tommy and Ryan were arguing about which of them was going to work the camera. ''Whoever it is has got to be sure to zoom in for the good parts.''

''What are the good parts?'' Jenny asked.

''Depends which you like better. When we blow up the drink or sauce the neon tetra.''

''The neon tetra? Isn't that one of your fish?'' Her gaze flew to the aquarium in the corner, where dozens of inch-long tropical fish swam.

"The neon's *my* fish!" Jason shouted.

"You can't kill a fish!" Crystal said only slightly lower.

Ryan had a taunting smile on his face. He grabbed the fishnet and headed for the aquarium. Jason snatched the net out of the bigger boy's hand.

"Give that back, Squirt."

"Make me!"

"Yeah, make him!" Crystal shouted in such a bloodthirsty tone that Jenny looked at the girl in surprise.

"Hang on," Tommy shouted into the din. "We aren't going to cook a real fish. It's part of our act. We're going to pretend with this." With a grin, he took a small fishing lure from his pocket and dangled it in the air. "From a distance, it's going to look like we're doing all that stuff to a real fish. Like, it's a joke."

"Really?" Crystal looked suspicious.

Aping her exactly, the little poodle cocked his head.

Jenny smothered a laugh.

Jason and Crystal insisted on being part of the commercial. That perplexed the twins for a moment, but then they got the bright idea that Jason could work the camera. Crystal could be the studio audience.

"Whoever heard of an audience of one person?" Crystal asked in disgust.

And so Jenny, Crystal and the dogs became the audience. Crystal held Silver, and the twins threatened Face-off with certain death if he didn't stay.

"This is great," Tommy pronounced after he managed to get Face-off to wear a knit hat from the hall closet. "Like a comedy."

"It's supposed to be a comedy, you dork," Ryan said.

"Well, whatever. I mean, there's funny and there's funny and Face-off is *funny*."

Face-off smiled.

Finally, the audience was seated in front of the counter. Jason panned the little crowd with his camera.

On the counter, a tray with a tumbler of vinegar and a wine bottle filled with water sat next to a wineglass filched from the china cabinet. For some reason, the wineglass was half-full of baking soda. Jenny was pretty sure the glass was an antique, and she hoped the kids wouldn't break it. A glass bowl held a small, glowing fish in water they'd drawn from the aquarium.

The twins donned white shirts and tall paper chef hats.

"Ready?" Jason asked, clearly itching to get to the filming.

"Ready."

"Lights, camera. Action!"

Jenny and Crystal applauded. That got Face-off excited and his hat fell down over one ear. Jenny straightened it while Jason was filming a close-up of Crystal. Face-off licked Jenny's hand, a big sloppy lick.

Tommy popped a tape into the tape player. An

instrumental version of "On Top of Old Smokey" played.

The twins had their own lyrics. In voices so off-key that they'd grate on a mule, they sang at the top of their lungs:

"On Olivers' Cooking Cor-ner, the food is so fine,
Tune in for an epi-sode, of cooking with wine."

On and on it went, silly rhymes, while the boys clowned in the kitchen. Face-off abandoned the audience for what was happening on stage, and Silver strained in Crystal's arms. The boys ignored the pacing dog, and Jason deliberately kept the camera high to avoid catching Face-off on film.

Holding up a wine bottle, Tommy poured liquid into a pan. He pretended to take the fish out of the bowl, but instead flipped the lure into the puddle in the pan.

"Lit-tle fish are more ten-der," they sang as they turned and sauced the lure. Jenny laughed out loud as Jason came in for a close-up. For that moment, she forgot her troubles, forgot how difficult the twins could be, even forgot the feel of Mitch's mouth on hers.

Forgot that tomorrow she was going home.

"The wine of the day is spark-ling…" Ryan sang, pouring the vinegar on the baking soda.

The brew erupted. Foam spewed over the glass, over the tray, over the counter, onto the floor. Face-off went wild, running, bumping, barking. Silver joined him, his high-pitched little puppy-yaps sounding above the din. Tommy yelled for Jason to get the dogs, Ryan yelled for Tommy to get the dogs, Jason yelled for Ryan to get the dogs, and everybody yelled for Miss Jenny.

Jenny ran for a towel. Jewels streaked across the counter, right through the mess, her tail puffed. Jason tripped over Face-off and landed on his back, video camera to his eye, presumably still filming.

Crystal was shouting something about a fish.

Jenny looked up to see the tiny tetra skidding across the counter, its glass container broken. She shrieked. Her sensitive stomach lurched.

"Jeez!" Ryan shouted, picking up the fish with the net. "Put a lid on it, you're going to scare this fish!"

Jenny's heart was pounding. She stood there with a towel in her hand, wondering what to wipe first, which kid to settle first. At that moment it was very hard to remember why she'd ever thought she could be a good mother.

"Hello! Hello!"

It was a new voice, barely heard above the din. Tommy opened the door to the garage, and a woman in a brown suit stepped into the room.

Face-off took off for her at breakneck speed. The woman held out her hands to ward off the dog, who pushed her into the door frame, reared up on his hind legs and licked her face.

"Get that dog!" Jenny shouted to Tommy.

Tommy made a grab for the dog and took him to the laundry room.

Oh, Momma, if you could have heard me shout just now! "Just a minute," she yelled to her visitor. Jenny then put every organizational skill she had into getting the kids quieted down. Slowly, things got back to normal. The fish went back to the aquarium. Silver quieted in Crystal's arms. Tommy and Ryan fought for a second over the video camera one of them had taken from Jason, until Jenny snatched it up herself.

Foam dripped off the counter.

Jenny put down the camera and smoothed her palms on her hips before hurrying over to the woman. "Lord, I'm so sorry about the dog. Really, I thought Face-off was a lot to handle too at first, but he's really gentle, though rambunctious." She made herself stop rambling. "Can I help you?"

The woman's face looked as gray as the permed curls on her head. But she brought herself upright. She did not hold out a hand. In fact, she kept both hands firmly on her purse, the way Momma had always said to do when walking in the big, dangerous city. "I'm Margaret Howard, from Social Services. I'm here to do a home study on Mr. Oliver."

CHAPTER EIGHT

FIFTEEN MINUTES LATER, Jenny was getting nowhere. "It was simply a school project that got out of hand," she said for the seventh time. "The kids are what my momma would have called 'high-spirited.' As a professional working with children yourself, you certainly know what I mean." She gave Ms. Howard a conspiratorial smile but got no smile in return.

They sat at the kitchen table, right where all the mess was. Jenny had suggested the living room, but not before Tommy, looking panicked, had offered the woman a seat at the table. If the house had been noisy before, now it was quiet in a way Jenny had never experienced here. The kids hovered, listening.

Tommy had offered Ms. Howard a glass of water. He'd put it in a plastic tumbler from a fast-food restaurant, and there was no ice. The social worker made no attempt to pick it up. The anxiety in the room appeared to puzzle Crystal, but she was interested because the boys were interested.

"As a matter of fact," Ms. Howard said, "I don't work with children anymore. Now that I have seniority in my agency, I assess homes. The state regulates how many bedrooms there must be, and there are health hazards I need to check for.'' She looked quite satisfied with herself.

Jenny tried one more time. ''But surely you study whether the children are happy and well adjusted.''

''Of course.'' Ms. Howard nodded vigorously.

''Well, these children are happy. Crystal is doing well.'' It occurred to her then that perhaps she shouldn't be defending Mitch. That this was a perfect opportunity to take custody of Crystal, to do what Kathy had intended all along.

After all, while she might understand his parenting better now, she still questioned his lack of discipline with the boys.

She opened her mouth to tell the truth, the whole truth, and let the social worker decide for herself. But at the last moment, she realized she couldn't.

There was no doubt that Crystal was doing well here. Crystal's very profanity the other day had showed that the little girl was adapting. Though Jenny generally deplored a lack of manners in a person, maybe it was better for Crystal if she could forget manners once in a while. That was a startling thought. After less than two weeks in this crazy household, was Jenny willing to throw over eighteen years of her momma's teachings?

Well, could she offer Crystal more in South Carolina? Crystal would certainly miss Jason. Taking the child home would just be uprooting her once again, and then Crystal would have another adjustment to make once Jenny's little girl was born. She heard a whine from Face-off and thought of Silver.

Mitch buying that dog had forever changed things, she realized. It was an unsettling thought.

"Are you happy, Crystal?" Ms. Howard asked.

Crystal said matter-of-factly, "Well, I miss my momma. She died, you know."

"Yes, I know. I'm sorry about that, and that's why I'm here. To see that you have a safe place to live." Her gaze swept the kitchen. "To make sure there are no dangerous objects around, like broken glass."

Tommy grabbed a paper towel and hurriedly began to pick up chunks of glass and put them in the garbage disposal.

Jenny winced at the fate of the disposal.

"Oh, it's safe," the little girl said. "I only cut myself once."

The social worker perked up.

Damn.

"Not on broken glass," Jenny said quickly. "Crystal was just playing."

"Did this injury occur while you were supervising?" The woman gave Jenny a pursed-up look that reminded her of the church ladies gossiping about her daddy. Weren't social workers supposed to be helpful and caring?

"Actually, it was before I arrived—"

"Nobody was here but Jason and Ryan and Tommy," Crystal said quickly. "It's not Miss Jenny's fault."

"No adult was here?"

"The twins are fifteen," Jenny said desperately.

"Age isn't important. What's important is how

mature the child is who is in charge." Her look Tommy's way said it all.

"Really, it was okay," Crystal said. "I stopped bleeding before Uncle Mitch came home."

Ms. Howard leaned forward. "How long did you bleed?"

"Gee, I don't know," Crystal said at the same time Tommy said, "Hardly at all."

"That's a lie," Crystal said indignantly. "Besides, the boys weren't supposed to play football with me and knock me down and hurt me so hard I bled and bled."

Jenny resisted the urge to put her head in her hands. She felt a spurt of panic as a new thought occurred to her. Obviously, Ms. Howard wasn't impressed with Jenny's parenting, either. The woman wouldn't do something like take Crystal away from *both* Jenny and Mitch, and put her in foster care, would she? At the thought, her hands got icy and her stomach flipped over, one big flip, as though the baby had reacted to the shock of the idea.

"Who left the garage door open?" Mitch asked, coming through the doorway at just that moment. "I've told you guys a million times not to leave that door up."

He looked casual and gorgeous. His hair was windblown, his cheeks ruddy, his khakis covering muscled legs, his leather jacket molding powerful shoulders. Jenny had never been so glad to see anyone in her life.

She jumped up from the table. "Mitch, come on in and meet Margaret Howard. The social worker who is checking on Crystal.'' She tried to give him a look that said things weren't going well. Out of the corner of her eye, she saw Ms. Howard sitting stock-still, her mouth open just a bit, as if transfixed. So Jenny wasn't the only one who thought the man looked good.

His eyes swept the kitchen and he gave Jenny an astonished look. Okay, since she had come here she hadn't let the boys mess up the kitchen this way. But she'd lapsed. At the wrong time.

Jenny caught the split second that comprehension dawned on Mitch, the realization that the social worker had come at A Very Bad Time. He strode across the room and put out his hand. ''Hello. I'm Mitch Oliver. I'm sorry I wasn't here to greet you when you came.'' He held the woman's hand just a mite too long.

For good measure, he gave her a wide, practiced grin, one Jenny hadn't seen since he'd tried it on *her* in South Carolina. ''I was at work. When you're running your own business, it's a struggle for a while.''

Ms. Howard lit herself in the glow of that dazzling smile. ''I've heard it is. You must work very hard. That's surprising, really. I've heard you were a professional athlete.''

''Yes, until I realized I missed my family.'' Another grin, this time as warm as just-baked peach cobbler.

''And now you're starting your own business. How wonderful.''

''I'm so glad you think so.'' A sigh. ''Of course,

it's difficult when you have home responsibilities, too. I'm sure you've noticed we don't manage to keep the house up as well as we might.''

This frank acknowledgment seemed to take the remaining wind out of the social worker.

Lord, it was effortless. Totally, completely effortless.

Jenny had gotten nowhere, but for *him* it was effortless. In fact, within ten minutes, he and the social worker had agreed about how difficult it was to work *and* raise children. In fifteen, they'd agreed that good cleaning help was hard to find nowadays. In twenty, Mitch had hung his head in an aw-shucks way when Ms. Howard told him how wonderful it was that he brought jobs to his hometown instead of taking his money and living someplace—here she pursed her lips again—like California.

In twenty-five, he had the woman feeling sorry for him when she discovered that in addition to his boys and his poor little orphaned niece, he had the responsibility for a feckless female houseguest.

That was about the point when Jenny realized she'd gone from supportive to furious.

It was also about the point when Mitch finally managed to steer the woman out the door.

''I do have to come back and see the bedrooms,'' Ms. Howard said, not sounding at all put out at the prospect. ''I'll call and make an appointment.''

''Please come when you have plenty of time for us to talk again.''

''Oh, I will,'' she promised on the way out the door.

Mitch shut it behind her and leaned his back against it. "Whew."

"Hard work being a hometown hero?" Jenny asked. She was glad Mitch had been able to get rid of the woman, but she hated his phoniness.

He shrugged. "It comes in handy sometimes."

His comment made her angry.

"Way to go, Dad," Ryan said. He strode over to his father and gave him a high five.

"Everything's okay?" Jason had been unusually quiet.

"It is now." Mitch whistled a tune fragment as he wandered into the kitchen. "Good thing I was early." He sniffed. "Something smells good." The twins had half cleaned the kitchen while Mitch and Jenny had sat at the table with Ms. Howard. Mitch ignored the rest of the mess.

He lifted the lid of the Dutch oven, narrowing his eyes in pleasure. "I'm surprised Jenny's ham didn't win Ms. Howard over. Obviously, the woman doesn't know good southern cooking." He smiled at Jenny, clearly extremely pleased with himself.

She said tightly, "I have to talk to you."

He turned from the silverware drawer, where he was obviously getting a fork in preparation to sampling her ham. "All right."

"I have to talk to you outside." She motioned him toward the sliding glass door. She opened it and marched outside.

He followed. She kept going, across the deck, down the steps, across the frosty grass toward the pond. She stopped by one of the big trees at the bottom of the hill. "Just pleased with yourself as all get-out, aren't you?" She hugged herself. Against the cold, against him.

He put his hands in his pockets. "Okay, you're mad. Even I can gather that. Want to tell me why?"

"Because you...you manipulated that woman into agreeing with you."

He looked nonplussed. "How about that look of yours when I first came home? Weren't you trying to tell me things weren't going well and you needed help?"

That cooled her anger a little. After all, she had intended to communicate exactly that message. But the way he'd responded— "Well, it surely wasn't right of you to use your...your smile, and your...your good looks to win her over."

He said in the most reasonable tone, "I don't know why you're so upset. I thought you and I were working as a team, like we'd do in a hockey game."

"Life isn't a hockey game. Life is serious business."

"Actually, hockey is serious business." He gave her a coaxing smile.

Anger burned in her again. "You know what I mean!"

He sobered. "I was just going with the flow. I sized up the situation and went with what I thought would work. Think about it this way. Was she being fair to us? To our family?"

"No, still..." She knew he was right. But for a few minutes there, he'd sounded like Delane. Manipulative.

She said, "Are you proud of using your status and your looks to get something you wanted? Are you proud that you let your kids see you do that?"

Ah-ha. She had him. He looked away, out toward the pond. She pressed her point. "Do you want to teach your kids that they can get whatever they want that way?"

There was a little silence. Finally he said, "The kids didn't realize what was going on."

"Ryan gave you a high five, Mitch. He knew."

He cursed, soft and low, and let out a breath. It steamed in the cold air. "You're right. I didn't realize they'd pick up on what I was doing."

"So it's okay to do it if the kids don't see? Or are you just sounding sincere so you can appease me the way you did that social worker?"

He put out a hand, snapped off a small twig. He studied it, thinking. Then he looked at her. "I can't ever win with you, can I?" he finally asked quietly.

She was being unfair, and she knew it. Mitch wasn't really like Delane. She shivered, suddenly cold. "I'm sorry."

"Ah, hell," he said, and took off his blazer and put it over her shoulders, wrapping her in it. "Better?" he asked. There was a note of rough comfort in his voice.

She nodded, the kindness of the gesture further undermining her anger. "I don't agree with your tactics, but I'm glad Ms. Howard's decided at least one of us is a fit parent. For a second I panicked, thinking maybe Crystal would have to go to a foster home."

He nodded. "I could tell you were upset the minute I walked through that door."

"It all worked out, I guess."

"Right. Listen, it's cold out here, but we do have some privacy. If you can stand it another minute or two, I want to ask you something." He put his hands in his pockets. "I've been thinking. Why don't you stay here? In Ohio?"

Elation leaped in her, but she ignored it. "My life is in South Carolina. How long can I keep putting it on hold?"

"How about you don't put your life on hold? Why not start a new life here, stay permanently?"

Permanently. It was something she'd never considered. She took a quick look at his face, at the stark, strong features, and knew if she had any sense, she'd go with her original plan, and get on that plane tomorrow. "I have my condo—"

"Your condo can be sold. It's only four walls— nothing more. You've become important to the boys, especially Jason. You've always been important to Crystal, and you could see her often."

Her heart ached. She'd give almost anything to be able to be near the little girl, but that was impossible.

"Look, I know it isn't easy to give up everything—believe me, I know. But Crystal's family to you now. If the person you love is elsewhere, is South Carolina really home?"

It wasn't, and she acknowledged what she'd known for some time. Hilton Head wasn't going to feel like home anymore. She had no job, her best friend was gone, Crystal was here.

She hugged his jacket to her. There was something about that big, warm jacket that was affecting her judgment. Because staying here, starting again among these fast-talking northerners, almost sounded like a good idea. "But all my business contacts are there…"

"You could get a job here." He'd gone still. He was very focused on her suddenly. When the man wasn't in go-with-the-flow mode, he could be relentless.

Well, why not get a job here?

Because…because she liked the feel of his jacket too much. Because she needed to stay with her plan. "Mitch, there's something I haven't really shared with you. Actually, I'm between jobs now, and I have prospects down there, good prospects—"

His forehead creased. "You're between jobs?"

"Yes, my employer went into bankruptcy." She explained what had happened.

"Well then, that's great. You can stay here." He looked pleased with himself, brashly boyish. "I've got a job for you right here. I was wondering how to bring it up. I know from these last two weeks that you'd be great at it, but I was sure you'd say it was a nothing job, compared to that fancy development firm in South Carolina. But now maybe you'll consider it. I'd like you to manage my store."

He paused. "I didn't bring up the subject before because I was concerned that you wouldn't think managing one store was good enough. But I've got

plans to make Serious Gear into the biggest sporting-goods chain in the Midwest.''

His eyes held their own vulnerability. She knew
Mitch was utterly serious when it came to his business.

He added, ''There are a hundred details you have
to pay attention to when you run this kind of oper-
ation. If I could get out from under them, I could
travel. I could meet with the coaches of the high
schools in other cities, explain what we could offer
in terms of uniforms, support. I could scout out new
locations. I could—'' He stopped, spread his hands.
''Well, you get the idea.''

If she managed the store, she'd see Mitch every
day. No, she wouldn't, she thought in relief. He'd
just said he'd be traveling. If she accepted the job,
at least her immediate worries would be over. Suddenly, she was no longer cold. She felt in control
again, and it felt good.

She could stay near Crystal! She could even see
Jason from time to time. It was perfect. She could
choose to stay.

He said, ''I'd pay you whatever you were earning
in South Carolina.''

She named the figure, then said, ''But I'd need a
raise.''

He winced.

''You can afford it,'' she said, and she couldn't
help smiling, she was so relieved that she had a job.
''Trust me, I'm worth it.''

''Done.''

''Just like that?''

"Yep."

"I'll need to find a place to live—"

"You can stay here."

"I don't think that's a good idea—"

"At least until you find a place you want."

She thought for a moment. Staying at his house for a while really was a good idea. She did her share by cooking the evening meal and helping the kids with homework and school projects. She could take the time needed to get her condominium sold, and use the proceeds to look for a small house, maybe with a nice backyard where she could put in a swing and sandbox. "Thank you for your hospitality," she said.

"Such as it is." He smiled again. He grabbed her hand. "Come on, let's go for a walk and settle the details."

"Aren't you cold?"

"Not anymore. You?"

"Not anymore." Mitch had dropped her hand as she'd fallen into step with him, and now she used her hand to keep his jacket closed as they walked.

As they talked about her hours, how the store worked, Jenny made plans.

First things first. When should she tell Mitch about the baby? she wondered uneasily. When she needed to, she decided.

He was pleased now, animated, talking about his precious store. He wasn't taking advantage of her— her request for a raise was proof she'd held her own.

But would he take advantage of her emotionally? Whether he traveled or not, she was going to be seeing a lot of him. She was staying at his house, and she was now working for him. After all, not twenty minutes ago, she'd dragged him out here to accuse him of using charm to get what he wanted from a woman.

She needed to be careful. It was one thing to risk her own heart, but she had her baby's happiness to consider.

They stopped at the edge of the pond. The wild ducks that stayed through the winter, thanks to regular feeding and the open water Mitch maintained, swam up to the shore. They quacked for food.

"I don't have any," Mitch said.

They quacked louder.

He laughed. He pulled out his pockets, showing the ducks the linings. She realized she'd never seen him quite so carefree.

Mitch said to the ducks, "If Miss Jenny Litton hadn't dragged me out here like she did, I'd have brought you some crackers."

The ducks milled around, swam, looked hopefully at Jenny.

They seemed so much like begging toddlers that she laughed, too. It felt so good to laugh!

Mitch continued to address the ducks. "She drives a hard bargain, Miss Litton does, and in her own southern way, she is very hard on people who don't measure up to her standards of behavior."

"No, I'm not," she said, even though she knew what he was saying was true. Well, she was harder on herself than anybody else. "I like your kids, but let's face it, they don't measure up to most standards of behavior, southern or otherwise."

"That is a fact," Mitch told the ducks solemnly. "Though I've caught Miss Jenny laughing quite a few times with Jason, so I wonder how much that sort of thing bothers her nowadays."

The mother duck darted for Mitch's feet, pecking with her bill.

"I thought you women liked to talk. Can't we have a little conversation before dinner?" Mitch asked the duck. "I was talking about Miss Jenny, explaining things to you. Another thing about her. She goes all prickly if you try to flirt with her. Don't you, Miss Jenny?"

Her heart gave one quick, hard beat. She tried to sound light as she said, "That shouldn't be a problem. You don't flirt unless you need to."

"Is that a fact?" Almost lazily, playfully, as slowly as the day was turning into an early-winter twilight, he put out a hand and grasped the ends of his blazer, tugging gently.

She actually took one step toward him, propelled by something deep inside her, something that hoped—that yearned—for his touch, his kiss. Heat bloomed in her as she looked up into his suddenly intent, handsome face.

Heat. Dangerous heat. At the last possible moment, she put her own hands on his and dislodged his hold on the jacket.

They stood looking at each other, that tiny distance between them. If she took one small step, she'd be in his arms.

He seemed to be waiting. When she didn't move, he shook his head, one hard shake. Then he turned abruptly and started up the hill.

Jenny waited a moment in order to give him a head start. Her heart was still beating fast, but she told herself she'd done the right thing in not taking that step. She had everything she wanted here. She couldn't afford to blow it by getting involved with Mitch.

Some of the ducks had grown discouraged and had scattered, swimming closer to the center of the pond. But one of the females struggled up onto the shore, and followed Mitch with a determined waddle. Females of every persuasion did that.

The trick was not to be one of them.

CHAPTER NINE

JENNY MADE a quick trip to South Carolina to arrange storage for her furniture, to list her condominium with a Realtor, to pack her clothes and to drive her own car back to Ohio. In the end, it wasn't that hard to say goodbye to her old life. The weather in Hilton Head was wet, cold and dark, a little warmer but not that much different from Ohio. She had lunch with two friends who promised to keep in touch.

But with Kathy and Crystal gone, the condo she'd taken so much pleasure in decorating really did seem what Mitch had called it: four walls and nothing more. She'd been so busy at Kyle Development, she'd never had time for a pet. She hadn't even had time for houseplants. Instead, her plants were silk. Easily boxed to wait until she had her own home in Ohio.

But maybe when she had her house, she'd put a pot of real ivy on a sunny windowsill overlooking her backyard.

She returned to Ohio, and spent the next couple of weeks focusing on her job as manager of Serious Gear. She liked the work. It was varied and interesting. Now that she was finishing her third month of pregnancy, she was less tired, and her stomach seemed less rebellious, too. It made working easier, which was a good thing now that the Christmas rush at the store was beginning.

The baby was becoming more real to her. At night, she'd lie on the big bed in the guest room and think about her child. She couldn't shake the feeling that it was a girl. Of course, she'd love a boy, too, but in her heart she was more and more certain it was a girl.

During the day, she found herself talking to her daughter, mentally whispering silly things like, *We're going to inventory the tennis rackets. We're going to play a counting game. Won't that be fun?*

But at the moment, she was trying to straighten out a snafu in the scheduling of the sales help. ''Excuse me?'' she said, realizing Robin Donovan was talking to her. She put the schedule down on the glass-topped counter and focused on the young woman.

Robin wore a tight black jersey dress that floated just above her ankles, square-toed black boots and eyeliner that made thick, smoky rims around her eyes. She looked fashionably moody. The tight dress showed the contours of her bra in a way that reminded Jenny a little of Stacey, who'd come to call at Mitch's. Jenny's momma would have called Robin brazen.

But Robin also worked very hard, and was one of Mitch's best part-timers. Today, however, she twirled a lock of her long blond hair around her finger and said, ''I can't work next Friday. The Lights are playing.''

"I need you here," Jenny said. "Tina has exams, and school has to come before dates." Dealing with a staff that consisted mostly of teenagers juggling school, work and active social lives could be trying.

"All right," Robin said finally. "I guess I can go out with David after the game, but I hate not being at the arena when he's playing. No telling how many girls will try to get him, you know."

Jenny made a note on the schedule. "If David likes you, he won't be paying attention to those other girls."

"You think?" The girl stopped twirling her hair and looked at Jenny. She looked so young and hopeful that Jenny's heart unexpectedly went out to her.

"If he's worth your caring about him, he won't be sucked in by those girls."

That was something her momma would have said. But Jenny's own experience had taught her differently. Besides, the way Mitch had described the girls who hung out at the rink, even a well-intentioned nineteen-year-old boy might not be able to resist. "You know," she said now, "maybe you should be thinking about other guys. Dating different people. You're only eighteen, not even out of high school—"

"I don't want to date other guys. I love David."

Did she really? Or did she love the chance to breeze by the waiting girls at the locker room? Jenny thought of Delane and sighed. Women were drawn to power, she guessed, and celebrity was power, in a way.

"Have you got a closed reel?" A customer was

standing in front of the case, peering down through the glass top at the fishing reels on the shelf beneath.

"Right here," Robin said with a smile, pulling out her key to unlock the case. "We've got a good selection."

While Robin showed the reels, Jenny stayed by the counter, using a pencil to juggle the schedule, listening with half an ear to the conversation. After the customer had chosen the most expensive one, Jenny looked up to thank her.

The woman smiled. "I used to buy from Mr. Oliver all the time, but he doesn't seem to be here very much."

Jenny explained that Mitch was often out of town and that she was the new manager.

"Oh, good. I'd wondered if there was a problem. I'd hate to think of Mr. Oliver having a problem with his business."

"No problem. Business is good," Jenny assured the woman. And it was true. Mitch had racked up impressive growth figures for Serious Gear in its first three years of business.

"A couple of years ago, Mr. Oliver donated some basketball equipment to our church league and even paid for the uniforms," the customer said. "I've been shopping here ever since."

"Oh, Mitch does lots of good stuff," Robin said breezily. "Last week Serious Gear gave some duffel bags to the YMCA, and this week we donated a trophy for the soccer camp tournament. Mitch does things like that because he has so much money."

"Robin—" Jenny interjected quickly, but the

customer just laughed and said, ''Plenty of people have money, but they don't share any of it.''

Now that she was at the store on a daily basis, Jenny was impressed by the extent of Mitch's giving. He had a regular budget at the store for donations. It was a nice gesture. Like the customer said, he didn't have to do it. It made him a fine man.

Of course, it was also good for business. Every item that went out was in a bag with Serious Gear printed on it. Did Mitch give to charities the way Delane and his family had sponsored charity golf tournaments and museum teas?

Mitch's motives weren't her business, she reminded herself, checking her watch. She was bone tired. And late. She needed to head home. She'd promised to quiz Jason on the continents for geography, and she'd planned to make chicken-fried steak for dinner.

She was still in charge of the evening meal and she was still helping the kids with homework and school. It was important to her that she do her share. She'd stayed at Mitch's a heck of a long time, and Momma had always said the hallmark of a good guest was knowing when to leave.

But in all honesty, Mitch didn't seem to be in any hurry for her to go. In fact, he spent most evenings after the little ones were in bed talking business with her. He seemed to laugh more than he did when she'd first come. He looked at her in a way that made her feel pretty, very aware that she was a woman.

It was a wonderful feeling, to have an incredibly handsome man look at you that way.

It scared her to death, that feeling. She knew she was wrong not to just say to Mitch, *I'm going to have a baby*.

But then she'd have to explain about Delane, about her own stupidity in choosing a man who wouldn't stand by his child.

You also aren't telling him because then he wouldn't look at you the way he does.

Of course, she should tell Mitch about the baby. She knew that. But if she couldn't bring herself to tell him, she had to make sure that she never gave him reason to believe that there would be anything between them.

That last was very hard.

THE FOLLOWING SUNDAY morning, Mitch awakened to a rare silence. The kids must be sleeping in, too. They'd all stayed up very late the night before putting up the Christmas tree. He stretched, got up and walked to the window.

Snow had fallen. It coated the branches of the firs, the big willow on the hill. It drifted against the picnic table. There was a hush to the outdoors.

Crystal had been waiting for it to snow. Not the few flakes they'd had the last couple of weeks that had quickly melted. She'd seen that in Hilton Head. What Crystal wanted was what she called a "sticky snow."

He hurriedly got into jeans and a sweatshirt and sneaked down the long hallway. His niece's door was open. He poked his head in and saw that she was up. Her back was to him as she stood looking out her window. Her red hair trailed down her back, she was dressed in a flannel nightgown and held her favorite doll. She must have heard him at the doorway, because she turned around.

She glowed more brightly than the fresh snow under the sun. "Snow," she said, sounding stunned, as if she hadn't really believed it was ever going to come, despite Jenny taking her shopping for a snowsuit, mittens and shiny red boots. As if snow was better than Christmas. "Real snow!" she squealed.

"Snow!" It was Jason, whooping in the hallway. There was banging along the wall as he came. "Ryan! Tommy! You dorks, get up! It snowed!"

They all crowded around the window in Crystal's room. Even Jewels was there perched on the windowsill. Mitch held Crystal up higher than Jason's head so she could look over the boys. She saw a cardinal at the bird feeder, the one that looked so bright red against the white snow. She saw dog tracks that traced crazy lines in the backyard. She asked Mitch if the tracks were made by a wild animal, and he said yes, they were made by Face-off. She asked why the snow didn't stick to the water of the pond, which wasn't completely frozen yet. She chattered in a way he'd never heard her chatter. It amazed him. It made something buried very, very deep in him, something sad and cold, melt a little.

"What's going on?" It was Jenny in the doorway.

The boys didn't hear her, but Mitch did. He put Crystal down and turned to look at her.

She was sleepy-eyed and mussed, bringing to mind visions of a warm bed. Her terry-cloth robe was modest, belted at the waist, and he could see a bit of her blue satin nightgown peeping out. Now he imagined the satin against her skin, the way the fabric would hug and cup her full breasts.

"Let's go sledding!" Jason yelled right in his ear, and Mitch was reminded in the strongest way possible that here and now was not the time for imagining satin and skin.

The kids ran pell-mell for the doorway. Jenny stepped inside the room just in time to keep from being run down as they struggled for passage. When they'd gone, Mitch asked Jenny, "How about it? How about sledding?"

Her forehead creased. "Sledding would be pretty physical," she said.

"Well, sledding is physical, but it's not exactly hockey. I think Crystal would like you to come." *I want you to come.* He imagined walking through a snowfall with her, kissing her cold nose, burying his own nose in the warm skin in the crook of her neck.

"I don't know...we haven't had breakfast."

"We've got granola bars, we can eat them on the way out. Look, I know you're not a morning person, but couldn't you be a little flexible?"

She flushed. "I—I haven't been feeling well. I need to take it easy with physical activities."

Alarm shot through him. A few times in the morning she'd looked pale. But he'd thought that was because she wasn't much for mornings. "You're sick?'' Memories of Anne's illness washed through him. He'd never be easy about illness again.

She must have caught his expression. ''I'm not seriously ill.''

''You've seen a doctor, then?''

''Yes.'' There was a little silence. Then she lifted her chin and looked so prickly and touch-me-not that it was as if she'd grown quills. ''The doctor says I'm fine. I don't need breakfast. I don't want to sled but I'll come watch Crystal and y'all.''

At that moment, the kids came back down the hall, talking about Luke not being here to sled, wondering where Mitch and Miss Jenny were, wondering where Jason's glove was, wondering if they could cross-country ski, and if so, wondering where the ladder was so they could get the skis down from the rafters in the garage.

He didn't really want to end the discussion with Jenny. There was a kind of tenseness in the air that he didn't like. But the kids were all looking at him expectantly. ''All right. Let's get dressed and go sledding.''

Ten minutes later, Mitch had Crystal sitting on the sled. He pushed her down the safe part of the hill, where there were no trees and she was unlikely to end up in the pond. She screamed with glee.

The boys went to the other run because it was steeper and therefore more fun. Crystal begged to learn how to steer the sled, so Mitch showed her, and she made a couple of curving, wobbly runs down the steep slope herself. Suddenly it didn't make a difference that she was a girl. Kids were kids. Crystal was as excited about her accomplishment as the boys were about theirs.

Jenny walked around, picked up handfuls of snow, sniffed them as though they were some strange flower. The cold and the fun seemed to have taken the last of Mitch's irritation. Instead, he enjoyed watching her playing in the snow.

The kids were occupied, and he didn't seem to be in danger of being called to fish one of them out of the pond any time soon, so he kept watching Jenny. Then he got an idea. He reached down into the wet snow and brought up a clump. It made a perfect, baseball-size snowball. He slung it at her. It caught her high on the shoulder with a burst of cold, glittering snow. She stopped and stared at it, as if for a moment she couldn't figure out where it had come from.

He grinned. There seemed to be so many things Miss Jenny Litton had missed in that uptight southern belle life of hers. Without a word, he made another snowball, sent it sailing. With the good aim of the professional athlete, it hit her other shoulder.

"Why, you…" She bent, started to make a snowball.

He chuckled in anticipation, knowing she couldn't possibly win this game. In fact, he got in two more hits before she managed to make her first snowball. She stood awkwardly, one booted foot in a snowbank, and reared back to fire her missile.

He took aim, fired at the same time she momentarily lost her footing. Instead of hitting her on the shoulder again, his snowball hit her smack in the face.

"Whoa, I didn't mean to hit you in the face!" In two strides, he was nearly upon her. She held out her hands to ward him off...

And fell backward into the soft, cushy drift. Her arms and legs stuck out at awkward angles; she struggled. He bent to help her up and lost his footing himself.

Okay, so he didn't exactly lose his footing by accident. But joining her in the snowbank seemed like a great thing to do.

He landed. She went still. Her hat had come off, and all that glistening blond hair spilled out over the snow. Her skin was china-doll pink, her eyes as blue as the pond, with big, perfect snowflakes caught on her eyelashes. His thigh wedged between her legs, and where he pressed against her he felt warmth. Cold and hot and sexy as hell. His face was inches from hers.

For a long moment, they stared at each other. He was breathing hard now, way harder than he needed to be. Her lips parted as she, too, seemed to take in a long breath of air.

He ached to kiss her. He bent his head. Her eyes drifted shut...

Suddenly she squirmed and twisted. *"Don't,"* she said with such vehemence that he stopped. She pushed at him, and he struggled to roll off and offer her his hand. She sat up.

"Would it be so terrible if I kissed you?" he asked quietly.

"It would be terrible," she said so quietly he wasn't sure he'd heard her. She turned to face him then. "You don't want me, Mitch. Believe me."

There was so much in her voice—regret, maybe, and certainty. All of a sudden he got a very bad feeling. "Tell me why."

She struggled to her feet. "I will. I know I have to. I mean, you'd know pretty soon anyway, but...but right now I...I've got snow in my boots and I..." She fled, awkward in her boots, hurrying through the snow to the back door.

What the...? He didn't have a clue. He sat on his cold rear in the drift and watched her go and thought about following her inside and confronting her.

He looked up and saw that Ryan had paused at the top of the hill and was watching her, too. So Mitch got to his feet and said, "Hey, what did you guys do with the toboggan?"

RIGHT AFTER CHRISTMAS, Jenny promised herself as she stood at the stove and browned meat for a stew. She would tell Mitch right after Christmas. She would also find another place to live right after Christmas, even though her condominium in Hilton Head hadn't yet sold. She'd rent for a while.

But she couldn't go yet. Crystal was so excited about the tree. They'd shopped for a pretend gift for Crystal's momma in heaven, and Crystal sent it to Kathy in a prayer. Jenny knew this first Christmas without her mother would be difficult for the little girl.

The season was working against Jenny. Instead of

traveling, Mitch was often at Serious Gear during this busy time. They were both putting in long hours on the sales floor; she was very tired most of the time, and she saw that Mitch too was strained nearly to the limit.

At the same time, she was looking forward to the holiday. This Christmas seemed more exciting somehow. Maybe it was because she'd had to buy so many presents. Maybe it was because it was cold and snowy and all the storybooks she'd ever read to Crystal pictured Christmas that way.

Maybe it was because she would be spending the holiday with Mitch. She quickly tried to think of something else.

She had just got home from the store a few minutes ago, and it was close to dinnertime. She washed carrots and peeled and cubed potatoes to add to her stew, and got the gravy bubbling.

Her feet were often swollen and achy these days, and she tried to make one-pot meals so that she could rest a little sooner. The twins were around somewhere, and suddenly exhausted, she called to them to keep an eye on dinner. She went into the family room, stuck a CD in the player and put her feet up.

Ah. Bliss. She closed her eyes and over the soft strains of the music, started the calming, inner dialogue with her baby, telling about all the sweet little outfits she planned to buy for her little girl next Christmas.

It was hard to relax, because the twins were in the kitchen, presumably watching her dinner, but arguing. The sound was an annoying overlay to "The Holly and the Ivy."

"Rats!"

"You ruined it, you dork!"

Crash!

Wearily, Jenny got to her feet.

"Big deal. It was your fault, anyway!"

She knew the drill by now. *Goodbye, stew,* she thought, heading into the kitchen. Another disaster was definitely not something she felt like dealing with today.

The pan of stew lay upside down on the kitchen floor. A small pile of silverware was on the floor, too; that must be the source of the metallic crash she'd heard a few seconds ago. *Stay calm,* she ordered herself. "Okay, what happened?"

"He was screwing around," Tommy accused Ryan.

"It was your fault. You tackled me, you dork!"

"Well, if you weren't trying to stab me in the neck with that fork—"

"Would y'all just...*grow up?*"

They both looked at her, then at each other. "Chill out, it was an accident. Hey, we can get a pizza," Tommy said, brightening. Ryan just looked at Jenny and glowered.

"How about an apology first?"

She got a say-what? look from both the twins. "An apology right now," she said again with real sharpness in her tone.

Ryan gave her an insolent look. "Dad will cough

up for a pizza. That ought to be apology enough. You don't have to cook again.''

''I don't have to cook at *all*. I'm not the hired help, and it's a good thing I'm not, because then I surely wouldn't tolerate your mess and disrespect.''

''Whatever,'' he said sullenly.

Tommy shot her a guilty look, but moved closer to his brother.

''A simple 'I'm sorry,' will do.''

Ryan shot her a look of open hostility. ''Forget it.''

Jenny clamped her lips shut and bent to pick up the pan. As she turned it over, she saw that her stew had burned even before it had all landed on the floor. All she'd asked them to do was stir it a few times, and those...*dorks* hadn't even done that. She looked down at the burned pan, and for the first time she really understood what Momma meant when she'd get mad and say she was ''seeing red.'' Weeks of hormones running wild, of tension with Ryan, of tension of another kind with Mitch, of secrets and plans and...and swollen feet sent her over the edge. She stood next to the glob of stew in the middle of the kitchen floor and burst into tears.

''Aw, jeez,'' Tommy said, putting out his hands as if to ward her off. ''Aw, jeez. Man...''

Ryan said impatiently, ''Come on, it's only stew.''

Tommy said, ''Jenny, jeez, don't cry. I would have said I was sorry if it hadn't been Ryan's fault...''

Jenny cried harder.

Tommy and Ryan backed away from her just as Jason and Crystal came into the kitchen. Crystal took one look at Jenny's tears and started wailing herself.

Jason watched, a look of pinched misery on his face.

Jenny tried to stop crying. She held out a hand to Jason and Crystal. The little ones huddled against her.

Jenny swallowed, choked on one big sob. The twins hovered, Crystal still crying openly.

AND THAT'S HOW Mitch found them.

"My God, are you hurt?" He dropped his briefcase and hurried over to Jenny.

She shook her head.

Jason, his voice shaking with outrage, told Mitch about the dinner.

Mitch looked down at Jenny. It was a shame about dinner, but could she be this upset—her eyes and lips puffy, red and swollen—over food? He didn't have a clue what to do—he'd never been good with crying women, and now he had two of them. Maybe he should start with the little one.

"Crystal, come on, honey, you don't need to cry." The girl shook her head and sobbed harder.

He gave Jenny a panicked look. *Help me here.*

He could see the effort it cost her to get control. But she managed to do it, finally, and hugged and shushed his niece.

Jenny whispered, "Look at this mess. I want an apology from Ryan and Tommy."

Uh-oh. That could be a problem. None of the males in the family were good at saying sorry.

Tommy said, "Hey, why don't I help clean up?"

Ryan said nothing.

Jenny repeated, "I want an apology, Mitch."

She had been crying and that hurt something inside him. He shoved his hands in his pockets. "Look, guys, I know you were just horsing around, but why don't you say you're sorry. Jenny worked hard on this dinner." It sounded lame and he knew it. But he could tell by the way the kids hung their heads that they were damn sorry.

"Sorry," Tommy mumbled, going bright red.

"Thank you," Jenny said. The silence got thick after that as everyone looked at Ryan.

"I won't," he said with vehemence.

"Look," Mitch started, "I know you didn't mean anything, but you weren't paying attention and—"

"Are you going to make me?" Ryan looked at him with open defiance. Mitch studied his son. There was a challenge in his eyes, and a kind of bitterness that seemed to go deep.

"I won't say I'm sorry!" Ryan burst out. "Not to *her.* Why should I apologize? I never asked her to come here! I have to eat, but I never asked her to make dinner! We were doing fine without her!"

"What's got into you?" Mitch asked, astounded. "Jenny has been good to us—"

"She's been good to *you,* you mean. You're always looking at her! Like…like *that* way. I know why you keep her here. I know what you want. It makes me sick, the way you can't hide what you want—oh, hell.''

Mitch himself went sick with embarrassment and more. He'd never dreamed he'd been that transparent. He glanced at Jenny. She looked as stunned as he felt. Her red cheeks matched her red nose. "Ryan, Jenny has never..." He trailed off as he realized that everyone, even Crystal, was listening.

"Well, you still want to jump—"

"That's enough!" he said sharply, bringing his fist down on the kitchen counter.

"Seems like a big shot like you could get it somewhere else, without bringing it home to Mom's house—"

"Enough!" he roared, in a voice he'd never heard himself use before. His hands were shaking. "Now, you *will* apologize to Jenny. I mean it. Right now."

A long, ugly pause as he and his son looked into each other's eyes and battled wills. Ryan finally said in the most insincere, defiant voice possible, "I'm sorry."

THIS WAS A BAD NIGHT. Crystal knew it in her stomach. Ryan was bad to burn Miss Jenny's dinner and then say bad things about her. Uncle Mitch wouldn't explain why they were bad things, and neither would Miss Jenny when Crystal had knocked on her door a while ago. But she knew Ryan had said bad things just the same.

After Ryan and Tommy and Miss Jenny had left the kitchen, Uncle Mitch had made Crystal and Jason each a peanut butter and jelly sandwich, but even Jason wasn't hungry and that wasn't a good sign, because Jason was always hungry.

Now she went down the hall with Jewels in her arms, past Ryan's room. Ryan was in there with the door shut, playing his music real loud.

Crystal went on by and stopped in the open doorway of Jason's room. He was lying in bed and had the TV on, but his head was turned toward the wall and he wasn't even watching the screen. He rolled over and looked at her when she said, "Jason?"

"Whatcha want?"

She went in and said it was a bad night, and her voice sounded funny when she said it. Jason sat up and got nice then and said it was a really bad night. Then he said, "Ryan thinks if we like Miss Jenny that's kind of saying we're not remembering our mom. But I can't help it. I like Miss Jenny a lot."

He looked as if he was going to cry, so Crystal looked away quick, because seeing Jason almost cry scared her. Because that meant she was right in feeling like something bad was going to happen. "Why didn't Ryan want to say he was sorry?"

Jason shrugged. "Because Ryan is a dork."

"If I said, 'Cut the crap,' I'd say I was sorry, and Ryan didn't even say anything as bad as that. Except he did burn the pan, and I guess that made Uncle Mitch mad."

"I think…" Jason paused. "I think maybe Dad really likes Miss Jenny."

"Well, sure. We all do."

"I mean, I guess Ryan thinks Dad's sort of like in love with her."

Oh. Now Crystal got it. That made her happy, Uncle Mitch in love with Miss Jenny. "That would be good."

There was another pause. "I think so, too. It seems weird, though, Dad like in love with a lady. He's so old. But it would be good."

"Why doesn't Ryan like Miss Jenny?"

"Because I think he wants Dad to still be in love with Mom."

"But your momma's in heaven, same as mine, and it's a wonderful place but you can't ever come back from there." If heaven was go great, Crystal didn't understand why she wasn't allowed to go there to be with her mom, but she'd given up trying to work that out long ago. At least Miss Jenny was still here in the world. "Do you think Miss Jenny's in love with Uncle Mitch?"

Jason got up then. "How'm I supposed to know? You're the girl. What do you think?"

"I don't know, either." She tried to puzzle it out. "I don't think so, I guess, because Miss Jenny was going back to Hilton Head, and even now she says she's going to buy a house with a backyard and I can come visit. So she isn't going to live at Uncle Mitch's and I think she would if she loved him."

She swallowed real hard. "But maybe she won't stay in Ohio, because Miss Jenny was really sad today." Crystal knew Miss Jenny was staying in Ohio because she had a job in Uncle Mitch's store, but maybe Miss Jenny wouldn't do that job anymore if she was mad at Ryan. She whispered what she'd wanted to ask right at first, but had been too afraid to say. "Do you think Miss Jenny will go home now?"

Jason gave her a look and she knew that's what he was thinking, too. "I don't know," he said, and she could see him swallow, too.

She stayed talking to Jason for a while, but finally she went to bed. She couldn't find Jewels, and she almost cried about that. But Silver got in bed with her, and she hugged him while she said a prayer that Miss Jenny stay. She felt her dog's curly fur and heard the beating of his heart, and she promised God to be good and asked Him to try to make the boys be good so maybe Miss Jenny would stay. After all, Crystal said to God, Hilton Head was closer than heaven, but it was still very, very far away.

CHAPTER TEN

DESPITE HER EXHAUSTION, Jenny couldn't sleep. Finally too restless to lie in bed anymore, she got up. She looked out the window for a few minutes, then decided to take a short walk. Though it was the middle of the night, the moon was bright, and maybe a bit of fresh, cold air would help her sleep when she came back to bed.

She put on her clothes. Ryan had embarrassed her thoroughly tonight. She was no longer as angry as she had been, now that she realized what had been bothering the teenager all along. It wasn't surprising that Ryan had trouble handling his feelings. Chances were, this was the first time Mitch had been involved with a woman since—

Well, not "involved," but it was the first time he'd looked at a woman *that* way—to use his son's words—since Anne's death.

No wonder she couldn't sleep!

She tiptoed downstairs. Once there, she put on her boots and parka, and realized no one had turned off the Christmas tree. The big tree was set up right in the middle of the family room's bay window. She left the lights on so she could see her way, opening the sliding glass doors from the breakfast area and going out onto the deck. There she stood at the railing, watching the glow of red and blue and amber and green light across the snow. She took deep breaths of cold air. It felt good. There was a hushed quiet about the farm that was unusual and pleasant.

She heard a noise behind her and turned. Mitch came though the sliding door, in jeans and a leather jacket. He looked so handsome. But her cheeks warmed at the memory of Ryan's comments.

"Hi," he said quietly.

"Hi."

"Couldn't sleep?"

She shook her head.

"Me neither. I heard you come down." He joined her at the railing, and for a moment they were both silent. His hands were bare, and he used one finger to make a lazy line in the snow that coated the railing. "Look, this isn't any easier for me than it was for the twins, but I want to say I'm sorry." A pause. "I *have* been looking at you as if I want to kiss you every second of the day, and I guess it showed."

She glanced at him. A fragment of green light revealed a quick, self-deprecating smile that came and went in a heartbeat. His breath made a cloud in the cold air. "I'm not sorry for wanting to kiss you." Then, more soberly, he added, "But I am sorry I let my son know that's what I had in mind."

She studied the sweep of lawn, the snow pocked with footprints and dogs' paws, and tried for a nonchalance she didn't feel. "Well, for a man who claims he doesn't like to apologize, that was pretty good."

"You think?"

"Yes. And I also think you're not the only one at fault. I haven't discouraged you enough."

He let out a short bark of laugher. "Lady, you could have fooled me."

"Mitch—"

"Wait." He held up a hand. "I just want to finish what I came out to tell you. I think you deserve an explanation for why at first I didn't want to make the kids apologize."

She was about to tell him to forget it, but something about his stillness stopped her.

"The thing is," he said softly, "when I played hockey, I was never around. You don't realize what it was like, because though I work long hours now, I'm home at night. You've seen how it is with Luke, how seldom he's here, and for me it was worse. We decided to live in Ohio instead of Chicago because Anne wanted to be near her family and her friends. The commute from Chicago to North Shore complicated things. I was lucky to make it home once every couple of weeks during the season."

"You must have hated that."

"Not really." His answer surprised her. "I mean, I guess I'd have rather been home, and I missed Anne and the kids, but I loved hockey. I'd get so wrapped up in the game. It takes so much concentration to play at the level of the NHL. I *couldn't* let anything interfere, and, as I told you, Anne agreed with my decision to focus on my career. I think it was one of the things I loved most about her. I felt so bad when she got sick and I didn't come home right away.''

"But she'd said it wasn't serious."

"Yeah, but the second I saw her I knew it was. She'd lost so much weight and she was so pale. If I'd have been here more often, if I'd have been paying attention, maybe I would have noticed earlier.'' His voice ached with regret.

"Would...would that have made a difference?" she asked gently.

He didn't look at her. "No, probably not. Her illness went fast, even with treatment."

Her heart went out to him; she longed to take his hand.

"That wasn't all," Mitch went on. "Just before she died, Anne made me promise that I'd take care of everyone. Like she felt she had to get a promise out of me to take care of my own kids. But at first, that promise was all that kept me from hiring a nanny and going back on the road.

"I really resented that I had to give up hockey. You know, I still dream at night sometimes that I'm out on the ice. But I love my kids, so I took over parenting. It was really hard for all of us. I know I'm not tough enough on them, especially about things like manners. I know you think I don't discipline them enough, and you're right."

He held up a hand when she would have spoken. "But it's been easier for me to be their friend. We had to start from where we started. It's tough for a person to apologize, and as their friend, I know that."

"I understand." It was hard to be angry with a man who loved his children as much as Mitch obviously did.

"Do you?"

She hesitated. "I know being a parent—especially a single parent—must be difficult. Sometimes when Crystal—"

"I think you do great with Crystal. You're relaxed around her, you laugh with her. I see you hug her."

"Crystal's easy to love."

"Now you do the same thing with Jason."

"Jason's easy, too."

"Not bad for a boy." They shared a smile, for once in perfect understanding.

He studied the paths his finger had made in the snow. "I thought you were awfully uptight there for a while, but I know now you're not. You're as vulnerable and as soft as anybody I know."

Her heart gave a little lurch. Very few people in her life had realized that. Delane used to praise her business skills, tell her how well she ran the office. She was so good he didn't have to be there very often, and she wondered—not for the first time—if that hadn't been her chief appeal to him.

He added, "I'd come home and see you in the kitchen. You'd be smiling at something one of the kids said, and it just seemed so pleasant in there and...warm. Once, I came home and you and Crystal and Jason were all rolling out piecrust and singing that silly song. Then I knew. I knew you were special."

Oh, my. *Oh, my.* "Oh, Mitch."

He turned to her. "So. Here we are. It's dark and there's a moon, and the Christmas-tree lights are making the snow look pretty. It's cold, but that's not a bad thing if you can find a way to keep warm."

She should go in the house. This minute. She knew it as sure as she breathed. Instead, she stood still, because he'd said she was special.

He said, "I told you before. I'm ready. I want some of that warmth, too."

His naked admission stirred her, brought something inside her to life. If only she could—

She couldn't. She couldn't let him kiss her. She couldn't let him think she was free, that she felt the same way he did. And she couldn't trust herself to stay away from him any longer. In two seconds she'd be in his arms...

He leaned toward her, through a streak of blue light. She said quickly, "I've got to tell you something. And I owe you a bigger apology than you or your family ever owed me."

He stopped short, obviously caught by something in her tone. "Jenny—"

"Wait. I've got to tell you." She hurried now, speaking quickly. Despite the night air, she felt hot with embarrassment and shame. *How long do you think it takes to make a baby? Five minutes? Ten on a good night?* Mitch's own words. He wouldn't understand. "When I was in Hilton Head, I was engaged." There. Work up to it.

He went still. "But you didn't get married?"

"No, he left me. But that was all right. By that time I knew he wasn't the right man for me."

"Then what—"

"Wait." She held out her hand. "His name is Delane Kyle, and he was the owner of Kyle Development, the firm I worked for in Hilton Head. He was nice-looking and rich and charming, and it was easy for me to fall for him. I knew better, I realize appearances don't mean much, my momma being a maid in a house full of rich people taught me a lot about appearances, but— Well, anyway." She stole a glance at him. He wasn't looking directly at her. Instead, his back was straight, and he was looking out at the lawn. Quiet. Listening.

Not judging. That gave her the courage to go on. "You know, not too long before I started dating Delane, I met your sister. Kathy and Crystal meant a lot to me, right away. Crystal was, well, you know what a neat kid she is. Kathy had made me realize what I was missing. A family. I'd proved I could be independent, make a success of my life, but I was…lonely." A little lump formed in her throat at the memory of that loneliness.

"Then Delane and I got together, and I started dreaming about a child of my own. A little girl like Crystal. And, Mitch, I—" She stopped, cleared her throat. "I—"

He looked at her, and when he spoke, his voice was gentle. "Just tell me what you want to tell me."

She was suddenly very conscious of the cold. She tried to steel herself for the loss of Mitch's respect, and for the moment when he no longer found her attractive. "Delane and I got engaged, and I thought it was all right, that we were going to get married andIgotpregnant." Her last words ran together as she rushed to say them.

"What?" In the act of reaching out to her, he froze.

"I'm pregnant, Mitch. I'm going to have a baby in June."

His gaze flew to her stomach, encased in a heavy jacket. "No. You're not...you don't look pregnant. A baby?" he said, sounding stunned.

"I'm not due until June," she said, noting where his disbelieving gaze was fixed. "I can feel it if I put a hand on my bare skin, a tight, bitty little mound, but it doesn't show when I wear something roomy."

"A baby," he said again. "I don't believe it."

He made no move toward her, but he didn't recoil, either. "I thought you were wearing those loose sweaters because you were modest."

Hurt stabbed her. "I *am* modest."

"You're a modest woman who got pregnant." His voice was still soft and shocked, but now there was the ugly undertone that she'd feared.

"I loved Delane. I was going to marry him," she cried. Another wash of shame bathed her. All right, it was a new century, babies were born to single mothers all the time. Even in Sweetspring, South Carolina, girls got pregnant. If you were from a nice family, it was gossiped over and forgotten in the round of baby showers and christening. If you were trash, well then, people shook their heads and said things like, *What did you expect? It's trash begetting trash.*

She'd worked hard to put a good distance between her and Sweetspring, South Carolina. But under Mitch's contemptuous gaze, she felt as if she'd never left.

"So you got pregnant." He said the word *pregnant* as though he couldn't quite get his tongue around it. "Why aren't you married to your nice-looking, rich and charming boyfriend?"

"Fiancé."

"Okay, fiancé. Why isn't he your husband now?"

"He didn't want the baby, Mitch." Tears gathered in her eyes, and she willed them not to fall. "He wanted me to have an abortion and I couldn't."

For a moment, his expression softened. He even said, "Oh, Jenny," and hope sputtered to life in her. But then his features hardened, and she could see his perfect mouth set in a strong, hard line. And when he spoke, his voice was hard, too. "So Kyle Development didn't go bankrupt. You weren't out of a job."

"Oh, yes, it did go bankrupt. It happened after Delane and I broke up. I was there the day they closed the door."

"You continued to work for the man after he refused to marry you?" His voice was harsh with contempt.

"I needed the work! Maybe if you'd ever been poor, you'd understand how I wasn't going to be poor again, how I'd never let my baby be poor if I could help it. I hated working for him. But I was afraid I couldn't get another job!'' Her voice rose, as if in volume she could get him to understand.

"Till you found a bigger fool who offered you one here.''

She clenched her fists. "That's not fair.''

"It's not fair for me to think you manipulated me into this job, when you lied about everything?''

"I didn't lie! I've never lied to you! I tried to tell you that I couldn't get involved, Mitch. I did say that. More than one time.''

Mitch stared at her. He couldn't really recall if she'd out-and-out lied, but not telling him amounted to the same thing, didn't it? In the low light, he wasn't sure if she was crying or not. He didn't want to know, because he didn't want to go all soft and helpless the way he always did when a woman cried.

It occurred to him then that it was cold out here, that maybe he should get Jenny back into the house. After all, she was going to have a baby. No, damn it! That baby of hers was not his problem. He thought of his kids and was sickened. "So you came here and befriended my kids, knowing I'd ask you to stay.''

There was a long, ugly pause. Then she said very, very quietly, "Do you really believe that?''

No. He didn't. Yes, he did. Hell, he didn't know. All he knew was that he felt betrayed. As if he'd been sucker-punched by one of his own teammates.

He stood with both hands gripping the deck railing, gripping so hard the knuckles hurt. She came and stood next to him. They were both quiet for a moment. Then she reached out and covered his hand with hers.

Her hand wasn't cold, but hot, and that startled him for a moment. Until he suddenly remembered that Anne had often had warm feet and hands when she'd been pregnant. He thought of Anne's belly, knew that Jenny's would soon swell.

He struggled to remember how it had been for Anne when she was pregnant. Truth to tell, he didn't remember that much. Jason had been born a long time ago, and he'd always felt funny about the details of Anne's pregnancies, anyway. Like it was some mysterious, feminine process that was beyond him. But he remembered how Anne was always sick in the mornings early on. How Jenny never wanted much breakfast.

He'd been a fool, all right.

"Mitch, believe me, I didn't want to hurt anybody. All my life, I've been a planner. Then when I got pregnant, everything seemed to fall apart. I was so scared, but I didn't know what to do, except try to stick with the plans I'd made. I didn't think I'd need to tell you at first. I didn't think we'd be involved, I didn't think I'd want to—'' She stopped. Then she said, "I never intended to hurt your kids. Believe me.''

He did. Hearing the sincerity in her voice, he really believed that the bastard she was engaged to had let her down and she'd just tried to keep her head above water.

She added, "You know how I grew up. I mean, I haven't wanted to dwell on it, but you know my momma was a maid. My daddy was kind of what, in Sweetspring, they called a 'no account.' They called us trash, Mitch. I—I thought maybe that's what you'd think of me, too, and I couldn't bear it if—'' She fell silent.

He was so confused. Every instinct he had said that Jenny was sincere. That the woman who had flown out here to check on Crystal, who had cheered Luke on in his hockey game, who had done her share in the house, who had helped with homework and listened to Jason's stories about his mother, would never use him.

But this was no time to go with his instincts. He had to remember how many years he'd tried to avoid manipulative women. He had to think of protecting his kids. He had to use his head.

He pulled his hand away.

There was a pause. Then Jenny said, ''I know things will change now. In every way. For one thing, I know this means I'm out of a job.''

''No, you're not,'' he said in surprise. A curious protectiveness mixed with anger at her deception.

Then a new anger spurted in him, this time at himself. He was like every other celebrity out there, duped and thinking with his— ''You don't deserve to be fired, but you're a bad influence on the boys.''

She gasped.

He'd said the most hurtful thing he could think of. Instantly, he wanted to take it back. But he didn't.

''I'll leave tonight,'' she said in a tight voice, and she turned and went back in the house.

Good. It was the best solution for all of them.

He stayed on the deck. In a few moments, her light went on upstairs, and it gleamed from the cracks in the blinds, and shone out over the deck. Mitch studied that path of light, imagined her packing. He was glad she was going. Glad! Dee-lighted. Brimful of holiday joy.

He stood there until his feet got numb with cold. He wrestled with a sense of loss that surprised him in its intensity.

He struggled also with a sense of justice, at how harsh his judgment of her was. He struggled with the thought that he'd thrown a pregnant woman out of his house in the middle of the night.

In the end, he found himself upstairs in the guest wing, still in his outdoor jacket, knocking at her door. "Look, I— Just listen for a minute, okay?" Silence on the other side of the door. "Look, you can stay a few days. It'll give you a chance to find someplace decent for you and your baby."

Silence. He knocked again. "Jenny? You don't have to go right now. You can stay here until you get on your feet. Did you hear me?"

"Yes. I heard you." Southern belle prim and cold as ice.

Well, what had he expected? Satisfied that he'd done his duty, he went off to bed.

He didn't fall asleep, but he never heard her leave the house. He never heard her car.

But in the morning, she was gone.

WELL, she wouldn't really have left. Not after he'd said she could stay here, not after he'd just about said he was sorry. She was at the store, he decided with relief. She must have decided to avoid him by going in to work early. That's what he told Crystal—leaving out the part about avoiding him—when she asked why Jenny hadn't joined them at breakfast.

He hurriedly showered and shaved. He got sharp with the boys when they screwed around and were almost late for the bus. He didn't have time to drive them to school today. He needed to get to the store and make sure Jenny was all right.

When he got to work, he saw her car in the parking lot. His hands on the steering wheel went slack, making him aware of how tightly he'd been clutching the wheel.

He headed up to the suite of offices that occupied the second floor. Jenny was in his office, putting a piece of paper on his desk. Another spurt of relief went through him. He told himself he was only worried about her the way he'd be worried about any woman under the circumstances. "Oh, you're here," he said stupidly.

"I'm leaving you this." She waved the paper. She looked too pale, with circles under her eyes.

"Okay." Whatever. "I'm glad you came to your senses and decided to stay at the house."

"I don't intend to stay. I left last night, Mitch."

Whoa. "Where did you go?"

"The Sunset Motor Court." Cool and tight, as prickly as the day he'd met her.

The Sunset Motor Court was one of the few in

town that would be likely to have an empty room in the middle of the night the week before Christmas.

"I told you that you could stay with us."

"How can I? I'm a bad influence on the boys." There was a world of hurt in her voice.

He winced, but he still didn't take back his words. "I don't kick out pregnant women," he said gruffly.

"I don't imagine it's something you have to do all that often, knowing your feelings on the subject."

He changed tactics. "What's that?" He gestured to the paper she held in her hand.

"My resignation."

Shit. "Well, I'm not accepting it."

"You can't do that. I'm resigning."

He adopted a wide-legged stance, folded his arms across his chest and remained where he was, blocking the doorway. "I need you here. It's almost Christmas. Are you going to let me down in the middle of our busy season?"

She bit her lip.

Ah-ha. "You agreed to do a job. You're in retailing, and in retailing Christmas is the make-or-break season. You can't quit on me now."

"Why on earth would you want me to stay?"

The sixty-four-thousand-dollar question, but all he knew was that he desperately wanted her to stay. He thought about turning on the charm, decided that wouldn't work. So he focused on her instead. Stood looking at her, holding her gaze. Slowly, the hand holding her letter lowered to her side. "I'll stay," she said quietly.

"Good," he said carefully. She was still in full porcupine mode.

"Just until after the baby is born. That'll give you plenty of time to find and train someone else."

"Fine," he said. "When I go to do the banking today, I can stop off at the Sunset Motor Court and get your things."

"I meant I'd stay on at work. I didn't say I was coming back to your house."

"Why not?"

"Because I'm a bad influence on—"

"Enough! I know what I said." Somehow, this situation had got to the point where *she* was in the wrong, but *he* was begging her to stay. He had no clue how that had happened, but he was not going to apologize.

"I've made my plans. I'll stay in the Sunset Motor Court until I can find an apartment to rent. I can visit Crystal. I can visit Jason if you decide I'm not a bad influence—"

"Forget the influence thing, all right?"

She flushed. "Thank you." Her voice softened to a near whisper. "I'd hate it if I couldn't see Jason again."

She wasn't a criminal, just a woman who was going to have a baby. Sure, she should have told him right away, but the worst part was that she'd hurt his pride somehow. It really bugged him—hurt his pride—to think of her carrying another man's child. But it wasn't right to take that out on her.

"Look, we'll tell the kids. I'll tell the boys, and you can tell Crystal." Now that he'd persuaded her to stay on at work, he pressed his advantage on the home front. "Crystal is really looking forward to your being at the house on Christmas Day. It's her first Christmas without her mother."

He knew that would get her to agree to come for Christmas, and it did. He felt a little better as she went back down onto the floor to make sure they were stocked for the day's Christmas rush. As he gathered the receipts and deposit slips, he thought again about how she'd turned the tables on him.

Was Jenny a manipulative female, or just one who was trying to do the best for her child?

It didn't matter. There was no hope of anything romantic between them now. Her baby had ended that for good.

"Wow!" Crystal said when Jenny told her about the baby. Jenny chose one of her visits shortly after Christmas to tell the little girl. They sat in the front seat of Jenny's car, in the parking lot of the local McDonald's.

The daughter of a single mother herself, Crystal asked no questions about the child's father. Jenny was relieved. There was time enough for that. Now Crystal leaned over from her place in the passenger seat, focused on Jenny's belly and asked, "Is it a girl baby or a boy baby?"

"Nobody knows yet. Unless I have some medical tests that the doctor says I don't need, we won't know until it's born. But I'll tell you a secret." She leaned toward Crystal's red head and whispered, "I have a feeling it's a little girl."

"A girl would be good. Can I feel where she's growing?"

Jenny chuckled, glad to be sharing this news with someone who was so happy for her. "Sure you can. Give me your hand. No, you've got to take off your mitten first, or you can't feel anything. The baby's still really tiny."

After Crystal had used her teeth to yank off her mitten, Jenny guided her hand under her sweater and the waistband of her slacks. "Feel that hard little knot?"

Crystal's forehead wrinkled as her hand pushed gently. "I guess. I can't feel too much."

"Soon you'll be able to feel her move," Jenny promised.

"Yes. I want to do that. You know, Miss Jenny, I think Jewels and Silver will be really happy about the baby."

"GROSS," Jason said when Mitch told him. Beyond that, Jason didn't seem too interested, even when Mitch told him that the father of Jenny's baby wasn't going to marry her.

When Mitch told the older boys, Tommy said the same thing. "Gross." He studied Mitch, then added, "The father sounds like an asshole. But it's her business, right?"

Ryan said, "Well, I guess I really was wrong, thinking you had the hots for her, Dad."

And Luke just gave his father a long, steady, measured look, and didn't say a word.

CHAPTER ELEVEN

LUKE WAITED a few weeks to bring up Jenny's pregnancy again.

Mitch had come to the Northern Lights practice on a cold, sloppy evening toward the end of January. He was on the ice, firing passing shots at Luke, who then slapped the puck into the net. Over and over they repeated the drill. Then Mitch skated past the centerline and passed so that Luke could practice a breakaway. The session got fast, a little rough. Luke was slamming shots into the goal.

When the coach called an end to practice, Mitch was soaked with sweat. Still he was loath to leave the ice, instead standing by the boards and talking strategy with his son. Finally, the Zamboni came out, and reluctantly, Mitch headed for the locker room.

There he showered, and when he finished, the place was nearly empty. He wandered over to the bench where Luke was putting on his socks. Mitch stood in his briefs, roughly toweling his hair dry.

"Dad?" Luke looked up from tying his sneakers. "Can I ask you something?"

"Sure."

"How do you really feel about Jenny?"

Mitch abruptly stopped toweling off. For a moment, he considered saying he'd never been interested in her, but he didn't. Even Ryan had been onto him back then. "What's to feel?" he finally said gruffly. "She's having a baby."

His son just looked at him. "You had no clue that she was pregnant?"

"How would I have a clue?" He didn't intend to be this sharp, but he couldn't help it.

Luke hesitated. "Well, when you…touched her. You know. Didn't you feel it when you made love?"

Mitch felt himself heat a little. "Uh, just let me get dressed before we have this discussion."

Luke smiled. "Sure."

Mitch took his time with his jeans. He knew Luke was grown-up now, but this was still some talk to be having with his own kid. He zipped his fly and then sat down on the bench. "Luke, Jenny and I never made love," he said quietly.

"Oh. I thought—" He shook his head. "You could have fooled me, but I guess I'm as bad as Ryan, assuming you liked her—"

"I like her," he admitted. "But as far as making love, Jenny didn't want that." Okay, there was an admission in there, that he'd have made love to her if he'd had the opportunity. But looking into his son's sympathetic gaze, Mitch decided it was all right to admit that. "Jenny didn't even want me to kiss her," he added.

"Hmm." Luke reached behind himself into the

locker, pulled out his duffel bag and set it on the floor. "Because she was pregnant."

"Or not interested."

"Give me a break. I could see her looking at you, too."

"Okay. Because of the baby, then."

A moment's silence. "And now you've decided you can't care for her anymore?"

"Son, she's having another man's baby. You can't exactly ignore something like that." He never forgot it, not for an instant. But the funny thing was, he still found her attractive. At the store when they'd be talking over inventory, he'd find himself focusing on her mouth. Wanting to kiss her. Wanting to hold her and feel her soft curves.

She'd found an apartment the week after Christmas. He'd hoped that having her out of his house would make him think about her less. But it didn't.

"Dad, I'm not saying forget about the baby. But doesn't it seem important to you that she wasn't interested in making love with you?"

Mitch leaned forward. "How so?"

"I mean, if she was going to use you, she'd want you as emotionally committed as possible. Wouldn't she sleep with you and try to pull you in?"

Obviously, Luke knew the kind of issues that made his old man tick. Actually, Mitch hadn't thought of Jenny's refusal that way.

"She said she'd been putting me off because of the baby," Mitch admitted.

Luke nodded. "I like Jenny, did you know that? From the first day I met her."

"When she was all uppity?"

"Even then."

"Well, then you could see something in her I couldn't."

"Maybe so. Maybe it's easier to see when you aren't as caught up in things."

"Maybe so."

"You know, Dad, it's been four years since Mom passed away. I think you're ready, and I think Jenny may be the woman you can love."

"She's carrying another man's *baby,* for Chrissake."

"Does it matter?" His younger eyes captured his father's, and he looked wise beyond his years. "You can love all of us boys. You love Crystal, she wrapped you around her little finger and we had a French poodle in no time flat. Can't you love one more baby?"

He stood, too restless to sit any longer. "That sounds noble and good, son. But this is the real world." He raked a hand through his hair. "You know me. I usually go with things. But not here. Not with Jenny. I just can't be flexible about Jenny's baby."

His son looked as if he was about to argue, when a locker clanged. Both Mitch and Luke started; they'd thought they were alone.

David Chandler came around the corner.

"David. I didn't know you were here," Luke said quickly, getting up and giving his friend a high five. Mitch looked closely at the young man's expression, and decided David hadn't heard anything. In fact, he seemed to be distracted. When Luke asked him if Robin was meeting him, he said no, but declined to go out for a burger with Luke.

"Can I talk to you, Mitch?" David asked. He cast a glance at Luke. "Alone?"

Luke picked up his jacket and duffel bag, and swatted David on the rear. "You're gonna miss out on some great-looking babes, and I was going to buy," he said good-naturedly. "But hey, if you'd rather talk to an old guy than look at babes with me, who'm I to stop you?" He chuckled as he headed out. The door slammed shut.

Mitch got a sweatshirt from his locker and pulled it over his head. He was bone-weary, and he found himself wanting to go over his son's words, repeat them to himself, think about how they'd made him feel. That was nuts, and so he was almost glad for the distraction that David provided.

"What's up?" he asked casually, shoving his wet towel into his duffel bag.

"Ah…well, Robin wants to get married."

Hell. Mitch's hand stilled on the towel. "When?"

"As soon as she graduates from high school in June."

Mitch tried to keep his voice relatively neutral. "That soon?"

"Yeah." David's eyes were troubled.

"What do *you* want to do?"

"I don't know. I say, what's the rush, but then she gets all pouty and won't speak to me for a couple of days, then I end up saying I'll think about it."

"It doesn't sound like you're ready. David, you'll be on the road even more when you're called up. And you're way too young for this kind of commitment."

Though Mitch suspected he was saying exactly what David wanted to hear, the young man's face got mulish. "Didn't you get married young?"

"Pretty young. And you're right, it worked, Anne and I had a good marriage. But it wasn't perfect, and it wouldn't have worked at all if I were still interested in other women when I got married. Which, my friend, you seem to be," he added bluntly. "You and Luke certainly talk about girls often enough, and you seem to get a real kick out of signing autographs for those women who hang around the rink."

"But I like Robin best."

"Like? Or love?"

David went red. "I don't know. She's a really great-looking girl. I like to, ah, kiss her. Besides, we talk, you know? I like talking to her. I tell her things I don't tell anybody else." He appeared honestly bewildered. "Is that love?"

Was it? Mitch, for the first time in his life, struggled to define love. "It's hard to say. Love's something special." He and David looked carefully away from each other. David's hand on the locker door was tight-knuckled. This wasn't the kind of conversation one man had with another, but David needed help and Mitch had to try.

"It's love when you want to spend your free time mostly with that person. When you tell her things, like you do with Robin, that you don't share with another living soul. When you want to hear what she has to say.'' He paused, thinking. ''When you walk into a room sometimes and she looks so good to you that it hurts you in the gut.'' He paused again. ''Yeah, when it hurts you in the gut, but the hurt feels fine, that's love.'' All in all, he was pretty pleased with himself for coming up with that definition. ''Do you love Robin like that?''

''Sometimes,'' he admitted after a moment.

''Then you have to think about this. If you do love each other, what's the hurry about marriage?''

David turned to him eagerly. ''Yeah, I know! I mean, I say that to Robin all the time. Like can't we just be together for a while?''

Mitch nodded. ''You have your answer then, don't you?''

David's eyes were troubled. ''Yeah, I do. I think you're right. Whether or not I love Robin, I'm not ready to get married. But when I say stuff like that to her, she gets so upset. She cries, and then when I call she won't talk to me.''

''If she really loved you, she'd want the best for you, she'd want you to be happy.'' He let that sink in for a few seconds, then he added, ''You've got to remember, you're going to be a major-league hockey player. Maybe even a star. You need to make sure Robin isn't just trying to get you to tie the knot before you make it big.''

David looked him in the eye. ''Robin wouldn't do that.''

"Are you sure?"

"Pretty sure."

"David, Robin might be the woman for you. But that doesn't mean you have to marry her in June."

When David left a few minutes later, he'd decided to tell Robin once and for all that he wasn't ready for marriage. Mitch was relieved.

He got the rest of his gear together and found his car keys. He was vaguely uneasy, even though David had made the right choice. The talk about Robin and marriage had Mitch thinking about Anne. That was expected.

What was shocking was that it wasn't Anne's face he was picturing now.

It was Jenny's. He recalled how, when he walked into his store in the afternoons, he felt tight in the gut, the way he did before a game. Anticipating. Then when he saw her, he got that good pinch that he'd mentioned to David.

That good pinch scared him to death, but it didn't stop him from making excuses to be near her, talking to her. While they chatted, he focused on the bloom in her cheeks, on her soft lips.

It wasn't love, of course. It couldn't be, because she was pregnant with another man's baby. But it sure felt—

Good thing David had his head on straight now. At least one of them did.

So THIS WAS Ohio in February. Jenny stood at the big window at the front of the store and watched the snow blow outside. The sky was gray and even the snowflakes were gray and hard. The wind made sighing and moaning sounds that made her shiver.

''This is a heck of a storm,'' she whispered to her baby.

Her little girl kicked. It felt like a swish, butterflies brushing little wings against the inside of her belly. For nearly a week now, she'd felt that swish, and a kind of pleased awe would make her smile. Now she touched her stomach. *There, baby. I feel you.*

It was quiet in the store. There were no customers; the storm had kept them away. She'd sent home her sales help—an older woman—while the driving was still relatively easy. The music that played overhead was muffled by the sounds of the storm outside.

She turned back to her task of organizing the inventory sheets, sitting down in a chair at the counter. Her feet seemed to hurt more than usual today. In fact, her lower back hurt too, and she felt a little clammy and sweaty. She ran the back of her hand over her forehead.

The door banged open, increasing the noise of the storm.

Mitch.

She looked up. It was ridiculous the way she couldn't help staring at him, and embarrassing to feel the skitter of awareness that went up her spine, feel the little hum of attraction that settled somewhere in her belly. A person would have thought she'd be too busy making a baby to have these feelings. ''Hi,'' she said when he had his coat off and was shaking it by the doorway. "How were the roads?"

"Rotten." He looked her in the eye. He did that a lot, to avoid glancing at her stomach. That annoyed her. She wanted to share some of what she was feeling—this excitement, this sense that the baby was real and with her all the time.

She was feeling less ashamed these days. Nobody at the store seemed to think ill of her. She'd explained the circumstances and people seemed to understand. Crystal and Jason didn't treat her any differently than before. North Shore, Ohio, in the year 2000 wasn't the Sweetspring, South Carolina, of her childhood.

Only Mitch treated her differently. Only Mitch never mentioned the baby, pretending that if he didn't see her stomach, he wouldn't have to acknowledge her baby.

That humiliated her.

Mitch set his briefcase on the counter. "Where is everyone?"

"I sent Louise home because of the storm. I didn't want her driving in it."

"You shouldn't be driving in it, either. Not with the…"

"Baby. You can say it, Mitch."

His face was ruddy from the cold, but still she saw a little red creeping up his neck. But he kept his eyes on hers. "You should get home and, ah, put your feet up or something. I can take over here."

"I've still got over an hour till quitting time." Going home sounded marvelous. She could have a cup of herbal tea and, as Mitch said, put her feet up. She was very tired, she realized. But she was determined that Mitch never have reason to call her a slacker. So now she said stubbornly, "I'll stay."

He looked out the window for a moment. "Yeah, maybe that would be better. I can drive you to your apartment when I close up here."

"I can drive myself. But thank you," she added belatedly. Momma would be appalled at the way Mitch seemed to make her forget her manners.

He shrugged and took some paperwork from beside the register. He stood slouching, with his rear end parked against a showcase, his legs crossed, reading in a pose that was graceful, and very masculine.

Jenny worked on some paperwork, too, then headed to the bathroom.

Mitch watched her go. She walked with a sway of hip that was very feminine. From the back she was sexier than ever.

From the front, well, her belly was growing with another man's baby. Ever since his conversation with Luke, he'd been stealing looks at her front when he thought she wouldn't notice. He'd swear her breasts were bigger. And that little mound in her belly was utterly feminine. He was confused as hell, because he wasn't turned off the way he ought to be.

When she closed the bathroom door, he went back to his paperwork. He could still feel the lustful smile on his face. It was a good thing she was so short with him these days, because if not, she'd probably notice the way he was hanging around, watching her.

The door opened. ''Mitch?''

At the odd note in her voice, he looked up quickly. Jenny's face was pure white and tense. The sight of it made him take a few quick steps toward her.

''Mitch, I'm bleeding.'' Her voice cracked, went high. ''The baby—''

Horror washed over him, and he broke into a sprint until he reached her side. ''Bleeding a lot?''

She was obviously trying not to panic. ''Just a little. It's brown, not bright red. But any bleeding's bad, isn't it?''

He didn't have a clue. ''You need to go to the hospital.'' He looked toward the window. The snow was piling up fast. ''I'll drive you. We can make better time in my Jeep than if we call 911.''

Sick with fear, but better because he'd thought of something he could do, he was hurrying her toward the door of the store even as he spoke. She didn't protest, and that made him realize just how frightened she was. He grabbed his coat as they passed the counter and wrapped it around her.

''You've had four kids,'' she said. ''Did Anne ever bleed?'' She gave him a half fearful, half hopeful look.

''I don't know,'' he said bluntly, too worried to think of a comforting lie.

''Oh, Mitch. I felt her move a little while ago. She can't be in trouble, can she?''

The wind hit them as they got to the parking lot, saving Mitch the need to respond.

JENNY LAY on her back in a hospital bed in the emergency room. Mitch sat with her, looking far too big for the small chair. He shifted in obvious discomfort. But he had chosen to stay with her instead of sitting in the waiting room. Jenny was grateful for his presence.

She needed somebody to tell her everything was all right. Mitch agreed it would be, though at some level Jenny realized he was humoring her.

Now he looked at the walls, the floor, everywhere but at the monitor or her belly. The monitor made regular, reassuring little squiggles, indicating the baby's heart was still beating. All the way to the hospital in the cold and snow, Jenny had been making bargains with God about that heartbeat. Now it was the sweetest sight in the world. She stared at the monitor, willing it to blip, letting out a breath of relief every time it did.

Finally, her doctor came in. She'd been seeing Ken Saunders for her prenatal care since moving to North Shore. He was hurried but kind. "Everything looks all right, as near as we can tell. Your ultrasound was normal."

Normal. If a blipping heartbeat on a monitor was the sweetest sight in the world, then the word *normal* from the lips of her doctor must surely be the sweetest sound.

She turned to Mitch. "Did you hear that? Dr. Saunders said my ultrasound was normal!"

Mitch shifted again. "Hey, that's great."

He did look happy. She thought about how nice he'd been in this crisis, taking care of her, how he'd sat with her despite obviously being out of his element. Something inside her went soft and warm and yearning. Her eyes stung.

"Yes, a normal ultrasound is a good sign," the doctor said cheerfully, turning to Mitch. "You must be very relieved."

"He's not the baby's father," Jenny blurted out, her cheeks reddening at the doctor's assumption.

Mitch shifted in the chair—yet again—but didn't say anything.

"Well, that's fine. That's not my business, you know." The doctor got very busy with his chart and didn't ask any questions about why North Shore's most famous widower was sitting in an ER with a pregnant woman who was carrying another man's baby. Jenny felt a half-hysterical need to giggle with relief. At any other time, the discomfort of these two men would have been very funny.

"Now, Jenny," the doctor went on briskly, "would you like to know the sex of your baby?"

She smiled. "Yes." If they were going to tell her things like this, the baby really *must* be healthy. "It's a girl, right? After a scare like this, I'll take any healthy baby. Actually, I've felt that way all along, but I've also been so sure it's a little girl in there. I'm right, aren't I?"

The doctor looked at the chart. "The baby was a little coy, its hand was placed rather modestly during your scan. But yes, the tech thinks there's about an eighty percent chance you're having a little girl.''

A girl. Yesss! Jenny gave herself a moment to revel in the knowledge. "I've picked out names." She wanted everyone in the room to share her relief and joy. "I'm going to name her Stephanie. Isn't that a lovely name? Beautiful and strong."

The doctor chuckled. "Sounds like she'll be a handful."

He gave her instructions that included lying down for a few days with her feet up. "Since we're not sure why you bled, we have to assume there's still a small possibility of miscarriage. We'll know for sure in a few days. If everything goes well, you can return to work in a week or so, as long as you take it easy there and put your feet up several times during the day."

"You mean I can go home?"

"Yes, we're releasing you now."

That sounded great. As if happy about the decision, too, Stephanie swished. Jenny put a hand on her belly, trying to hold her baby.

Mitch had been quiet. When the nurse came in with a few maternity-size sanitary pads, he took one good look at what the woman held and mumbled that he'd wait outside.

The nurse said, "You probably won't need these, but just in case..." as she handed Jenny the package.

Jenny thought of Mitch on the other side of that curtain. The big, bad hockey star was scared of a sanitary napkin! Once again she fought the urge to giggle.

That urge fled when she was back in Mitch's Jeep and she realized he wasn't heading back to the store. "Mitch, I have to get my car, I left it at the store."

"You're not driving," he said flatly. "Luke or I will bring your car back to your apartment in a few days."

"Thank you." He didn't say too much after that, and neither did she. The heat of the car, together with the tremendous sense of relief, had her drowsing a little.

She awoke when Mitch braked for a stop sign. "Wait." She sat up more fully and looked around. The light was dim; the snow swirled, and they weren't anywhere near the city limits of North Shore. "I thought you were taking me to my apartment."

"I'm taking you back to the farm."

"Just like that."

His mouth was a grim line. "Just like that."

"I can go back to my apartment. I can take care of myself!"

She'd never forget Mitch's angry, cutting words about her being a bad influence on the boys. He couldn't want her back at the farm, and he'd been noble enough for one day. "Listen, I appreciate your being there for me today—I really do. I didn't have anyone and I was so frightened and you helped, and I was—" She made herself stop before she blurted out how she'd felt that rush of tenderness for him. "You don't have to do this," she finished lamely.

He didn't answer, just turned onto the road that led to the farm.

"Mitch, really, you've done your duty."

He kept his eyes on the road. "That's what you think I was doing back there? My duty?"

"Well, and giving me your friendship. I'm grateful for it, but now you can take me—"

"How are you going to take care of yourself when you're not supposed to be on your feet? Do you want to be alone in an apartment in the middle of a snowstorm if you start to bleed again?"

"Lord, no—"

"Then quit arguing, okay? When you're sure you're okay, you can go back to your apartment. And by the way, when you do go back to work, you can just forget about trying to prove something by working your tail off day in and day out."

He sounded a little angry, and she had no idea why. She knew she shouldn't impose by going back to the farm; it was the sort of thing Momma would have frowned upon. But what was she going to do? The baby's well-being came first. "Thank you. I accept with gratitude," she said, falling back upon the old-fashioned manners she'd been taught.

Even through the falling snow, the house gleamed brightly at the top of the hill as they approached it. The boys and Crystal must have every light on.

When they got inside, there was a huge commotion. As usual. But Jenny realized she rather liked the noise. Crystal squealed, and the dogs barked, and Face-off tried his very best to lick her face, then settled for a grin instead. Jewels pranced around, her tail in the air. Jason said, "Hi, Miss Jenny," in a shy, happy way that melted her.

Later, lying fully clothed on the bed, so tired she couldn't muster the energy to put on the bathrobe she'd borrowed from one of the boys, she thought she knew the word for how the farm had felt tonight. *Home.* That thought should have scared her, but somehow it didn't.

And later still, Mitch stood in the doorway and asked if she needed anything. She said no, but still he lingered. Then he said, "You know, I like the name Stephanie."

She smiled and touched her stomach.

CHAPTER TWELVE

OVER THE NEXT FEW DAYS, Jenny focused on her baby and on healing her body. She slept long and often. When she was awake, she stayed in bed, her feet propped up on pillows. While the kids were at school, the house was quiet, and it was peaceful to have Silver or Jewels lying at her feet as Jenny listened to the soft creaks of the old house.

At night she joined the rest of the household for the inevitable fast food. After dinner, Mitch usually headed to his study, and Jenny sat in the big family room—her feet up on Mitch's recliner—and watched television with the boys. It was all a dream, the farm she'd once thought so chaotic now an oasis.

Almost a week went by, and she was sitting in Mitch's recliner again one night and realized rather abruptly that it was time to go back to her apartment. The crisis was over; her baby was fine.

She owed Mitch a thank-you. The man—who clearly wasn't happy about the baby—had helped her protect it. The man—who'd said she was a bad influence on his children—had brought her to his home nevertheless.

She waited until the kids were in bed, and then she headed to his study.

She paused in the doorway. The study was rather dark, lit only by the dim hallway light and the glow of Mitch's laptop computer.

"Hi," she said softly.

He sat up straight with a squeak of his big leather desk chair. "I thought you'd be in bed."

She smiled a little nervously. "A reasonable assumption, considering I've been lying down for a week. But now I'm well enough to go back to my apartment."

He didn't move for a moment, then he nodded.

She glanced at the computer. "I'm sorry that I left you in the lurch at the store."

"It hasn't been a problem. We aren't that busy in February, and Louise and the others are more efficient than they used to be, thanks to your training. Everything's fine." He gestured toward her. "Come on in."

She took a few steps into the room. She'd seldom been in this room. Even though she'd stayed at the farm before, she'd always been conscious of being a guest, so she hadn't thoroughly explored the huge house. The study seemed even more masculine than the rest of the house. Pictures of Mitch's glory days with the Great Chicago Fire adorned the walls, including one of him shaking hands with the president of the United States. She'd seen the picture once in the daylight.

Trophies and awards were lined up on shelves, and these were all his. Out in the family room, the more public space, he'd chosen to showcase his kids. Only here in his own sanctuary was there evidence of how hockey had once consumed him.

"Are you working on the store financing?" *Quit dawdling and tell him how grateful you are.*

"Not *the* store, exactly. The next two stores, to be exact."

"Mitch! You've finalized plans for some stores?"

He grinned at her enthusiasm. "Two. One in an existing center that will open this spring, and one freestanding superstore I'm building, right on the edge of a new suburban development in Old Fort, about fifty miles from here."

"My goodness. When did this happen? Why didn't you tell me?"

He cocked his head and looked at her. "Well, you know I've been working on it. But I didn't want to bother you with work while you were recuperating."

"Congratulations. You've earned it." And now he'd just handed her the perfect opening to say what she'd come to say.

"About that recuperating." She swallowed. With anybody else, she'd just say what was in her heart, that she was grateful. With Mitch, she couldn't say all that was in her heart, and she knew she had to be careful not to say too much. Not to embarrass either of them. "I've been pretty zoned out these last few days."

"You shouldn't have been working so hard. It was obvious you were very tired." He looked at her face, not her belly.

"I know. I thought I could do everything, but now I realize I have some limits. I don't like that."

"I never liked facing my limits, either." He smiled at her in sympathy, and his understanding made talking even harder, because she felt a connection with him that thrilled and scared her.

She took a deep breath. "Thank you for everything."

He waved her off.

"No, really. You always hear about southern hospitality, but who would have thought you northerners have it, too—" She broke off as she realized that there was no way to make light of what he'd done. "When I was in danger of losing my baby, you stepped in despite your feelings, and I'm so grateful."

He got up then and stood looking at her from behind the desk. "It occurs to me that if you hadn't been so worried about my feelings toward that baby, you might not have been working so hard."

"My bleeding was not your fault."

He looked her in the eye. "No? Well, maybe it wasn't, just like my wife's illness wasn't. But I've been selfish again. I never thought about how you'd feel with me as your employer, after the things I said. After I found out you were pregnant, I—"

Mentally, she finished his sentence. After he'd found out she was pregnant, he wasn't interested in her anymore.

But he'd made it clear from the beginning that her job wasn't in jeopardy. If she'd worked extra hard it had been for reasons of her own.

"It's not your fault. I work too hard. I always have. But that will have to change."

He was still looking at her. "Is the baby really all right now?"

"Yes."

"Good." He paused, cleared his throat. "I don't know too much about babies."

She smiled. "That's apparent. Even though you had four of them."

"Anne had them. I didn't even make it back in time to see Jason born."

She gasped.

"I know." His mouth was set in a line. "I tried, but there wasn't a plane out of L.A. in time to get back here when she went into labor early. I missed so much, but you already know that. I tried to make it up to Anne... What does it feel like?" he asked abruptly. "What does it feel like to be pregnant?"

She felt heat in her cheeks. His back was tense, and she was grateful for the desk between them. "Well, at first, all I felt was sick to my stomach, and tired. All the time I'm conscious that there's a baby growing inside me. Lately, I've started to picture my little girl more. I can sort of see her face, and I imagine her swimming in this place I have for her, a place that's as warm as the tidal pools on the beach when the sun is shining."

Her embarrassment left her as she talked. It felt so wonderful to share this. "I feel like Eve. Like the first woman in the world who's ever done anything so incredible. I can put my hand right here—" she paused and put a hand on her stomach "—and feel her move. She's been moving quite a bit tonight."

His gaze focused on her belly for the first time in months. There was a curious tenseness in his expression. He lifted a hand, put it down as if he didn't quite know what to do with it. "What does it feel like when she moves?"

"Like little fish brushing against your hand."

Somewhere, a clock ticked. The house was quiet. "I remember that. I remember touching Anne and feeling her babies move. It seemed like a miracle."

Her gaze met his. There was an odd sort of expression on his face. A sort of reluctance, a sort of confusion, yet a yearning that made her ask, "Do you want to feel her?" She held her breath as she waited for his response.

He came around the desk toward her. "Since you came back, I've been thinking about so much. About the boys being small."

She took a step toward him. He held out his hand, and she took it. It felt warm and strong. Big. Definitely a man's hand. Her heart beat hard and fast and her throat felt suddenly thick. He stood very, very still. She guided his palm onto her belly.

The baby kicked.

"Here. Oh, right here." Quickly, she moved his hand over to where the baby was kicking. "Feel it? Like butterflies?"

"I don't know. It just feels tight... Yes," he whispered. "Yes, there she goes."

She didn't know how long they stood there, a little, careful space between them, his hand on her stomach. Stephanie liked the attention; she put on a good show, swimming and swishing and kicking.

It was so quiet that when he swallowed, she heard the sound.

And she thought, *I could love this man.*

Oh, my Lord. She stood there, afraid to move, afraid to call attention to the tender feelings washing through her. She wanted to prolong this moment when he touched the baby he hadn't fathered, but that he'd protected.

Finally Stephanie quieted.

Mitch removed his hand. For a moment, neither moved. Then he cleared his throat again and said, "If we didn't know it was a girl, I'd say there's a hockey player in there, the way she was moving."

He made her smile, and his comment took some of the tension from the air. "I talk to her, did you know that? We make plans together."

"That sounds like you, making plans."

She smiled more broadly. Once the comment might have hurt. Now it warmed her that he knew her so well.

Somehow she ended up talking to Mitch as she hadn't to another person since Kathy had died. They sat on the couch together. She told him about selling her condominium, about how she wanted her little girl to have a real house to grow up in. An old house that already had good memories.

When she ran out of steam, Mitch said quietly, "Maybe you'll marry someday."

She didn't look at him, and she sensed he was careful not to look at her. There was tension in the air again. "No."

"You could change your mind. Stephanie could have a father—"

"She doesn't need one," she said quickly. "I can do it all. I can't take the chance, Mitch. I'm not good at picking men."

"Because you had one bastard of a fiancé."

"You don't know the half of it," she said, and there was a bitterness she couldn't hide.

The clock ticked. Finally he said carefully, "You could tell me about it."

She'd told his sister some of it, but she'd never told another living soul all of it. She turned to him, studying him in the dark. He was leaning back on the sofa, his powerful legs extended, his hands linked behind his neck, a relaxed pose. But he wasn't relaxed, and neither was she.

She took a long breath. "Let me tell you about my family, my life," she said slowly. "You already know my momma was a maid, and my daddy was a 'no account.'"

She took another long breath. "My momma left him when I was small, to become the maid for the Talbots. I think she took the job mostly because it came with a nice apartment over the old carriage house. All the time I was growing up, I used to hear what a fine man Mr. Talbot was, to take in a woman with a child and give us a fine, clean, respectable place to live. But the main house was so much more beautiful. I used to study the art on the walls and listen when Mrs. Talbot played music, and I learned a lot about gentle living in that house." She paused.

"Go on," he said softly.

"Momma thought Mr. Talbot walked on water, so I did, too. Momma was a snob, but Mr. Talbot *was* nice to us. Mrs. Talbot was polite but distant. But Mr. Talbot would compliment Momma on her biscuits, discuss what the minister had said in his sermon that Sunday. Momma always said he had class, and that was Momma's highest compliment. He was nice to me, too. He'd ask me how school was going, give Momma a little extra money for my clothes. Sometimes, when I was small, I pretended Mr. Talbot was my daddy.

"Anyway, the Talbots had a son. Jeffrey was two years older than I was. He was away at William and Mary, but he was home summers."

The story was getting harder to tell now, so she made light of what came next. "The long and short of it is that he came home the summer I was sixteen, and I became...infatuated. He was so worldly and exciting. He'd kiss me."

She blushed and she hurried with the rest. "I was too naive to realize he wasn't going to settle for just kissing. He...groped me. I was frightened by it. I mean, I liked him, but I...wasn't ready, I guess. He started pressuring me. For—for more." She stole a glance at Mitch. He hadn't moved, but there was a kind of coiled awareness in him that told her he was listening intently.

"I remember how hot it was that summer. I was always sweating from the heat, from nerves, from having to know where he was all the time. Then one night when there wasn't anybody around, he grabbed me—" She swallowed and stopped.

Mitch leaned forward. "He didn't—"

"No. No, he didn't. But he said he could make his daddy fire my momma if I didn't change my mind."

Mitch cursed.

"But I didn't say yes. Instead, I told Momma. She went straight to Mr. Talbot. After all, she wasn't just the maid to Mr. Talbot, not after cleaning his house for fourteen years. She was special. He always told her so."

"Why am I not liking where this is going?" Mitch muttered.

She sighed. "Mr. Talbot hit the roof. He told my momma he'd take care of it. She was pleased as punch he was taking the situation seriously."

"And he didn't take care of it."

"Oh, yes, he did. And Jeffrey never bothered me again."

Mitch let out a long breath, as though he'd been holding in some air. "Good."

"Yes. But…it was the way Mr. Talbot did it." This was the truly terrible part. "I heard what he said. He said to Jeffrey that the Talbots didn't mess around with the help. All right, that's what we were. Then he said—" tears pricked her eyes, even after all these years "—he said, 'Why are you messing with that trash?'"

Mitch turned to her and gripped her arm. "Listen to me and listen to me good. You are not trash."

The tears threatened to overflow. She blinked. "Don't mind me, I'm just so emotional these days." She sighed again. "I know I'm not trash. Here."

She touched her forehead. "Here, too, most of the time," she added, touching her heart. "But it was a lesson I never forgot. I learned to be independent, to stand on my own feet and not idolize people and expect them to take care of me. And I learned I have a—a character flaw. I seem to be drawn to beauty and charm. To handsome, charming, rich men. Mr. Talbot, Jeffrey, Delane."

Mitch said very, very quietly, "Most people are attracted to nice-looking people with manners. Rich doesn't seem to hurt, either."

She heard the faintest bitterness in his voice, too, and thought of the groupies. Maybe his own experiences made him a kindred spirit of sorts, one capable of understanding. Maybe that's why she'd been able to tell him. "I can't take a chance, don't you see? I've made so many mistakes." Her voice gained strength. "I'll never trust another man again. Because I can't trust my judgment. Because I have Stephanie's happiness to consider now, just as my momma had mine."

Her words seemed to hang in the air. Finally, he said, "You can never trust a man again?"

"No."

LONG AFTER JENNY had excused herself and gone to bed, Mitch stayed on the sofa, staring into space. The computer's screen saver moved and bobbed, making a shifting play of light over the desk. Otherwise, the house was still.

He was going nuts.

Because his palm was still tingling. It was as if

he could still feel Jenny's hard, warm stomach and the faintest movement of baby against his palm.

And he was going nuts because all the time he'd been touching little Stephanie, he was thinking how beautiful, how somehow right it was that Jenny was having a child. He wasn't thinking about it being Delane Kyle's, just that it was Jenny's, and that it was the neatest thing he'd ever felt.

And he was going nuts because he was imagining lifting his hand, that very hand that she trusted to cradle her child, lifting it to her breasts and cupping and stroking. They'd be tender from her pregnancy—he remembered that part now—and her nipples would be large and extra dark. He remembered that part, too. He'd just put his tongue lightly on the tips, tease extra gently, be so careful with her because she was making a baby—

He was going nuts.

He shifted, trying to ease the heaviness in his groin. His feelings for Jenny had always been so complicated.

But now he seemed to have crossed some kind of line. The minute he'd put his hand on her belly, he'd realized that Jenny's child was part of her and precious because of that.

His son was right. *Does it matter? Can't you love one more baby?* He could, he thought, if he was in love with the mother. Long before he knew she was pregnant, he'd wanted to explore what was happening between them. Now he realized that he still felt that way.

So he was going nuts. He'd waited four years to

fall in love again and then it had to be with a woman who didn't trust men.

She'd said one word, with two letters: "No."

He'd like to take those men in her past, starting with Delane Kyle and ending with the Talbots, and show them what an ex–hockey star could do with his bare hands to their rich, charming faces. That was the proper guy thing to do—avenge the honor of the woman he loved.

He wanted to show her that they were jerks, that not all men were like them. But he understood with a sudden clarity that she feared he was.

After all, he was a celebrity, he lived in a big, rambling house that still showed the signs of the decorator he'd hired once upon a time. He'd never really thought of himself as handsome, but women seemed to feel differently, and he knew just what kind of smile to use when he had to. No wonder he scared her. Add to that the lousy things he'd said to her the night she'd told him about the baby—

But he was different. He knew it.

How would he ever get her to believe that?

THAT SUNDAY AT LUNCH, Jenny learned that everyone was going skating on the pond.

Neither she nor Mitch had brought up the subject of her leaving. Jenny knew she should go. It was dangerous to stay here. Dangerous to her heart, but she seemed unable to leave.

"Plus, we're gonna roast wienies on a bonfire for dinner!" Crystal shouted. Jenny was having trouble getting used to Crystal's volume these days. But that volume was good; it meant the little girl was really learning how to live in a household of rambunctious boys. Jenny smiled. ''That sounds like fun.''

''You can watch me skate. Luke can, too, can't you, Luke?''

Luke had a rare weekend home, and now, as he got up from the table, he ruffled his cousin's hair and said, ''Sure, Squirt Two.''

''Uncle Mitch has been teaching me to skate,'' Crystal went on. Mitch, with Jenny's help, had selected a pair of pom-pom-adorned figure skates for the girl for Christmas. That gift had gone over far better than the mitt and baseball he'd sent the year before.

''I can't wait to see you. Now, why don't y'all get your hats and coats and gloves. I'll clear up. No, you go ahead and get the wood for the bonfire,'' she said when Mitch offered to help her. ''I feel fine and I like earning my keep.'' She got up and started stacking dishes.

With the usual arguments, the mob poured out the door, followed more slowly by Mitch. Jenny watched through the kitchen window and saw bright mittens and hats racing toward the pond below. Mitch followed, skates over his shoulder, firewood in his hands. The snow was almost gone, but it was still cold and the ground was frozen hard. The iced-over pond glittered like a diamond under the blue sky.

She'd been careful not to be alone with Mitch these last few days. If she wasn't ready to move out, the least she could do was stay out of temptation's way.

Behind her, someone coughed. She whirled around.

Ryan stood in the kitchen.

"Oh, sorry," she said. "You startled me. I didn't realize you didn't go out with the others."

He opened the dishwasher and picked up a couple of plates. "I thought maybe you could use some help."

What? Ryan volunteering for chores? "Well... thank you."

"No problem."

No problem?

Jenny started rinsing plates, which Ryan jammed into the dishwasher willy-nilly. About to say something about that, Jenny clamped her mouth shut.

"I want to talk to you," he said finally.

"Shoot." Shoot was one of what the twins called "southern words," and they teased her about using it. And about her accent. But now Ryan ignored the chance for a jab and instead said, "What I wanted to talk about...well, there's this girl." A pause. "Colleen Hart. And I...like her, you know?" Under his sandy thatch of hair, he went brick red.

When he didn't say any more, Jenny said, "I take it she doesn't appreciate your good qualities."

"She doesn't think I have any," Ryan said in an injured tone. "I scored more points than anybody on the team at the basketball game last weekend, and she wasn't even at the game."

"She doesn't like sports?"

"Nah. She likes to read, and hang with her girl-friends. On Friday I was talking with her, and she pulled this huge book out of her locker and said, 'So, like, what are you reading now, Ryan?' What could I say? You know how much I read."

"I see." Jenny couldn't quite imagine what Ryan found attractive about a girl who didn't like sports, but who could ever figure out why two people liked each other? "Well, what *did* you say?"

"Well, I was glad she was talking to me. A few months ago she would just ignore me." He sounded extremely disgusted. "So, I'm like, 'I've been too busy with practice to read much,' and she turns up her nose, so I say, 'Maybe I'll read what you're reading.' And I looked at the book. Charles Dickens. I mean, can you believe she's reading Charles Dick-ens for *fun? A Tale of Two Cities.* Jeez."

He shook his head. "She said, 'Oh, it's so ro-mantic, all the sacrifices the men make for Lucy.' I thought I was gonna puke." He put a glass into the dishwasher so forcefully that Jenny winced.

"Maybe she's not the girl for you."

He straightened slowly. "She is. That's the prob-lem. I can't get her out of my mind. So I thought—" He swallowed, looked away. "Look, I know I haven't been real...friendly to you. I said...that stuff. But I'm...I'm sorry about that. You haven't been too bad to us and you're not that bad, you know?" He looked at her with an earnestness that unexpectedly touched her.

"Thank you," she said softly.

"It's just, you're a lady, and Dad never brought any ladies here... But you're okay. Really okay."

She touched his arm. "I know you guys aren't into saying you're sorry, but you gave me a sincere apology just now and I surely appreciate it." She paused, studying him. His face was averted, and he still was pink from the effort his apology had cost him. "I think we could be friends."

He busied himself with the dishes. "Well, if that's what you want."

Jenny smiled to herself as she handed him a glass.

"So," he said after a few minutes, "I figure, Colleen's a girl and you're a girl, and Colleen is always reading and you read a lot, so maybe you could tell me how to get her to like me."

Ah... "Maybe you should try actually reading *A Tale of Two Cities,*" she suggested. "Show her you're interested in what she's interested in."

"I thought about that. I thought of getting the Cliff Notes."

"Or reading the whole book," she suggested gently. "Do you like Colleen or not?"

He thought for a moment. "Yeah, I guess I could read it, but I'll probably barf on the parts she thinks are so romantic."

"That's it!" Jenny said. "She likes the romantic parts. You could do all sorts of romantic things. Read the books she likes, get her a few little romantic gifts."

"Okay." His forehead creased. "Say I read this book, though it'll probably take till I'm dead before I finish. What could I buy her?"

"Well, you're not dating or anything, so the gift shouldn't be too personal. But it has to be personal in a way, too, so that she'll realize you were thinking romance."

He gave her a blank look.

"Really, it's easy. Momma always said the only appropriate gifts for girls were candy, flowers and books. Actually—" she was enjoying herself now "—I always suspected Momma got that out of *Gone with the Wind*. And I'll bet you any amount of money that Colleen's read *Gone with the Wind*. When you're done with Dickens, you might want to tackle reading that."

"One book at a time," Ryan muttered, looking beleaguered.

"Right. Maybe we'll pick out a book together that you could give her. A romantic classic. I could take you shopping. Power shopping. We could pick out a book, but also we'll buy one fresh flower—a rose—that you can give her."

"You've got to be kidding. I give her one lousy flower and all of a sudden she likes me?"

"It's a little more complicated than that, but yes, if she sees you're sincerely interested in her and making an effort to be romantic, I think that'd go a long way toward getting a conversation started, at least."

"Maybe you're right. Can you take me to the mall?"

"Sure. I'll take you after school tomorrow."

"I hope none of my friends see me there, buying

flowers and *Gone with the Wind,*" he muttered darkly. "Are you sure this'll work?"

"Well, I can't promise, but if somebody went to that trouble for me when I was Colleen's age, I think I'd fall in love." A certain wistfulness had crept into her voice, but Ryan didn't seem to notice. Ryan might be choosing the most obvious of gifts, he might be taking a stab at being, well, charming, but he truly liked this girl and wanted to please her, and that made his gesture touching. "Tomorrow after school," she promised. "I only work until two nowadays."

"Okay, I'll do it," Ryan said.

A FEW MINUTES LATER, Jenny put on her coat and hat and went to watch the kids skate. It was a beautiful day and she enjoyed hearing the shouts of the boys and Crystal's high, happy laughter as they circled the pond.

Mitch was on the ice now, and she stared openly.

Dazzling was too mild a word for Mitch on skates. He seemed to glitter on the pond. His legs pumping, he sped out toward the center of the pond, did an ice-spraying full stop, and then came skating backward at breakneck speed, heading straight toward Jason.

She opened her mouth to shout a warning, but in the time it took to blink, he did a graceful, perfect high-speed pivot around his son, snatching Jason's hat off in the process. "Hey," Jason shouted.

"Do mine! Do mine!" Crystal yelled, standing still with one hand on her hat to keep it from Mitch.

So Mitch did a breathtakingly fast circle around the little girl, but instead of pulling off her hat, went for her unoccupied hand and snatched off her mitten. Crystal squealed with delight.

Face-off was pacing at the edge of the ice, barking every once in a while. Silver had taken a few tentative steps out onto the ice. Now, hearing Crystal's shrieks, the puppy broke into a run. He lost his footing and did a belly slide toward her. "Silver!" She reached out and promptly fell on her rear, her feet in the air. Mitch grabbed her and hugged her. Watching, Jenny felt a prick of tears.

She got to the edge of the ice, and Mitch skated over. He was smiling. His nose was red with the cold, his teeth flashing white. He wasn't even breathing hard. He looked so good it was hard not to show she was staring. "You're really wonderful at this," she said, realizing how lame the words were.

"It was something I did for a living, remember?" he said with a flippant grin that had her insides humming. "Now, watch Crystal. She has Oliver genes, too."

"Watch me, Miss Jenny. Watch me!"

So Jenny watched Crystal's earnest figure eights, her wobbly spin, and all the time she was conscious of the man beside her. In her peripheral vision, she could see the steam from his breath.

When Crystal finally stopped spinning, Mitch said quietly, "Want to try going out on the ice yourself?"

Oh, how she'd like to. How the girl in her, the

one who had never seen real snow before this winter, the one who would like a boy to give her one pink rose, that girl wanted to try it. To glide on the ice under a blue sky. "I can't. I don't think it would be good for the baby."

"I know you can't race and spin. Or even skate. But you could glide in your boots. I'll hold you. We'll go slowly."

"I don't know…"

"Luke can help me." He whistled for his eldest son. "Neither of us falls at the speed we're going to be going. Trust me."

Trust him. She hesitated. "All right." Very gently, Mitch put his arm around her thickened waist. On her other side, Luke held her hand. Skating was as easy—maybe easier—for these two as walking. She felt safe as they glided her into a wide, slow turn. Safe and cherished and as if she belonged. She lost herself in the glittering, cheerful, cold world of the pond, with a man's arm around her, guiding her, protecting her, sharing the ice with her. She closed her eyes. *Look, Stephanie, we're skating.*

She opened her eyes when Mitch said conversationally to Luke, "You know, I bet the kids would like to make their bonfire now."

Luke and he exchanged glances over her head. "Yes, I just bet they would. Want me to get them started?"

"That'd be a real help," Mitch said mildly.

"No problemo." Luke let go of Jenny's hand and skated off.

Some kind of masculine code had just been exchanged here. Mitch and Luke never used those careful tones with each other.

But as Mitch glided across the frozen pond, she was so caught up in the feel of freedom that she let go and enjoyed his closeness. When they got to the far side of the pond, she could see the kids at the bottom of the hill and large flames coming from the barbecue pit. "Is that safe?"

"Sure. Luke's there. That's just the kindling burning." They watched as the fire went down quickly. "There's nothing a kid likes more than fire," Mitch said with the authority of four years of parenting. "See how happy they look. Even Crystal."

"You've worked to make her happy. You bought her Silver and gave her skates."

"Maybe those things are helping. But what's really helping is your being here. You were the one who nudged me on Christmas Day to talk about Kathy. You were the one who insisted I make some time for her."

"If I helped, I'm glad."

"The boys are pleased that you're here with us."

She thought of Ryan in the kitchen, telling her she was "really okay."

"The thing is," Mitch added quietly, "they aren't the only ones glad you're here."

Stephanie kicked, one nice kick. Or was that her insides flipping a little at the serious note in his voice?

"I want you to stay. Permanently."

Permanently. How heavenly that sounded. To belong, to stay. *To be with the man she loved.* She was so conscious of his arm around her shoulders.

"Jenny." He turned her toward him, took both her hands. "I love you."

Joy rushed in her, hot and fast and so all-encompassing that she wondered if she'd ever felt such happiness before. She felt it in her blood, along her nerves, right to the tips of her fingers.

The wind picked up, ruffling his hair. "You can say something," he said finally.

"I…"

"'Oh, Mitch, I feel the same way.' Or, 'Sorry, you're a nice guy, but I'd rather be just friends.' Either way, just say it." He was looking down into her eyes, a little smile on his face. But his eyes didn't mirror the smile. Instead, they seemed vulnerable.

"I'm having a baby," she whispered. "It's not yours."

"I don't care. I touched her. I love her mom. I can love her, too."

Could he? Could a man really love another man's baby? She searched his eyes. They were sincere. He stood under a blue sky, and everything about his taut, blunt features spoke of sincerity.

He put his lips to her forehead. "Trust me, Jenny."

Oh, how she wanted to! But did she dare?

She was separated from him by a little distance, linked only by his hands in hers, the whisper of warm breath on her forehead. Stephanie was still.

The wind died. Even the children across the pond were momentarily quiet. Waiting.

"Yes," she whispered. "I think I can trust you."

He let out a whoop that caused the kids at the bonfire to start for the ice. He waved them off. "Sorry. Here we have a moment alone, and—" He broke off, searched her face. "Wait a minute. You *think* you can trust me?"

"I love you, Mitch. I really do. Can you live with that?"

"For the moment. For the moment, Miss Jenny Litton, I guess I can. But soon I want you to say you trust me, and mean it without *thinking* all the time. Till then—" he slid her toward him and put a warm, wet kiss right on her lips "—till then, we're gonna have *fun*."

CHAPTER THIRTEEN

FUN WAS ALMOST a foreign concept to Jenny. Life had always seemed to be serious business. Now she relaxed and found out what fun it could be to be in love with a great guy who laughed and teased.

They were seldom alone. He made a joke of his frustration, and she loved him for that, loved that he wanted to be with her, but didn't resent his kids.

Once when she was in the back room of the store, he caught her behind some huge cardboard boxes and pulled her close for a long, warm kiss. "Wonder what the boss would think if he caught us here," he whispered wickedly as he drew her toward him.

"Mitch!" But she couldn't help laughing as she leaned into him and put her arms around his neck.

"Well, it's hard to do this at home." He kissed her soundly again.

Because nothing about their future had been settled, both were careful not to be too obvious about their affection in front of Crystal and the boys. They wanted to set a good example for the kids so Jenny went demurely into the guest wing each night at bedtime. There she tossed and turned because she wanted to be in Mitch's bed. Judging from the amount of time Mitch spent looking at her over the dinner table with a hangdog expression on his face, he shared a similar longing.

It was thrilling to be wanted by such a vibrant, sexy man even though she was six months pregnant and her ankles were swollen.

Just how thrilling, Jenny found out one night about a week later. She couldn't sleep late one Sunday night, and she went quietly downstairs for a snack.

She had the refrigerator door open and her head inside when a voice nearby said, ''Which is it tonight? Sour pickles, a glass of lemonade, or a grapefruit?''

''Mitch!'' she said, startled.

''That's my name.'' She shut the refrigerator door and looked at him lounging in the doorway, barefoot, bare-chested...and mouthwatering. ''Well,'' he said, ''what's your craving tonight?''

You. I have a craving for you. ''I couldn't sleep,'' she said.

''Me, neither. I think,'' he added solemnly, ''in my case that's due to sexual frustration.''

She felt heat on her cheeks. She'd never been with a man so frank.

He stood up straight. ''And you couldn't sleep because...''

''Because I wanted a grapefruit?'' She squeaked out the last syllable as he approached.

He chuckled and grabbed her. ''Why do pregnant women always want something sour when there's something so much...sweeter available?'' He kissed her lightly, then more deeply. His tongue probed.

Through her thin robe she could feel the warmth of his chest. Her breasts went heavy and her nipples got stiff. It was hard not to rub up against him like Jewels did, to moan her pleasure.

"Sweet," he murmured in a husky whisper.

It was sweet. It was wonderful to be in love. "You," she said with a surge of sudden boldness. "I don't want a grapefruit. Just…you."

He pulled back to search her face. "Well then," he said, low and urgent. "Let's find someplace to neck before one of the boys decides he needs a peanut butter sandwich." He caught her hand, tugged her toward the family room. In the doorway, he stopped.

There was a wide opening between the kitchen breakfast area and the family room, and there were no doors. "Hell. Okay, come on."

"Where are we going?"

"To a place where nobody can find us for a while." He led her through the family room to the doorway of his workout room. Once they were through it, he reached behind him and closed the French doors. The doors, though glass, were fitted with fabric panels. She looked around. It was so dark. Even when her eyes adjusted, she could barely make out the shapes of the equipment.

He said, "I know it's not romantic, and maybe I'm over killing the privacy problem, considering it's 2:00 a.m., but…" He led her to the exercise mat on the floor by the big windows. He sat and helped her down.

"I wish I could take you upstairs," he said as she

moved to make herself more comfortable. He put his arm around her. "Ah, blessed privacy. Are you okay?"

"I'm fine."

"Nervous?"

"A little," she admitted.

"I'm nervous, too, but maybe we can just take it one step at a time." He turned to her in the dark and smoothed a lock of hair off her face. "Is this really okay?"

His asking gave her some reassurance, a sense of control. "It's a little awkward, I guess, but it's all right. I'm just glad it's dark." She tried not to giggle with nerves. "My stomach's so big now, and I noticed some red streaks there that I'm afraid are going to be stretch marks—" she broke off, embarrassed. How sexy of her, to be alone with the man she loved, and be discussing stretch marks!

He paid no attention, kissing her gently on her eyelids, her nose, her cheeks. He eased her down, pressing her into the mat. He lay by her side, his head propped on an elbow. His other hand went to the tie of her robe. "This is slinky and thin. I like it better than that thick terry-cloth thing I saw you in once before."

"I'm too hot for all that fabric," she said. "With the baby and all." No matter what, she kept coming back to the baby. Of course, her baby was constantly on her mind, but she was really giving Mitch every chance to be reminded of her pregnancy and back out.

He paid no attention, instead pulling open the tie

of her robe. "Look out," he whispered. "Things are about to get a whole lot hotter." When he slid off the straps of the nightgown, she discovered with a warm shiver that he was right. His hands were hot. And when he leaned over to kiss her, she felt his chest on her bare skin, and that seemed hotter yet. A fire lit within her. She moaned, shocked at how out of control and needy she was.

She slid her hands up his chest, feeling taut skin and the ridges of muscles. He was so powerful, yet so gentle. He bent down and touched her nipple with his tongue. Her back lifted from the mat. "Oh, my!"

He chuckled. "I never realized how much fun it would be to make love with a prissy southern woman." His "prissy" comment had once hurt; now it felt good. Like his hands and mouth on her.

He continued his lazy exploration of her breasts and neck, and when finally he slid a hand up under her nightgown and along her thighs she was trembling. He touched her between the legs, and she gasped.

He groaned. "You feel better than I ever imagined…"

The praise went straight to her head. She forgot her self-consciousness then, forgot everything, sensed everything. Bold now, yet not planning her approach, she reached out and stroked his erection through his sweatpants. His husky groan emboldened her. She pushed beneath his waistband and grasped him.

He sat bolt upright. "Much more of that… It's been a long time, sweetheart." And indeed, when he bent to kiss her again, she felt his whole body quiver as he struggled to maintain control.

She swallowed. Her mouth was dry. He was so strong, yet she was making him quiver and tremble. It was like nothing she'd ever experienced.

"Jenny?" His whisper was ragged. "Just how far can we go?"

Forever. We can go forever, Mitch. "I..."

"It's okay? With the baby?"

Oh. Oh, yes. "I think so. The books say so." She struggled to think. "Of course, I've never asked the doctor." Despite his attentions and the readiness of her body, his words caused a prickle of anxiety.

She must have stiffened, because he said, "Relax... We can stop when you want, but let's just try this..."

His hand was still on her, *there,* experienced and knowing, and she was glad for that experience because his hand felt so good. He set up a relentless rhythm, stroking with his fingers. In a few moments, she was lost. She twisted in his arms. He held her tight, touched her, stroked her, kissed her, urged her to let go.

And she did then. She let go as she never had in her life, squirming and moaning and begging. She closed her eyes and was suddenly on the pond again, where the sun made the ice look like sparkling diamonds. The sparkle grew and grew, and she and Mitch glided across the ice, freewheeling, fast. He spun her into a turn, faster and faster yet, and suddenly the ice exploded and the world was all glitter and light.

"Oh, my," she murmured when at last she became aware of her surroundings again. "Oh, my." She lay on her back, and he was on his side next to her, one leg thrown over her thighs, his face buried in the crook of her neck.

He sighed, his breath against her damp skin. "You have no idea how sexy a southern accent is when you say those words." Though he teased, his voice sounded strained.

That strain was a reminder that although she was satisfied, he wasn't. She reached for him, and touched him again. He was so...big. "Oh, my." Well, her vocabulary was certainly limited. She gave a tentative stroke and was rewarded when his whole body jerked.

"You don't have to do this," he muttered. But he thrust into her hand just the same.

"I want to," she whispered. And she did. She wanted to take him to the same place she had gone, to that incredible, free, glimmering, gliding place. So she stroked again and again until he was panting.

When he came, he grabbed her shoulders and held her tightly to him as he groaned. She flung her free arm around his neck so she could feel every inch of his quaking body, experience and revel in his pleasure.

A couple of minutes later, he whispered. "Oh, my."

She smoothed his hair. "I never knew how sexy a northern accent could be."

She was so happy it scared her.

They lay together for several minutes, locked in

each other's arms. But eventually, they had to return to their own beds. Mitch stopped her in the family room and kissed her. He stopped her at the bottom of the stairs and kissed her. He reached for her at the top of the stairs, too, but she pulled away, conscious that they were in the upstairs hall in their nightclothes, with the scent of sex clinging to them both. He smiled and put his finger lightly on her lips before she turned away from him into the guest wing.

Jenny's body still hummed, her lips and breasts were still delightfully tender from Mitch's kisses as she got into bed a few minutes later. Her arms still ached to hold him, and it scared her how much she wanted him in her bed.

As she listened to the creaking of the old house, she relived every moment of their lovemaking. She thought about how she'd completely let go in his arms, how good it had felt. But then she recalled how she'd begged him so shamelessly for release. How she'd opened for him so completely.

That scared her, too.

WHEN SHOULD he ask Jenny to marry him? Mitch wondered almost daily.

The time never seemed to be right.

Ryan came home one evening and gave a startled Jenny a high five, telling her that it had worked—whatever "it" was—and the teenager smiled and turned pink when Jenny told him she'd been sure he could do it.

"Well, it's just the movies, and just with a bunch

of other kids,'' he said, but he still looked mighty pleased with himself. Obviously, Jenny had done something for Ryan. That was great of her, after what the kid had put her through. He figured maybe he'd ask her to marry him that night. But he didn't.

He thought maybe he'd ask her to marry him when she helped him go through the paperwork needed for the real estate closing on his new store. She was as enthusiastic as he was, and that gave him a good feeling, and he thought, Tonight. I'll ask her tonight. But he didn't.

When he came down one morning to see that Jason and she had made grits for breakfast, and Jason was actually trying to eat them just to please her, he thought how his youngest was treating Jenny like a mother. Mitch decided he'd take her out for lunch and ask her then. But he didn't.

He had every reason in the world to ask her. Every reason but his instincts. Those instincts told him that somehow, despite that incredible lovemaking in the exercise room last week, she was holding back.

For one thing, they hadn't made love again. Of course, that could mean nothing. They had little time together, and zero privacy. He'd thought about renting a motel room, but was afraid he'd be recognized by someone, and he was old-fashioned enough to be concerned about Jenny's reputation. Besides, Mitch could just imagine her southern belle horror of a quickie in a motel room.

Several nights in a row, he decided he couldn't sleep and went down to the family room. He was like a hormone-driven teenager, one who'd got a taste of sex and now couldn't get enough. Surely, he thought, after the way she'd come in his arms, she wouldn't be able to sleep, either. But Jenny never joined him.

When he caught her in the back room of the store again, she kissed him with passion, so he told himself she was just too tired at night for lovemaking. That she was a pregnant woman who still—for his liking anyway—worked way too hard. She probably went upstairs every night and just fell asleep until dawn while he sat downstairs and waited for her.

He said he loved her, and she said she loved him. That ought to be enough, but somehow it wasn't. She was being cautious. Maybe she was still afraid to trust him.

What kind of marriage could they have if she could never fully get over her fear?

On Thursday afternoon, the social worker made a return visit. She toured the house, checked the bedrooms, took Crystal for a walk alone to talk with the little girl. Mitch was charming, but not *too* charming; he remembered Jenny's criticism. The effort to do it all just right made him tense.

The social worker said everything was fine, that she'd send a report to the agency in Hilton Head, recommending that he be given full and permanent custody of Crystal. Mitch figured they ought to celebrate.

When he came back from showing the social worker out, he found Jenny in the family room.

"Isn't that great? We've been looked over by a professional, no less, and found socially acceptable."

"Wonderful."

He frowned. "Hey, socially acceptable around here is terrific, better than anybody could ever hope."

She gave him a ghost of a smile and seemed distracted.

"I think we should go out to dinner tomorrow. All of us, in honor of Crystal being officially a part of the family."

"That sounds nice. I'll bring the camera and take some pictures." She smiled again, but it seemed a little forced.

"You don't sound that happy."

"Of course I am." She got up and put her book away.

He caught her hand and drew her to him. He tipped her chin up. "Come on. You're not thinking about the first time that old biddy came, and you got mad at me, are you?"

She shook her head, but her eyes didn't quite meet his.

He pushed. "That social worker coming had you thinking again about my—my *charm quotient,* didn't it? Are you comparing me with that asshole Delane Kyle?"

She bit her lip. "No." She hesitated just a fraction of a second. That fraction of a second hurt him. "I know you're not him."

"Damn straight I'm not." He kissed her then, a little desperately, somehow trying to communicate with his mouth what she meant to him. But a part of him was angry that she didn't seem able to see him as he was, after all this time. What if she never could?

JENNY WAS HAPPY, she told herself for a week straight. She really was. Her pregnancy was going fine; her baby was active and kicking. Crystal was allowed to stay with them now permanently. She had a wonderful man who loved her, a family in a house that more and more was coming to seem like home and a job she enjoyed. Everything was perfect.

So what was wrong with her? Once she thought with a sinking heart that maybe she was one of those women who was designed to throw away every opportunity for happiness. That idea upset her, so she tried to distract herself with cooking one afternoon: fried chicken, mashed potatoes—she'd make milk gravy to go with them—greens that were shiny with grease, sweet-potato pie. Enough cholesterol to kill a mule.

While she was measuring flour, Tommy came barreling through the kitchen and screeched to a halt when he spotted her. "Hey, what's for dinner? Fried chicken? I sure hope you made enough. I'm starved."

Despite her mood, she smiled at his enthusiasm. "I did. Have you got homework?"

"Nah. We're just going to play football. Over at the Cannons'. Ryan's already there. He rode the bus home with Kevin."

"Football?" It was awfully wet for sports. There

had been a March thaw, and the level part of the yard was awash in mud. Great puddles of brown water marred the gravel driveway and splashed up over her tires every time she drove in. She was forever reminding the kids to take off their shoes in the laundry room.

The sun didn't shine much these days, either. Maybe that had something to do with her mood. "But it's so muddy," she said, taking note of the obvious.

"So?"

She sighed. "By the way, do you know where Crystal is? I don't think I've seen her since she got home from school."

Tommy took the lid off her pot of greens, checked out the contents and made a face. "No clue."

"I hope she's not still upset about Jason and that hamster."

The day before, Crystal had decided—without Jason's permission—to feed Nosy. The hamster had escaped, and there had been a Keystone Kops–like chase around the house before the little animal had disappeared. He still hadn't been found, and Jason wasn't speaking to Crystal as a result.

Jenny had hoped the hamster would turn up this afternoon, and she'd braced herself to catch it if it did. In fact, she'd brought a bucket in from the garage that she planned to pop over the little guy, assuming he decided to show. But he hadn't, and she'd forgotten about Nosy as she'd gone about her cooking.

When the hamster had first disappeared, Jenny

had urged Crystal to apologize. In fact, Crystal was as upset as Jason, and had given the boy an apology that would melt a heart of stone. As long as that heart didn't belong to an eleven-year-old boy, that is.

Jenny bit her lip. "I guess I'd better go find her and make sure she isn't still upset." She expected to find Crystal in her room, but she wasn't there. Jewels was curled up on her bed. Crystal's school clothes were in a heap on the floor, so she must have changed and gone out. *Strange,* Jenny thought. *Usually Crystal tells me where she's going.*

Jewels saw Jenny, yawned and stretched, flexed her claws and went back to sleep. But now that she thought of it, Jenny realized Silver was nowhere to be found, either. The puppy shadowed his pint-size mistress. Maybe Crystal had taken Silver for a walk.

But that didn't seem likely. Crystal hated the mud as much as Jenny; she said it grossed her out. Now Jenny was worried enough to ask Jason if he'd seen the girl.

Jason was lying on his stomach on his bed, sorting through his Pokémon cards. "How would I know where she is?" he asked belligerently when Jenny inquired. "I don't follow her around, you know. Maybe if I did, I woulda caught her before she lost my hamster."

"Crystal is sorry. Besides, your daddy said that cage door isn't the best. In fact, he said Nosy has gotten out before."

Jason studied his cards and didn't answer her.

By now, she was worried enough to look for

Crystal outside. Her boots made sucking sounds in the soft ground as she walked all the way to the pond. When she got to the edge, she looked out over the gray water. Crystal knew she wasn't allowed by the pond alone. The water was too deep. She wouldn't have come down here in the mud, would she? She wouldn't have fallen in.

Alarm flooded through Jenny, though she told herself it was a big farm and the girl could be any number of places. Trying not to panic, she headed back to the house, calling for Crystal as she went. She finally phoned Mitch, who said he was coming right home.

She checked out the basement and the guest wing, then headed out the front door. She had some notion of walking to the road, in case Crystal had gone all the way out there. The fear that she'd been holding back suddenly struck her, a white-hot stab of it. "Crystal! Crystal!" she called, hurrying across the driveway, slipping a little in the mud.

Barking. Faint. Not Face-off. Silver!

"Silver! Here boy!" *Please bring Crystal with you.*

The barking continued, still faint. She was up over her ankles in mud now as she crossed the barnyard. Her sneakers were soaked. Her feet got heavy and she started to pant. *If Silver is here, so is Crystal.* She had the baby to think of, so she forced herself to slow down.

She opened the pasture gate. The barking was coming from the barn. She slid the big barn doors open and stepped inside. It was dark in here, thanks to the overcast sky. She'd seldom been in here before. There was an animal smell about it, and her stomach gave a heave. Ignoring it, she cocked her head and listened. Some bangs and snorts from the ponies. Another banging sound. Barking, too, from the far end.

The tack room was attached to the barn, and she hurried to the door. It was locked, and she yanked on the latch. The door opened and Crystal almost fell into her arms, sobbing. "Jason locked me in!"

JASON WAS DEFIANT as he faced his father. "She probably got Nosy killed."

"That's not the point, son." Mitch raked a hand through his hair and looked beleaguered.

"Crystal was wrong, but that doesn't make what you did right," Jenny said quietly. Crystal was taking a warm bath. Tommy and Ryan had not yet come back from the football game. Jenny's dinner remained on the stove, cooling.

Jason put his hands on his hips. "I didn't hurt her, did I? I just wanted to frighten her some so she wouldn't get into my stuff again."

"She could have been hurt," Jenny said. "It was cold."

"The tack room is heated," Mitch reminded her.

Mitch wasn't going to take Jason's side on this, was he?

"There's no food or water there," Jenny pointed out.

"I think we'd have found Crystal before she needed food or water," Mitch said quietly.

She turned her ire on him. "So this isn't a big deal?"

"No. No, I mean I didn't say that. Jason was wrong."

Jason was looking toward his father hopefully. "Tommy did it to me last year."

"That doesn't make it any more right this year, son."

Jason looked defiant for another moment, then suddenly crestfallen. "I know," he mumbled. "I remember I didn't like it. I was gonna let her out for dinner."

"Don't do it again," Mitch warned.

"I won't."

Mitch looked relieved. "Good."

Jenny couldn't believe this. "That's it? Don't do it again and that's it?"

Mitch turned to her. "What do you want?"

Consequences, Mitch. I want some consequences so the boys will behave better. It was an old issue between them. Mitch's discipline of the boys wasn't her business, she reminded herself. But she cared about Jason, and she was sure it wasn't right for him, for the person he was learning to be, to get out of things so easily.

She made one last try at reasoning with Mitch by speaking with Jason. "Jason, you not only scared Crystal, you scared me about half to death when I couldn't find her. Also, you lied to me. When I asked you where she was, you said you didn't know."

"I didn't lie. I said, 'How would I know?' when you asked me."

"And that really makes a difference?" she asked quietly, looking him in the eye.

His wouldn't meet hers. "Sorry," he mumbled.

She turned her gaze on Mitch.

He put a hand on Jason's shoulder. "I know you didn't intend to scare any of us, but that's what happened. Besides, you know we don't lie in this house. Locking up Crystal was bad enough, but the lying makes what you did far worse." He paused. "So you're grounded for the rest of the week."

Jenny realized she'd been holding her breath; she let it out in a long sigh.

"I said I was sorry!"

"That's good, but it's not enough this time. So you're grounded."

Jason tried arguing, but Mitch stood firm, and the boy finally stomped up the stairs.

Jenny and Mitch were left alone in the family room. "I think you handled that very well," Jenny said softly.

"Well, thanks for the vote of confidence." There was an edge to his voice.

She'd been scared, then angry, and she felt herself flare at his tone. "What's that supposed to mean?"

"It means I must have passed the test."

"The test?"

"The fatherhood test. Isn't that what this discussion with Jason was all about? To see if I could discipline the boys properly when the occasion called for it?"

She stared at him, her mouth open. Sure, she'd wanted Mitch to discipline Jason, but she wasn't testing him—

"Isn't that what everything's about these days?" There was anger in his voice, and a deep hurt she couldn't miss. "You watch everything I say, everything I do, for signs that I'm not measuring up. That I'll turn into a jerk, a bastard, one of those guys who've done you wrong."

Dear Lord, that wasn't what she was doing. "I was concerned that Jason learn from this episode," she said primly.

"Sure, go prissy on me," he said bitterly. "Tonight with Jason. The other day with the social worker. Would I be too charming with the social worker, a cardinal sin? Would I take Jason's horrible transgression tonight seriously enough? Or would I go with the flow with my son, an even worse fault than being charming?"

"Mitch, I—" Goodness. Was she really testing him that way all the time, finding him wanting?

"Jenny, I care about you. I care about your baby. I don't even think about not being her father anymore. I take care of my kids, I take care of my business. When you were sick, I took care of you and your baby. Look at me," he commanded.

She was looking. He was huge, a head taller than she, and he was looking down at her with a single-minded intensity.

"I'm just a man," he said tightly. "Just one of the guys. Maybe that's the worst thing of all, that I'm a guy. Because in your mind, men can't be relied on. Well, lady, here's a clue." He stabbed his chest with one finger. "This man can."

She knew suddenly, knew in her heart—in her soul—that he *could* be counted upon. Her mind flashed to his wonder the day he'd touched her belly. To the other night, when he'd been so aroused, but he'd still asked if lovemaking would hurt the baby. He was right. He'd taken her to the hospital, he'd taken her home and put her to bed to get well, to save her baby. He couldn't have taken better care of Stephanie than if he'd fathered her himself.

And before that, he'd taken Crystal into this noisy, messy household and he'd done everything he could to make her happy. Silver was only a part of all the things he'd done for Crystal.

And long before even that, he'd promised a dying wife to take care of his children, and he'd started from scratch and made a family. Maybe not a traditional family, maybe not a disciplined family, maybe not a neat and tidy family, but a family nonetheless.

He was right. His actions spoke for themselves, spoke of his character and told her in every way that he could be trusted.

Her eyes filled with tears. "I'm sorry. I haven't been completely fair to you. I was afraid to trust you. Oh, Mitch, I love you so much it scares me."

His scowl softened. "I know, honey. But how can I ever prove to you I won't run out on you? That you can trust me?"

She put her arms around his neck. "You already

have. Oh, Mitch, I understand that. I believe it. You already have. I trust you.''

He pulled her to him roughly, yet tenderly, and kissed her long and deep.

CHAPTER FOURTEEN

MITCH WAS PLEASED. Everything was going to work out. All he'd had to do was allow Jenny time to make up her mind. She trusted him. Heck, last night they'd even talked about marriage.

He whistled as he drove the Jeep into the parking lot at the rink, whistled as he got out and locked it, whistled as he half walked, half sprinted up the steps to the door. Even his bad instep wasn't hurting tonight.

"Mitch?" David Chandler was waiting in front of the doorway, still in his jeans and leather jacket.

"David, hi." Mitch glanced at his watch. "You're late suiting up for practice. What're you doing still out here?"

David looked around as if not wanting to be overheard. "I wanted to talk to you."

Something in the teenager's tone penetrated Mitch's good spirits. "Sure. What's up?"

"I can't talk here. There were some girls hanging around a minute ago, and I could hardly get rid of them. Can we go somewhere?"

"Sure. Right after practice."

"I'm not going to practice."

"Okay," Mitch said carefully, very concerned

now. "Why don't we get a cup of coffee and a doughnut? You can ride along with me. I'll just go tell Buddy that you're not feeling well and that I'm taking you home, okay?"

"Yeah. That sounds good." There was a curious tenseness about David.

When Mitch came back from talking to the coach, David followed him to the Jeep. They got in, but before Mitch could put the key in the ignition, David blurted out, "Robin's pregnant."

Mitch's hand froze. *No.* He'd told this kid time after time— "Are you sure?"

"She says so. Why would she lie?" His voice sounded high and desperate.

Mitch forced himself to sound casual. "The baby's yours?"

David gave a short, bitter bark of laughter. "Who else's would it be?"

The kid needs you. Take it one step at a time. "Okay," Mitch said, managing to sound calm, but not feeling calm at all. "Have you told your parents about this? Has Robin told her parents?"

"Robin just found out today, so she hasn't told anyone but me. I'm not going to tell my father." The Chandlers were divorced, and David's father had never been very interested in him. "And I *can't* tell Mom. She'll kill me."

Mitch turned to him. "You've got to tell your mom right away."

"I'm an adult," David reminded him. "I have my own place." Then his bravado collapsed. "I know I have to tell her." David leaned back against the seat and closed his eyes. "Telling Mom's the least of it. What am I going to do?"

Mitch thought. "What do you want to do?"

"I don't know. I can't, you know, tell Robin an abortion is okay. I just can't do that."

"That's not what she wants either, is it?"

"No. No, no way. We didn't even mention it, you know?"

"Good." Mitch leaned back in his seat for a moment. He'd figured out right away that an abortion wouldn't be on Robin's agenda, but he needed to be sure. He tried to think over the instant suspicion, the instant resentment that bubbled in him.

"Well, it seems you've got some thinking to do," he said finally.

"Thinking's all I've *been* doing. I mean, how could this happen to me?"

"If you were going to sleep with her, you needed to use something, David. You didn't, and that's how this happened."

"Robin was taking care of it. Oh, man," he moaned. "A baby. And now she wants to get married right away."

Mitch's ugly suspicion grew. Why couldn't the kid have kept his pants zipped? Mitch thought on a wave of frustration and anger. "David, listen to me. If Robin was 'taking care of it,' how did she end up pregnant?"

"Hell, I don't know. How would I know? What flaming difference does it make now?"

"It makes a lot of difference in what you want to do."

There was a small silence. Then David turned to him abruptly. "Are you saying she *planned* this?"

Well, a pregnancy certainly seemed convenient. Robin had ended up pregnant when she was supposedly on birth control. And she must have got pregnant pretty soon after David had said he didn't want to marry her. Mitch's mind flashed to a picture of Robin hanging around the rink, her clinging to David. It sure wouldn't be the first time a woman had used sex—and a baby—to snare a professional hockey player.

"I don't know if she planned it." But Mitch was pretty sure he did know. He decided to let David think about what he'd said.

He took him to a small coffee shop where they weren't likely to be recognized or interrupted. David ate four doughnuts, one after the other. Watching him, Mitch knew one thing for certain. No way was this kid ready for marriage.

"I don't want to get married. Not when I'm just going to the NHL," David said around doughnut number five. "But what can I do?"

"You can think about giving the baby up for adoption, for one thing."

Emotions played across David's face. Relief, a touch of sadness.

That sadness suddenly made Mitch swallow hard. Adoption wouldn't be an easy solution. There would be problems as David and Robin adjusted to the fact that they'd given up their child. But it was a good solution. The baby could go to two parents who desperately wanted a child. And David's life wouldn't have to change.

David put down the doughnut. "I...don't know. That seems so..."

"You can think about it, talk it over with Robin." But even as he said it, he knew what Robin would decide.

David put both hands down flat on the table. "You don't think I should marry her, do you?"

"No," he said bluntly. Out of every confusing, angry emotion David's news had brought out in Mitch, he knew that marrying Robin was the last thing David should do.

David swallowed a mouthful of doughnut. "Well, you seem to feel pretty strongly about that."

"I do."

"Well, then..."

"But you can't just walk away. If the baby is yours, if you and Robin don't give it up for adoption, you need to take responsibility. That means child support. Hefty child support, when you start making big bucks."

He leaned forward. "I have a good lawyer. The settlement will be fair to you and to Robin. After she realizes that child support's all she's going to get, she'll be happy with how much money she gets, I guarantee it."

"Really? You can fix this?" David looked suddenly very young. And eager to have a solution handed to him. That eagerness didn't sit right with Mitch, and he wasn't exactly sure why. Then he thought of Robin's baby, a little kid who was being brought into this world because its mother had an agenda, and he pushed his own, untouched doughnut aside.

ROBIN MUST HAVE MISUNDERSTOOD, Jenny kept telling herself over and over. She repeated the words when Mitch came home from a day out of town and gave her a smacking kiss and patted her tummy to say hello to her baby. And again, when she saw Mitch ruffle Jason's hair and pick Crystal up and hold her high so that the little girl could get something off a shelf.

Once, Jenny might have jumped to conclusions, but now she had to give Mitch the benefit of the doubt. But they needed to talk.

It took forever that night for the house to quiet down. Because it was a Friday night, the kids had been allowed to stay up late and watch the Great Chicago Fire play the Philadelphia Flyers on television. Luke was home, and watched the game with Mitch and the kids. There had been popcorn and pizza, mess and noise until Jenny's head hurt. She longed to go to bed and put her feet up.

Finally, the little ones had gone to bed, the twins had gone to their rooms, and Luke had left with a group of friends. Jenny caught Mitch in the family room as he was picking up an empty popcorn bag.

"I need to talk to you," she said without preamble.

He gave her a smile. "I thought since the kids were in bed, maybe you'd rather neck."

"I'm serious!" she said sharply.

He straightened slowly. "Okay," he said carefully, the way men did with women they were humoring.

His tone made her grit her teeth. She stood by the doorway, watching him closely. "Robin came into work today."

Mitch's face fell. "Oh, hell, you talked to Robin."

"Yes, I talked to Robin. She works for us. You must have figured at some point I'd talk to her, didn't you?"

He crumpled the bag in his hands. "Well, she hadn't told her parents as of Wednesday night, and I didn't know if she had yet. I guess I figured—well, I didn't think about this part, but now I can figure—that she won't have to work at Serious Gear much longer."

"Meaning?"

"Meaning after the baby's born, she probably won't have to have a job for the next eighteen years."

She reflexively touched her belly. "You sound very cynical."

"Yep. Cynical about cuts it here, doesn't it?"

"Because Robin is having a baby?" Anger was growing in her, though she told herself she owed it to Mitch to hear his side of the story.

He held the bag clenched tightly in a fist. "Because she's pregnant. Because a few months ago, she couldn't get David to marry her. She was supposed to be using birth control, and somehow she got pregnant.''

Oh. Jenny studied him. Robin hadn't mentioned birth control when she'd burst into tears at the store and told a disbelieving Jenny that she was pregnant and David wouldn't marry her. Thanks to his talk with Mr. Oliver.

But who had or hadn't used birth control wasn't really important. ''What does it matter now, Mitch?'' she asked. ''Robin's going to have a baby, and according to her, you convinced David not to accept responsibility for the baby he fathered. I told her she must be mistaken.'' *Please let her have been mistaken.*

''Oh, honey.'' His expression changed, he dropped the bag on a side table and came swiftly toward her. He put a hand gently on each of her shoulders and looked down at her. ''I didn't tell him not to accept responsibility. Listen, I've been upset by this myself. I was going to talk to you about it, it's just that I...well, I hadn't yet. But I didn't really think about how adoption might sound to you.'' His eyes were sincere and concerned.

Adoption. Robin hadn't mentioned adoption, either. Jenny felt her knees give with sudden relief, because adoption did sound like a possible, even a caring, thing to do. ''You told David they should have the baby adopted?''

''I told him they should consider it. They're not ready to be parents, and I know from the newspa-

pers, from TV, that there are all these couples looking desperately for babies.''

She went into his arms. ''Oh, Robin didn't tell
me about adoption. Yes, that does sound reasonable.'' She laid her cheek against Mitch's chest.
''Robin is just so upset, I guess she embroidered on
things, or maybe she didn't really understand. She
seemed to think that David was only offering to see
a lawyer and negotiate money.''

She felt him stiffen.

She pulled away slightly as her old fear washed
over her. ''No! Mitch, that wasn't your idea, was
it?''

''I said adoption first, but if Robin didn't agree,
David should take responsibility for the baby.''

''Responsibility how? By seeing some lawyer?''

''They'll need to work out child support.'' He
sounded stressed now. ''Look, Robin trapped him
and now he's got a baby. I told him he's responsible
regardless.'' She looked into his eyes and saw pure
stubbornness there.

''And then he just goes on to the NHL, has the
support deducted from his paycheck, and gets on
with his life?'' She could not believe what she was
hearing.

''Well, when you put it that way it sounds rotten,
and that's not how I meant it, exactly, but...'' His
voice trailed away.

Stephanie kicked hard. Oh, Jenny would like to
do the same to Mitch! ''Responsibility for a baby is
more than child support.''

"I realize that! But she trapped him—"

"You don't know that!"

"It's a likely scenario! It's not like it hasn't been done before about a million times! I've told you all about it!"

They had both raised their voices, and Jenny made an effort to calm down. "Mitch, the kids are upstairs," she said more quietly. Lord, her own volume had picked up in the months she'd been in this house.

She tried to think. Just last week, she'd vowed to trust this man. She'd put her happiness in his hands. If she really trusted him, she'd try to see his point of view, though she felt like sitting down in the chair and bursting into tears.

With effort, she said, "You've been working hard for four years to be a parent to your boys, and look how hard you've worked to understand Crystal. You, of all people, should know that a father is not some guy who pays child support and gets on with his life."

Her voice strengthened. She *knew* Mitch wasn't that kind of man. "When you lost your wife, you stepped in, learned to be a real father. Are you saying your attitude about fatherhood is only reserved for the families of women men choose to marry?"

Emotions crossed his face. Guilt, then a hardening of his mouth, and he looked away.

She was losing him, and her world was about to come crashing down. A couple of big, hot tears rolled down her cheeks. "Delane blamed me for my pregnancy, too. It takes two people to make a baby. Mitch, how long will it be—'' she swallowed ''—how long will it be before you decide I've tricked you like Robin tricked David? That I came here and saw your wealth and fame and decided to get a convenient father for my own baby?''

''No, honey.'' He turned back to her, his eyes concerned. ''Honey, this isn't about you. Damn, it's not about you. You didn't ask me for a thing, you've always made your own way, and I love that about you. You're an adult, I'm an adult. We aren't a couple of high-school kids.'' He grasped her upper arms. ''We've gotten to know each other, we love each other. This thing with David and Robin, don't make it about you and me.''

His words, their sincerity, made her want to cry harder, to go into his arms, to gain comfort from the very man who was making her miserable. She looked up into his eyes, dark with caring, and realized that he was doing what he thought was right, and that he was so very, very wrong.

He said, ''I thought you trusted me.''

Anger flared in her anew. ''You know,'' she said, ''you accuse me of not trusting you. But you've got some problems in that area yourself. You think that the rules are different for some people. For men who are professional athletes. For one thing, nothing so trivial as a family ought to stand in the way of a hockey star's success, should it?''

''Listen, that's not what I—''

''No, you listen. Isn't that what your career in the

NHL was all about? You've said yourself that you were so totally bound up in your career that you missed Jason's birth, for heaven's sake. You loved Anne. All right, I believe that. But at least one of the reasons you loved her was because she made your career so easy. You've admitted it. Nothing came before hockey. She ran your household and took care of your kids and nothing interfered. Despite everything that's happened to you, on some level, you still think that's how life ought to be, isn't it?''

"I came home when Anne got sick, I gave up everything for her!" His face was white with anger. "That was the season the Fire was probably going to the Stanley again, I was in line to smash the goals-scored record, and I still came home, and I stayed home.''

"How willingly, Mitch? Sure, you made the right decisions, but you've admitted that you resented having to leave hockey. You know what? I think there's a part of you that still resents it, or you wouldn't be so darn sure you're right about David.''

An ugly silence fell. Jenny felt numb, drained, exhausted. She could tell she wasn't getting through.

They'd moved away from each other as they'd talked. Now a little distance separated them. It might as well have been a mile. Mitch's back was straight, his hands clenched at his sides.

"Oh, Mitch, you made exactly the right decision four years ago." Tears rolled down Jenny's cheeks; she could no longer control them. "You have it all, but unless you can see that, you're…you're not the man I thought you were.''

Emotions warred on his face. Guilt, confusion, anger. She watched as anger won, and his perfect mouth settled into a hard, stubborn line.

''So…'' Her voice was quavering. ''It's a good thing we didn't tell the kids we were getting married, isn't it?'' She turned on her heel and left the room.

CHAPTER FIFTEEN

LUKE, Tommy and Ryan cornered Mitch in the kitchen.

Ryan leaned against the counter and said, "Okay, Dad, it's been over two weeks since Jenny moved back to her apartment, and you still haven't made up with her."

"You guys have marked the date on your calendar, huh?" He stood with the refrigerator door open, a bottle of milk in his hand. His sons were arrayed along the counter that separated the kitchen from the eating area, like a bunch of defensemen putting the squeeze on him.

Tommy said, "I don't need to mark the date on the calendar. You've been a crab for two weeks."

Luke added, "You're back to going to the rink every night. Even Buddy asked me what was wrong."

"Buddy gossips more than an old lady." Mitch didn't want to talk about this, didn't want to talk about his misery, his sleeplessness, his conviction that he'd blown it so bad he could never make things right again. He put the milk on the counter. "Okay, you must want to say something here. Better just say it."

"We want you to make up," Ryan said. "We want Jenny back."

"You sure have changed your tune," he said sarcastically, then dropped his act. What had happened was his fault, and he wasn't going to take it out on them. "Look, guys, I know you miss Jenny. I do, too, but it's over. I told you that."

"Why, Dad?" Luke asked the question softly.

Mitch paused. What had happened between him and Jenny was private, something between two adults. But he studied the earnest faces before him. He'd always been able to count on Luke. The twins—well, they were fifteen. They acted like half-grown puppies most of the time. What kind of explanation could they handle?

"She...said some things. And I said some things she didn't like..." He shrugged. "You know women."

"Nope. Not gonna work, Dad," Tommy said. "Somehow, you screwed this up, and we decided you need help. But we can't do it until you tell us what the problem is."

Mitch started to beat a retreat. The boys moved closer together, blocking the narrow passage between the counter and the wall.

He looked at his sons and thought how much he loved them. His throat tightened as he thought about how much they'd learned together. How Mitch had had to adjust, but they'd had to adjust, too. How they'd survived four years together by loving each other. Jenny's words rang in his head. *You have it all.*

"All right," he said finally. "I'm going to tell you, but I've got to be able to trust you. Some of this I've been told in confidence, so I'm going to trust you to keep it quiet. And I'm going to tell you some things about your mom and me. Can you handle that?"

Three heads nodded solemnly.

"Okay," he said. "Let's sit down."

When he was done speaking a few minutes later, there was silence. There was so much silence that Mitch could hear the clock in his study ticking. He didn't ever remember hearing that before.

Tommy spoke up. "But you've changed, Dad. I remember when Mom was alive, you weren't here much, and when you were home, you were always at the rink helping Luke with hockey. It's not like that now."

"Yes, I did change."

"So why did you say those things to David? Why did you say those stupid things to Jenny?"

Luke turned to the twins. "Dad told you that part. It's complicated. Because he felt two ways about Mom. He loved her, and he didn't want to come home, but he did want to come home, to take care of her."

Mitch folded his hands on the table. "I thought I'd put everything behind me, got on with my life, but maybe I didn't. Maybe I still was angry somewhere inside that I never got my biggest chance in hockey."

"Jeez, Dad." Tommy shook his head.

"You guys don't understand what it's like," Luke

said. "You're on the basketball team at school, but basketball has never been everything to you guys, the way hockey was for Dad. You've never practiced with a broken collarbone, or practiced when you have the flu and every fifteen minutes you've got to come off the ice to puke. You've never missed things you wanted to do because you had to practice or travel. I have. I know what it's like. After you've done all that, you think you deserve whatever success you can get. I understand, Dad."

Mitch cleared his throat. "Thanks."

"Hockey screws up your head if you let it."

"Guys, I did screw up. Not in the choice I made four years ago, but in the things I said to David. Then when Jenny called me on them, I got stubborn. The thing is, Jenny is harder to love in some ways than your mom was. She's more independent, she won't let me get away with things. I wasn't ready for that kind of love before, but now I am."

He leaned forward. "You kids made me start to change, to learn what was important in life. But it was Jenny who made me finish the whole thing. She made me be a better parent to all of you, and now she's wanting me to…to acknowledge, I guess that's the word—to acknowledge what's important to me, and to live my life according to those values."

There was a short silence as his kids worked through what he'd said.

Then Ryan put his head in his hands. "Dad, I can't believe you told a *woman* that hockey was more important than babies."

"In a way, I guess I did. And I don't think that, I really don't. Not anymore."

Ryan shook his head, and looked at his brothers. "Can you believe this?"

"Well, what makes you such an expert on women all of a sudden?"

"Since he got Colleen Hart to speak to him," Tommy said.

Ryan gave his brother a shove. "Well, so yeah, but she wouldn't have if Jenny hadn't showed me how to get her to pay attention to me."

"Can you discuss things with Jenny, Dad?" Luke asked quietly. "Just tell her like you told us?"

"I've tried. As soon as she spots me at the store, she finds some excuse to go to her office. I called her, and she said she didn't want to talk. I think she meant it."

"A woman who doesn't want to talk. That *is* bad," Tommy said in utter, complete seriousness.

"You've got to soften her up. Get her ready to listen to you," Ryan said.

"How?" What an oddball conversation to be having with your kid, he thought. But his own efforts had come to nothing. He had plenty to say to Jenny, but how could he say anything if she didn't want to listen to him?

Ryan snapped his fingers. "We're gonna shop. Power shop."

"Huh?"

"Give her romance." Ryan stood, went into the hallway and shouted up the stairs. "Jason! Crystal!

We're all going shopping to find stuff that Dad can
use to get Jenny back. Come on!''

Pounding feet on the stairs and questions. Mitch
stood. ''I don't know, guys—''

''Trust me,'' Ryan said confidently. ''This'll
work.''

Mitch was out of ideas, and Ryan's enthusiasm
was catchy. What better way to show Jenny he'd
changed than to do something so outlandish, so out
of the ordinary, so un-guylike that she'd have to pay
attention to him?

She loved him. All he had to do was get a real
chance to explain what he'd learned about himself,
and she'd forgive him, and she'd take that fragile
trust of hers and give it to him again. For good.

He hoped.

AT THE MALL, Ryan took the lead. ''Now look. It
takes a while to power shop, see? You've got to buy
just the right thing. You know, something that re-
minds you especially of her. But if you can't do that,
then you go with what Jenny calls her 'momma's
standbys.' Standbys are flowers, candy and books.''

''We've got two hours till the mall closes,'' Mitch
said, jingling the keys in this pocket.

''Not enough time,'' Ryan said. ''But I'll do my
best.''

''It's plenty of time.'' It was about twice the time
he'd ever spent in a mall. How long could it take to
buy candy, books, flowers and an engagement ring?
Of course, he'd seen women in Serious Gear chew

over buying a tennis racket for the longest time, but that was sports equipment.

On the way over, Ryan had suggested they all dress up in tuxedos if Mitch was really going to ask Jenny to marry him. Mitch himself owned a monkey suit from the days he'd had to go to charity dinners, but he'd have to get the boys outfitted. Fortunately, there was a place at the mall that rented wedding tuxes. Crystal loved the idea. The little girl was so excited, it was hard for Mitch to keep from smiling himself. This was going to work.

They stopped at the tuxedo store first. There the salesclerk had the boys try on jackets, and pronounced Luke and the twins "too big" in the shoulders.

"Do your best," Mitch instructed him. "We have an hour and fifteen minutes."

"I can't fit huge guys like you in that kind of time."

Mitch whipped out a couple of twenties. "Will this help?"

"We...ll. If I'd get started right away... They may not look that great, but I'll try."

"Good. Okay," Mitch said, turning to Ryan. "We still have over an hour. That should be twice the time we need."

But it seemed that there was more to this power shopping than he'd figured. For one thing, the mall was crowded. With so many shoppers looking at everything, it was hard to work your way over to the good stuff.

They stopped in the bookstore first. "The classics,'' Ryan said. "The stuff we have to read in English class.'' Luke wandered off, but the rest of Mitch's group headed over to the fiction section. Ryan reached up and pulled out a bright red, tooled-leather book. "Here. This says—'' he was reading the big cardboard promotional ticket. "'One of the World's One Hundred Greatest Books, Packaged in Real Moroccan Leather.''' He peered down at it. "Hey, I think I saw these advertised on Sunday-morning cable television. They were cheaper there.''

"What's the title?'' Mitch said.

"The Three Musketeers.''

"The Three Musketeers? For Jenny?'' That didn't sound right at all.

"It's a classic,'' Ryan said with confidence, turning the book over. "And even if they were cheaper on TV, this looks good for nine ninety-five. It is real leather. A deal.''

Mitch didn't care about the deal, but he was caught up in Ryan's confidence. The book did look pretty. "Okay.''

"I'll give her this,'' Ryan said, taking the book from Mitch.

"Hey, how about this one?'' Tommy had been browsing in another section, and now held out a book. Mitch read the title. *One Hundred Rules for Business Success,* by some guy he thought he'd seen on a talk show. "Okay, that looks better.''

"Good,'' Ryan said, taking the book. "Now we just need flowers and candy.''

And an engagement ring. Mitch asked for the books to be gift wrapped. Unfortunately, the clerk was out of what she called her "women's" paper, but the roll she had left was pretty nice—some golfing stuff printed on it. Well, the sports theme would remind Jenny of him and the boys, and that might look as if they'd selected it just for her. He was pleased with himself.

Luke went off then, and came back with another book that he said was his present for Jenny. The author was a woman, a name he'd never heard of.

"This author's on the *New York Times* bestseller list," Luke said.

One Hundred Rules for Business Success, still sounded better, but he decided to humor Luke. "It sounds fine, son." Luke passed on the gift wrap, just asking for a bow.

"All right," Mitch said when they were back out in the mall. "Candy, right?"

"Chocolate." Ryan sounded completely confident again, but for some reason, Mitch found himself looking to Luke.

"Chocolate's good, Dad," Luke confirmed.

Unfortunately, the candy shop at the mall was closed on Sundays.

"Well, that sucks," Jason said as they stood in front of the closed shop, peering in at the gold foil-wrapped boxes of mixed chocolates.

"Yeah, that sucks," Crystal repeated. "I know! We could go to the drugstore."

With great relief, Mitch herded his brood there. He didn't want to blow this. If for some reason any one of his gifts didn't suit, he'd get enough so that *something* would touch Jenny, make her listen to him.

The drugstore was huge, and they had a lot of candy. Unfortunately, it was all candy bars or Easter candy. "Don't they have boxes of chocolates?" Mitch asked in bewilderment. He finally found a clerk, a boy of about eighteen with a silver hoop in his ear and a tattoo of a bloody dagger on his arm.

"Heart boxes?" the kid repeated, chewing gum. "We get boxes like that for Valentine's Day, but it's almost Easter, man."

"A chocolate rabbit!" Crystal squealed. "Oh, Uncle Mitch, can I get Miss Jenny a chocolate rabbit?"

His eyes met Luke's. What was he going to do? They were about out of time, and chocolate was chocolate.

He got a little hurried, saying yes without thinking too much about it when Jason persuaded Crystal to add a big plastic bag of saltwater taffy in four pastel colors to her gift.

His own idea was perfume. At the cosmetic counter at the drugstore were a lot of tester bottles on a mirrored tray. "I'm not gonna spray them on me," Tommy said. "You know what I'll smell like."

Crystal volunteered to do the testing, but after they'd sprayed nine scents on her arm, Mitch could no longer tell the difference between them.

"How about this one?" Ryan pulled a giant bottle from the tray. He squirted some perfume in the air.

Mitch sniffed. It smelled like flowers. Jenny always smelled like flowers, and this perfume smelled even stronger than what she usually wore. He was pleased.

Ryan looked at the price and pronounced it a deal at nine ninety-nine.

Now that he was going with this idea of Ryan's, Mitch had an almost desperate need to finish, to go to Jenny and tell her he loved her. To show her their girl gifts, to put that ring on her finger. To tell her what he'd learned about love.

"Okay, what's next?" he asked the boys.

"Flowers," Ryan said.

At the flower shop, Mitch asked for red roses. The shop owner said they were out of red.

Ryan and Mitch looked at each other. Now what? Luke grinned and said, "You guys are on your own. I always buy red." Every man on the planet knew flowers had to be roses and roses had to be red. Obviously, a lot of men had got to the store ahead of Mitch.

Now unsure, he wandered over to the refrigerator case to look at some arrangements displayed there. "Hey, I see some red roses," he said, looking into the case. The clerk must have forgotten about these. Mitch felt lucky.

"Those are a little old," the clerk said. "I'd hate to sell you those. They won't last—"

"I'll take them," Mitch said.

By the time they got to the jewelry store, Mitch only had ten minutes. Now that he thought about it, he realized maybe he should have shopped for the ring first. There was a bewildering choice. He eye-balled the biggest diamonds.

But they didn't seem quite right.

When the clerk saw that Mitch was looking at the larger stones, he went in the back room and got the owner. The owner told Mitch that it was all right to stay a little past closing time. That was a relief.

The boys and Crystal all had opinions, and after a few minutes, Mitch was totally confused. He knew that this decision was important. If Jenny agreed to marry him, she'd be wearing this ring the rest of her life. Of course, he could let her pick it out, but that didn't fit with his plan. Jenny was big on plans; surely she'd appreciate all the planning that went into these gifts.

The boys were arguing, and Luke was trying to settle them down. "All right," Mitch said finally. "Can you all go out in the mall for a couple of minutes and give me a chance to think?"

"Sure, Dad." Luke hustled the group out into the mall.

Once the store was quiet, Mitch started wandering, not sure what he wanted. He wanted to get Jenny a big ring, but he thought of her pearls, and those little gold earrings she wore, the ones he really liked. He wondered suddenly if she'd really like a big diamond. Or a diamond at all.

Another stone caught his eye. He was pretty sure it was an opal. "Could I see this opal?"

The owner pulled it from the case. It was a large stone, and there were diamonds on either side of it. He peered more closely at the opal. It looked cloudy white on the outside, but there were all kinds of glowing colors in there, like a fire.

It reminded him of Jenny—cool on the outside, warm if you looked deep enough.

"It's an exquisite ring," the owner told him. "It's rare to find an opal this large that has this much fire in it." There was a pause as Mitch studied the ring. "You have good taste," the owner added.

Mitch grinned.

"No, I mean it. This ring's special."

Jenny was rare and special. "Can I get a wedding ring to go with this?"

"We can make you one," the owner promised. "Maybe one with diamonds."

"Can we do six diamonds?" He was on a roll here. For the first time since choosing the book, he felt this was perfectly right. "We've got six kids between us. Well, when Jenny's baby girl is born, we'll have six. My four boys, and my little niece— I'm raising her—and Jenny's baby. So six diamonds, six kids—see? And I don't know if she'll marry me, because I said some things—" He stopped abruptly and felt the red creeping up his neck. A guy didn't bare his soul to another guy. This shopping was messing with his brain.

Or maybe his palms felt suddenly damp because, despite all his efforts, Jenny might not say yes.

And he honestly didn't know if he could live without her.

JENNY TURNED OFF the television with a sigh. Sunday was her day off. But she'd been restless all day.

Though her feet were swollen, she'd taken a short walk. That had got Stephanie kicking up a storm, and so it had been hard to concentrate on her book when she'd returned. All day Jenny had been like that, going from one thing to another. Waiting. Waiting for nothing.

She glanced at the telephone. It hadn't rung, though she'd imagined it might; Sunday was Mitch's day off, too.

What difference does it make? she asked herself impatiently. She'd been avoiding him; she'd refused to talk to him, and now she wanted the phone to ring? He'd said all she needed to hear two weeks ago.

Don't cry, it's bad for the baby, she scolded herself. She got up to make a cup of tea. The little apartment was beginning to seem like home. Her condominium in Hilton Head had finally sold and she'd had her furniture shipped north. She'd brought a few pieces over to the apartment, and she'd bought an ivy plant at the supermarket. But she was waiting. She was waiting for after the baby to make her permanent plans. She was waiting for the phone to ring. She wasn't!

When the doorbell rang, she was actually startled it wasn't the phone. She was losing it, she thought grimly as she smoothed down her smocklike top to cover the elastic panel in her jeans. She pulled open the door. Mitch stood there, in a tuxedo.

Her mouth fell open. A tuxedo? And he was holding a bunch of half-dead red roses, of all things. And...and there was Luke, and *he* was in a tuxedo, and he had a package in his hands…and Mitch had a couple of parcels, too.

"Hi, Miss Jenny!" Crystal's voice, high and excited, and there was jostling, and she saw that Jason, Ryan and Tommy were there, and they were all— all except Crystal—in tuxedos and they all had packages.

She put her hands on her cheeks.

"Hi," Mitch said softly. "Can we come in?"

She blinked once more, then held the door open. They came in with a bit of shoving. The room was suddenly very crowded. They stood rather awkwardly in the middle of the room, and nobody said a word for a moment. Then Jenny noticed that Ryan's tuxedo had a sleeve so short it barely covered his elbow. Oh, and Tommy's jacket was so small, it wouldn't meet in the middle by a foot. Mitch's tuxedo fit perfectly, and she had to swallow when she looked at him. There wasn't anything better-looking on God's green earth than a trim, athletic man in a tuxedo.

"Are y'all going out somewhere?" she asked stupidly.

"We came to talk to you, Miss Jenny, and to bring you stuff," Jason said.

"Oh. Well. Goodness. I…maybe y'all would like some lemonade?"

Four young voices answered. "Sure."

"Yeah."

"Why not?"

"Sounds good."

"No, thank you," Mitch said.

"No thanks."

"Never mind."

"I'm not thirsty."

"I'll get myself some water later."

Luke smiled and rolled his eyes.

"Okay," Mitch said, sounding nervous. "I came to see you because you wouldn't talk to me at the store, and we brought all these things." He held out the roses.

"Thank you. Maybe I'll just go and put these in water…" But she stood still, holding the roses. A couple of bright red petals fell off and wafted gently to the floor.

"They do look like they might need some water," Mitch said ruefully. "Actually, they look done for. They looked better in the shop, but not much better. We had to buy them—they were the only red ones."

"I see." She didn't see at all, of course, but the earnest, desperate expression on his face was melting something inside her, something that had been cold for two weeks. Maybe something that had been cold all her adult life.

"You'll figure out what we're doing right away," Ryan said eagerly. He thrust a package into her hands.

She laid the roses on the couch and looked down at the gift. There were golf balls on the paper.

"Open it," Ryan urged.

She opened it, her hands shaking. It was a book. *The Three Musketeers.*

"It's Real Moroccan Leather," Ryan said proudly. "See, it says so right on that card."

"Thank you." Her response was automatic. Puzzled, she turned the book over in her hands.

They were all looking at her as if they expected something more. She struggled to think. "Oh, I see! You're giving me *The Three Musketeers* to remind me of y'all, you four boys. The Three Musketeers and their friend, D'Artagnan. How clever and sweet." But that still didn't explain why the kids were giving her presents at all.

"Yeah, that's why we got it," Ryan mumbled. He and his father exchanged pleased glances.

"Open mine, open mine," Crystal begged, thrusting a package into her hand.

"Sure, sweetheart." It took her a moment, because there was an awful lot of tape holding the paper on. When she finally got it off, she pulled out a chocolate rabbit. "Thank you for my Easter present," she said to the little girl.

"It's not an Easter present," she said indignantly.

"Oh." Her eyes met Mitch's. He was looking at her, his own eyes almost begging her for something. Something Jenny was supposed to get out of dead roses, a chocolate bunny and *The Three Musketeers*.

"Now mine." Jason solemnly handed her a package and stood there, pulling at his starched collar. His was the most bizarre of all. It looked like an alien spaceship. Inside, she found a large bag of saltwater taffy.

Luke gave her another book, a bestseller she'd been wanting to read. "Thank you, I was just thinking today how hard a time I've had concentrating on reading. This book—these books," she corrected, remembering Real Moroccan Leather, "will get me interested again, I'm sure."

"Wait! If you want books, here's more." Mitch looked at her very expectantly. He handed her what must be another book. Totally bewildered now, she opened it. *One Hundred Rules for Business Success.* She raised her eyes to his.

"Isn't that great? I picked it myself."

"Yes. It's wonderful." Lord, this was worse than meeting up with someone and not remembering their name. Because somehow, she'd got the notion here that if she could just figure out what they were up to, she'd learn something terribly important.

Tommy gave her a present, too, and when she opened it, the teenager took it from her. "Perfume, see? That wasn't part of the plan, but Dad said to get it. Here, smell." He squirted a long stream from the bottle, right in front of her nose.

Jenny coughed and quickly put a hand to her mouth, trying to stifle the urge. The perfume smelled garishly of flowers, strong and deep with some horribly musty undertone. Her momma would have called it "streetwalker perfume." "How nice," she managed to say.

"Because Uncle Mitch says you smell like flowers," Crystal informed her.

Uncle Mitch had said that? She looked at Mitch. He was standing on one foot, and then the other, and she realized again that something major was expected of her. In fact, they were all looking at her. "Where did all these lovely things come from?"

"The mall," Ryan said airily. "We all went."

She visualized Mitch and this stampeding herd of kids descending on the mall, apparently to buy presents for her, and she was touched. In fact, suddenly she was blinking back tears. "These are wonderful gifts," she said sincerely. "I...thank you so much."

Luke caught her eye. "They're very romantic, don't you think, Jenny?" he prompted.

Romantic. Ah... Something started to dawn on her. "Why, yes," she whispered. "Romantic."

"I told you so!" Ryan said triumphantly to his father. "I told you what her mom said. Flowers and books—"

"And candy. *Gone with the Wind,*" Jenny said, and more tears fell. A great happiness welled in her.

"When you want to get a girl to listen to you, you do romantic things to soften her up. That's what you said." Ryan was grinning from ear to ear.

It wasn't exactly what she'd said, but it was close enough. They'd gone to so much trouble, just for her. She suddenly felt cherished. Loved. She looked at Mitch, and as his eyes searched her face, he broke into a grin. "You can't tell a woman you've blown it unless you can get her to really listen and believe," he said softly.

Oh, my goodness, she was going to be blubbering in a minute. "Oh, Mitch."

"Out." Mitch turned to his gathered children. "Please. Out so I can talk to Jenny alone for a minute."

"We want to watch," Jason protested.

"Yeah, we want to watch," Crystal repeated.

"No watching. I'll tell you how it goes."

With some arguing, they filed through the door. Just before Luke passed through, he gave his father a thumbs-up signal.

A moment later, Mitch shut the door on utter silence and stood leaning against it.

"It's too quiet. You know they're listening out there," Jenny said nervously.

"Probably. We never have had much privacy. Look." He moved away from the door. "I want you to know that this afternoon's the longest time I've ever spent in a mall in my life."

She wasn't sure what she was supposed to say to that, so she settled for yet another "Thank you." He took a few steps toward her and nerves skittered up her spine. He looked so big and dark and gorgeous, and the intent yet uncertain expression in his eyes made her fall in love all over again.

He stopped in front of her. She focused on his broad chest, the pleats of his crisp, starched shirt. The pearl studs. He said, "I spent all afternoon in the mall, I stopped off home to drag out this suit and put it on, and I did all that stuff so you'd know I was capable of at least trying to understand you. Now I'm asking you to listen to me. All right?"

She swallowed and nodded.

"I was wrong."

Her gaze flew to his face.

"I was wrong about David. I realized I wasn't really giving him good advice, because I wasn't thinking real clearly on the subject myself. So I changed my advice. Yesterday, I told him that I would recommend taking him off the team unless he and Robin saw a professional counselor to help them decide what to do about the baby. They're going to have to think long and hard about what's best for the child they *both* created."

"Oh." Her insides were humming, on full alert. Mitch's advice sounded perfect. Could that mean—

"You were right," he added now, his eyes still locked on hers. "I thought I'd done right, coming home for Anne, and I did do right, but maybe my attitude wasn't the best. I loved her and I wanted to come home, but at the same time I felt cheated. Just like you said."

He stopped and seemed to be waiting for something. So she nodded.

"Okay." He let out a breath. "The thing is, that was so incredibly wrong. No wonder Anne felt that she had to make me promise to take care of my own kids. See, I've been thinking, and what I've decided is that the last four years have been tough, but I wouldn't have traded them for anything in the world. Not for the scoring record or another Stanley, or even ten more years in the NHL. Because nothing is as important as my family. Nothing. Believe that."

She did believe it suddenly. He'd gone to so much trouble, trying to talk to her, to "soften her up," as the boys would say. When she wouldn't talk to him, he'd tried to reach her without words, with all these silly, wrong presents, presents—with the exception of Crystal's—that were chosen by clueless men but that had turned out to be just perfect because those same clueless men had hearts that were pure gold.

"Jenny, if I had it to do over, even if somebody could tell me that I'd have a Stanley ring and endorsements and a career that was all a guy could want, if I had it to do over, I'd never even *begin* to play hockey if it meant I couldn't be a father. A real father, one who's home for his kids, focused on his family."

There was a little pause. "So what I'm trying to say is, I love you, and I think I know what it means to love a woman and have kids with her and raise them. I want you to be able to trust me. I want to be worthy of that trust. And every time I get screwed up in the head, I want a strong, independent woman who shares my values to set me straight."

She put her arms around him, held him as close to her as she could, with her baby between them. His arms came around her and cradled them both. "Yes," she said. "I trust you. I do. I love you."

He pulled another package out of his pocket.

"Another gift?" She smiled through her tears.

"Open it," he urged.

In the box was the most beautiful ring she'd ever seen. "Mitch!"

"You like it?"

"It's beautiful! It's so…"

He grinned. "So I got *something* right here."

"You got *everything* right."

"Marry me?"

"Yes. Oh, yes."

From outside the door, there was a whoop. "All *right,* Dad," Ryan shouted.

Mitch and Jenny looked at each other. Mitch shrugged, smiling, and Jenny laughed out loud.

EPILOGUE

MISS JENNY SAT UP in the hospital bed, holding her new baby. Miss Jenny was Aunt Jenny now, but Crystal could never remember to say the aunt part, and Miss Jenny said it was okay for Crystal to call her whatever she wanted. Uncle Mitch was here, too, and he sat on the edge of the bed, looking down at Miss Jenny and the baby with a sort of goofy, soft look on his face.

"Crystal!" Miss Jenny smiled when she caught sight of her. "Come here, sweetheart, and have a close-up look."

So Crystal came up to the side of the bed, and Miss Jenny pulled back a little white blanket and showed her the baby. An ugly baby, Crystal thought, all wrinkled, with red skin.

Miss Jenny gave Crystal a big smile. "Isn't this the most beautiful baby you've ever seen in your whole life?"

"Yeah, sure," Crystal lied. What could she do? Miss Jenny worked real hard to have this baby, Uncle Mitch said, and he would know because he was there in that room with Miss Jenny all that time. Plus, Jason said you had to love that baby because Miss Jenny had it and so what if it was ugly.

Then the baby's eyes opened and they were the prettiest blue. Like the sky. Like the pond when the sun was shining real hard. Gee, maybe that baby would get beautiful someday to match those eyes. It could happen.

After all, Uncle Mitch and Miss Jenny were married and sometimes it seemed like they were her new daddy and momma. Like Crystal's momma had had to go to heaven so God gave her a pretty good family because Crystal wasn't grown up yet by the time her momma had to go. And that was a miracle, wasn't it? So if Crystal could have a miracle, maybe this baby's face wouldn't stay all ugly and red.

"I'm so happy," Miss Jenny whispered to Uncle Mitch, and he leaned forward and kissed her so softly, and Crystal knew that was love.

"You're still happy, even though the baby's a boy?" Crystal asked. She still couldn't quite understand why Uncle Mitch and Miss Jenny were so happy about a boy when Miss Jenny had kept saying it was a girl. When Crystal had asked Uncle Mitch why it was a boy when that lady at the hospital had said it was a girl, Uncle Mitch just shrugged and said the lady got it wrong, like it didn't matter at all. Of course, Uncle Mitch had a lot of boys, so maybe he didn't care, but Miss Jenny was so happy it was a boy, too. That didn't make sense, but everybody knew a lot of stuff didn't make sense.

Miss Jenny pulled the blanket down farther. "If you put out your finger, he'll take it," she whispered.

So Crystal put out a finger, and the baby's tiny,

tiny fingers curled around it. His fingernails were so small and sort of perfect, much neater than the fingernails of her dolls. The skin of his hand was so soft, it was the softest thing she'd ever felt, softer even than Jewels's fur or Silver's ear.

Suddenly she thought, *Maybe this ugly baby is beautiful after all.*

"It's like he's shaking your hand," Uncle Mitch said. "Crystal, meet Stephen."

#924 BIRTHRIGHT • Judith Arnold
Riverbend

Aaron Mazerik is back. He isn't the town's bad boy anymore, but some people still don't think he's good enough—especially not for Riverbend's golden girl, Lily Holden. Which is fine with Aaron, since he's convinced there's even *more* reason he and Lily shouldn't be together.

Riverbend, Indiana: Home of the River Rats—small-town sons and daughters who've been friends since high school. These are their stories.

#925 FULL RECOVERY • Bobby Hutchinson
Emergency!

Spence Mathews, former RCMP officer and now handling security at St. Joe's Hospital, helps Dr. Joanne Duncan deliver a baby in the E.R. After the infant mysteriously disappears a few hours later, Spence and Joanne work closely together to solve the abduction and in the process recover the baby girl—and much more!

#926 MOM'S THE WORD • Roz Denny Fox
9 Months Later

Hayley Ryan is pregnant and alone. Her no-good ex—the baby's father—abandoned her for another woman; her beloved grandfather is dead, leaving her nothing but a mining claim in southern Arizona. Hayley is cast upon her own resources, trying to work the claim, worrying about herself and her baby.... And then rancher Zack Cooper shows up.

#927 THE REAL FATHER • Kathleen O'Brien
Twins

Ten years ago, Molly Lorring left Demery, South Carolina, with a secret. She was pregnant with Beau Forrest's baby, but Beau died in a car crash before he could marry her. For all that time, Beau's identical twin, Jackson, has carried his own secret. Beau *isn't* the father of Molly's baby....

#928 CONSEQUENCES • Margot Dalton
Crystal Creek

Principal Lucia Osborne knows the consequences of hiring cowboy Jim Whitely to teach the difficult seventh graders. Especially when Jim deliberately flouts the rules in order to help the kids. Certain members of the board may vote to fire Lucia and close the school. But Lucia has even graver consequences to worry about. She's falling in love with Jim...and she's expecting another man's child.

#929 THE BABY BARGAIN • Peggy Nicholson
Marriage of Inconvenience

Rafe Montana's sixteen-year-old daughter, Zoe, and Dana Kershaw's teenage son, Sean, have made a baby. *Now what?* Rafe's solution—or rather, proposal—has Zoe ecstatic, but it leaves Dana aghast and Sean confused. Even Rafe wonders whether he's out of his mind.

CNM0600